THE FIVE

By Vic LeClair III

Also by Vic LeClair III

First printing 2015
ISBN: 978-0-9963028-1-4

Printed in the United States of America

"Write the book the way it should be written, then give it to somebody to put in the commas and shit."

Elmore Leonard   *1997*

To my wife Joy…she seems to like me.

THE FIVE

1

Bernie Tennison stood in front of his office window. The dim parking lot lights burned through the snow that fell softly from the dark sky. His eyes were transfixed on a Styrofoam cup that swirled in the wind outside his company's new office building. The cup seemed stuck in a never-ending whirlwind, unable to escape the three brick walls that held it captive.

The connected manufacturing structure displayed no artistic imagination. Bernie had bought the building years ago to begin his business.

Bernie's modern office, however, was innovative and futuristic, inside and out. The brick exterior was much like any other building, though the pattern was striking. He instructed his bricklayers to do their job in a most interesting way. The walls became endless patterns of zeroes and ones. The structure belied his company's work in software, almost digitized in its form.

The offices were made to reflect some of the company's current products and prototypes. Each room's sensors controlled everything from lighting to smoke detection. The employees were not always thrilled about it, especially when Bernie had new toilets installed with flushing software.

They never knew what might happen. Bernie, on the other hand, loved to try new prototypes, even if they malfunctioned now and then.

Of late, Bernie found himself annoyed with many of life's displeasures. The fact that it was snowing on the first day of May was just one more irritation.

It had been a decade since he and his wife, Marcie, had started the company. The small electronics assembly company they'd called Phenco, Inc., now employed over four-hundred people. In his opinion, he'd done a remarkable job keeping the place together under the recent world-wide economic struggles. There had been lay-offs, but not many.

A few years ago, before the slowdown, Bernie had turned down a lucrative buy-out from a large firm in California. Then, he had been in the middle of new construction and felt that the timing wasn't right. Now, with his company struggling and his twenty-three year marriage in trouble, he stared out the window wishing he had taken the deal. It was of some consolation that his two boys were older, in college, and no longer had to bear witness to their fights. This weekend he was walking on eggshells. The boys were taking a break before prepping for finals. Bernie had taken them everywhere when they were small. He'd hoped to take them golfing this weekend, so this snow had hit a nerve. Hitting a white ball would have been much better than going home and waiting for the bickering to start. He didn't want to see his boy's shuttle off to their rooms to get away from the drama.

Bernie could hear the whistle of the cold wind fighting for supremacy over the hiss of warm air from his radiator. His office smelled of new paint, carpeting, and freshly stained baseboards. He wondered how long it would be before that newness disappeared. His eyes were still focused on the parking lot when he noticed one car near the back of the otherwise vacant spaces. *It must be someone in payroll...it's always someone in payroll on a Thursday night, he thought.*

Why did he feel he needed to be the last one to leave? That damn Styrofoam cup was still out there, spinning, unable to get out from its predicament. *The earlier I go home, the sooner the old lady starts bitching. I'm with you little cup...I know how you feel.*

He turned from the window. A sudden chill seized him, a presence. Before he could comprehend what was happening, he was hit with a spray of liquid across his eyes. Pain burned through him immediately and excruciatingly. There was no thought of what was happening to him or who was responsible. There was only pain.

2

Bernie had been right about one thing. Someone else was still in the building. Sheryl Norwitz was the payroll accountant. One floor down, she heard the wailing above her so distinctly, it was as if it came from the next room.

Sheryl was not one to take chances. She had been asked to finish the payroll spreadsheet report—a task that would take hours. The thought of going out in the dark, empty parking lot alone didn't thrill her. For that reason, only moments ago, Sheryl had called her husband and asked him to come and escort her to her car when she was ready to leave. The city of Granite, Wisconsin, has a population of thirty-thousand and is not known as a violent place. Green County's seat is about as safe a place as can be found. That made the scream even more surreal to Sheryl.

She sat frozen to her chair. *Should she call maintenance or 911?* Somehow her fingers found the phone and pushed the 911 sequence.

"I hear screaming, long horrible screaming. Yes, this is Phenco Incorporated."

Another scream echoed through the building.

"No, I don't think I can stay on the phone."

She put the phone down and found her hands shaking. Her first instinct was to sit tight. *I've done my part; let the professionals take it from here.* But, the screams wouldn't stop.

Sheryl cautiously broke from her tensed state. Still shaking, she crept up the stairs. *The pitiful noise was one of pain, not fright, she thought.* She began to move with more urgency. *Someone could be hurt. Maybe I could help.*

Closer now, she realized the noise came from the president's office. She ran to the door and reached for the knob. Marty, the night shift maintenance man was already running from the opposite direction. They reached Mr. Tennison's office at the same time, but it was locked. Marty fumbled with his keys, finally locating the right one.

Inside, the man before them stood, crouched over and wreathing in pain. Bernie Tennison's hands covered his eyes. His scream became garbled, a pitiful sort of hurt-dog sound as if his discomfort had subsided just a bit.

Sheryl heard the sound of an ambulance and police were outside the office window that had been curiously left open on this cold evening.

"My eyes…what happened? Who would do this?" He clenched his fist in rage. "I'll find who did this. This won't stand."

Bernie dropped to his knees and as he did, Sheryl got a glimpse of his face. His eyelids were tightly, painfully shut, wrinkled by burns. It was as if someone had cinched him ruthlessly with a hot poker.

The door pushed open again as an EMT and two patrol officers rushed in. The ambulance crew flushed Bernie's eyes with water, bandaged him, and strapped him to a stretcher. They injected him with something Sheryl figured was a sedative. It worked fast because he stopped making any noise at all. He didn't even complain as his stretcher got banged around as they carried him out and into the ambulance. She knew one thing, however, very few people in Green County were as well known, rich, and powerful as Bernie Tennison. This attack would bring a quick response from those that were responsible for the safety of Green County.

It didn't take long for the Granite Police Patrol to round up the response team. Sheryl was not surprised by all the detail and attention. She wondered if this much action would have been afforded her if she had been the victim.

She watched as the team's supervisor was followed by an Investigative Services Unit. This included three investigators and two evidence technicians. Heading the investigation team was eight-year veteran, Lieutenant Marion Patrick. Sheryl heard of this woman, but never met her.

Lieutenant Patrick was a solid no-nonsense woman. Though short and pudgy, she had a commanding voice and a scary facial expression that, at times, could make people cry. Her department wasn't far from Phenco and it only made sense for her to take the call.

Moments later, Green County Sheriff Department's Jason Barthus arrived at the crime scene with his underling, Sergeant Jim Ruferd. Those who knew Lieutenant Barthus as a friend or co-worker called him Jay.

The air blowing through the open window made Sheryl Norwitz shiver. She looked outside and wondered if she would need to scrape frost off the windows of her car. Then she scolded herself for thinking of such things at a time like this.

A technician snapped on rubber gloves. He carefully removed a plastic bottle from a tin trash can. Smoke fumed from the small spray bottle because of the contents that seemed to be eating away at it. The officer dropped it quickly back into the trash can before the liquid penetrated his gloves.

"Take the whole can, Kyle. It looks acidic," Lieutenant Patrick reasoned.

Jay Barthus knew that Phenco, Inc. was technically just outside the city of Granite. This would fall under his jurisdiction, but in small town America you helped each other out.

"Thanks for your help, Marion."

"No problem, Jay. I know you're spread thin on Friday nights, but Bernie's a pretty big fish. I'm here if you need me."

Jay scanned the office and looked back at Marion. "You would think we had a homicide the way the Captain wanted us to approach this. I guess it pays to be important."

"Doesn't it always?" Marion snickered, her pudgy face contorted. She took in the scene in front of her. Everything was neat and tidy. No muss no fuss, just do the job and get out. "It sure looks premeditated, doesn't it?"

Jay called across the room to Sergeant Jim Ruferd. Jim was his pal, but stood about a mile shorter. Like everybody else at the department, Jay didn't know his partners real first name. Everyone just called him, Rufe. He tended to finish his sentences. "Rufe, station a body at each exit and start an inside search. Find out how many workers were in the plant at the time. See if we have any witnesses."

"Already have the exits covered, Jay. Only two others were here at the time." Rufe pointed at them. He glanced down at his notes and continued. "Sheryl Norwitz was downstairs doing some accounting. Marty Kozloski was sweeping floors. He's from the maintenance department. When Mrs. Norwitz heard a scream, she called 911 and ran upstairs where she met up with Mr. Kozloski. Neither of them saw anybody go into or out of the room."

Jay looked out the window. There were no shoe prints on the surface below. The recent snow wouldn't have been enough to cover them. There were no signs of wet shoe prints on the office carpet or in the hall.

"I think that whoever did this opened the window to try and throw us off. Take plenty of pictures and check for prints around the window and especially on the handle. Then close it...it's cold," Jay said.

3

Jay Paul Barthus was not a fat man, nor was he skinny. His blond hair changed color depending on how much summer sun he was exposed to. Some years his driver's license gave his eye color as green, other years, blue. The way Jay figured it, the discrepancy is a combination of both hues and from a scale of one to a thousand, he didn't give a shit.

It was by virtue of his past that helped him get his current position. He called upon his experience for much of what he did and tonight was no exception. Jay's personality, likes, dislikes, and rules to live by revolved around an ever-changing cycle of three distinct groups of people and interests. His early years consisted of family, friends, and school, in that order. His high school days started with friends, family, and sports and evolved into girls, drinking, and sports. His first couple of years in college became drinking, girls, and more drinking. By the time his fifth year of college came around, Jay was sick of school, sick of drinking, and, at times, sick of chasing girls.

His grade point average sunk lower every year of college. Like many of his contemporaries, he put off declaring a major until the last possible moment. Jay struggled through his classes, having to study twice as long as most of his classmates. He had precious little to show for his efforts and the harder it got, the more he drank. The more he drank, the lower his grades were. Finally, near graduation, he found himself walking the imaginary straight line for the second night in a row. "Is that you again, Jay?" The cop knew him from the previous night. Back then, cops were more concerned with how to straighten people out, not how many tickets they could write up.

On that night, Jay sat behind the wheel of his beat-up Chevy and looked at himself in the rearview mirror. He didn't like the face that looked back. It was tired. The eyes were slits. The breeze that pushed into his face could no longer slow down the process of decline. Unlike the night before, he didn't have the capacity to call up his sober twin. His line walking was sad and though he didn't have any problem closing his eyes, touching his nose at the same time became impossible. The officer had Jay park his car and then drove him home. He gave Jay his card and told him to call him the next day or he'd give him a ticket.

Everyone, at some point in their lives, needs an event or a person to help them get back on the right path. That cop was Jay's pathfinder. He hadn't gotten lost since. Though he was still capable of straying from the path, he always had found the way home.

When time permitted, he would think back...back to times that were tough and other times that fell nicely into the puzzle that became Lieutenant Jay Barthus.

While the team scanned the room for evidence, the Lieutenant's pager beeped. A patrol officer in the back of the building was on the phone.

"Jay, we found footprints leading out of the south end."

It was the closest exit to the office where the crime had taken place. Jay ran down and borrowed the officer's flashlight to check out the tracks. Covering his short blond hair with his black-leather pilot's hat, he followed the prints. He turned around for an instant and saw a technician taking photos of the prints. They were large and smooth. No grooved patterns were visible and they looked oval shaped, as if the person who made them had large ostrich eggs in place of his feet.

Jay followed the odd prints through a short path between trees that led to a park-and-go. There, the footprints became mixed with a host of others. Car tracks, old and new, crisscrossed the lot. It was congested at this time of night due to a change of shift for the paper plant about a block away. Jay and the patrol officer peered into every car window, but found nothing.

The officer stood with Jay and looked up at the light on top of the parking lot post. The snow had stopped. He shook his head. "We don't have a long enough winter as it is and now it snows in May."

Jay nodded his head. "Let's hope this is the last of it, though it always helps when looking for footprints." He headed back into the Phenco building, leaving orders to write down every license plate in the lot.

Jay looked down at a report he received on the victim, Bernie Tennison. His employees knew him as an honest, albeit demanding boss. In Granite, the Canadian mix dialect was strong. You could hear it in any words that ended in o-u-t. Bernie was a different story; he would not have fit at all in the cast from the movie "Fargo". Though he was born in Minnesota, his parents came from Boston. Bernie's accent was a strange blend. The other thing about him is he was never one to shy away from telling it like it was. *He's an interesting fellow,* Jay thought.

4

A 1985 coupe rambled into an unattached garage. The motor stopped. A short man with gray, curly hair left the garage and headed directly to the basement. There, he retrieved a gallon jug, half-full with clear liquid. He walked back to his garage, carefully placing the jug in the trunk of his car. Closing the garage door, he returned to the basement. He reached into his pocket and pulled out a pair of thin shoe covers along with latex gloves, and tossed them into a metal tub. He squirted them with lighter fluid, lit a match, pausing to stare and smile at the sputtering flame, and then dropped it in the tub. He did the same with some notepaper. He then opened a small window, trying to let the smell of sulfur and burned rubber escape, but it didn't help much. He returned to his car, drove a few blocks to a wooded lot, and with attentiveness, emptied the hissing contents of the glass jug onto the snow covered ground. He glanced around for any intruders, and was happy to see a vacant street. Returning home, he stripped naked, putting each piece of clothing, including his coat, into the washer. His grin was short and modest as he flipped the machine on. He then went upstairs and enjoyed a hot shower.

5

"The sulfuric acid ate away any chance we had to save your sight, Bernie. I've checked with some of the best people in the country."

The doctor was a friend of Bernie's and would do anything to help his golfing buddy, but there wasn't any glimmer of hope.

It had only been a half day since the attack. Bernie was feeling the effects of the pain medicine and the IV made him feel trapped.

He heard his two sons whispering defiantly in the hospital room, and his wife tensely trying to quiet them. The boys still held on to the hope that their father could see. They were confused by the attack and angry that someone would dare hurt their father.

Bernie was being fussed about by a hoard of nurses and doctors. One of them mentioned that an officer was waiting to ask some questions. They were all well aware of his status on the Monroe Hospital Board of Directors. This hospital sustained itself largely through his sizable donations.

The medical team left and Bernie now heard his wife talking to Lieutenant Barthus as they entered his room. He didn't know his two sons followed behind. "This is crazy. Who would do something like this, Bernie?" Marcie asked her husband. She sounded tired to Bernie. Not angry or protective, just tired.

"Lieutenant, who did this? Was it an accident? He doesn't have any enemies. Everybody likes him."

"You okay, Dad?" Bernie's eldest son, Thad went to hold his hand. He was close to both of his sons, but Thad was quite special to him. He knew Thad didn't care for his mother's constant screaming matches at home and would side with his father during such times.

"I'm extremely angry right now, but I'll figure it out, Thad."

The lieutenant chimed in. "Nothing yet, Mrs. Tennison. Can I talk to Bernie for a while?" Bernie heard a ball-point pen click.

Bernie sensed his wife Marcie looked down at him from the other side of the bed. He could smell her perfume. Was she wondering what his eyes looked like behind those bandages? Did she care? His mind flashed back to younger, happier days, but not for long. The last few years had been exhausting and a huge waste of time. He knew she blamed him for that. In the last year, rarely a day had gone by without an argument. Before the attack they'd fought about all the time he had been spending on the golf course. Would she feel any measure of guilt in the realization that he might never again be able to play the game he loved so much.

Jay asked his questions quickly and efficiently, though many of them were previously answered during his ride to the hospital. Are you sure you didn't see anything? Is the back door locked? Any idea who might have been angry with you? Bernie didn't have anything new to say and Jay could see he had enough meds in him to calm a charging black bear. He made a few notes and told Bernie to get some rest. That was it...for now.

Bernie didn't feel the need to stay in the hospital and arranged to finish recovery from home. He was a man who was used to getting what he wanted. Education came easy to him and it didn't hurt to have parents who could afford to pay his way. This was the first time in his life someone had taken something from him that he couldn't get back, and he was enraged. For the most part he held his anger in, but Marcie could feel it. Bernie had avoided talking with her before the attack. Since he returned home from the hospital, they didn't talk at all.

Bernie had connections within the police force. They kept abreast of anything new on the case. In the days following the attack the city and county police investigation drew blanks. The owners of the parked cars in the park-and-go had been interviewed. Evidence technicians tried to match the strange footprints to workers who might have worn similar shoes or shoe covers, but without luck. No one at the park that night remembered seeing anything odd. Any prints that were left at Bernie's office were those of employees or family. All were removed as possible suspects.

Like his office building, Bernie's home was architecturally very contemporary. Rectangular forms and curves sometimes took strange angles. Bernie Tennison majored in electronic engineering and minored in business. Over the years, his home had become a test lab for new technology. From any device with internet access he could monitor everything – visitors, heating, plumbing leaks. Bernie believed that since his company could design and build the products, it was his duty to try them himself before giving the green light. His wife, Marcie, stood on the other side of the spectrum. Her wish would be a simple light switch and a remote for the television. But in the house of *Bernie,* things didn't quite work that way.

Lieutenant Barthus invited himself to Bernie's home to have another talk with him. When Jay pulled into Bernie's driveway, he was being monitored. Bernie had rigged his software to audibly describe the approaching car.

Jay's approach to the door triggered music throughout the house. Music that changed based on Bernie's mood. Cameras in the home picked up facial expression. It wasn't always perfect, but it was close. It was set to only pick up Bernie's face. He wondered what type of music would play if it was set to his wife's moods. In this case it was Coffey, from the soundtrack of The Green Mile that filled the room.

Marcy led Jay to Bernie's office and quickly disappeared. "Bernie, whoever did this, planned it out perfectly. This person left nothing behind except a plastic spray bottle of sulfuric acid, until the acid ate away at the bottle. This lunatic had everything figured out, from the time he reached your empty hallway, to the amount of time needed to use the bottle of acid before it disintegrated. No worries about fingerprints. Nothing left. Are you sure we have everything you remember from that night?"

"Lieutenant, you almost sound like I'm hiding something."

"Are you?"

Bernie turned his head slightly. "Of course not." Changing the course of the conversation, he continued. "So you have nothing. This prick walks into my office as pretty as a painted piss pot, takes away my sight and walks out. You sit there and tell me...you don't have a thing. I'm not happy with that. That's not going to cut the muster with me, Barthus."

Despite the lack of light in Bernie's home office, Jay could see Bernie's jaw tighten under the dark sunglasses.

"We're not done, Bernie. We're checking into recent purchases of sulfuric acid and are still conducting interviews. This is a small county and the people in it tend to get on each other's nerves when something happens without an answer. We're getting calls from neighbors accusing the other simply because he doesn't cut his grass. I'm here because I'm looking for your help. We know he or she was probably short. The spray was shot upward and the prints outside were from a smaller foot."

Bernie turned his head away from Jay and started to process things.

"Listen, Bernie. We'll find whoever did this. I would rather that it was sooner than later. Remember, it's only been a day. Are you sure you don't know anybody in your past that had something against you? What about your list of layoffs? Did anybody take it especially hard?"

Bernie shook his head. "If you find him…I still won't see, but damn it I need to know who did this. Listen, Barthus, it's like I told you. I don't know anybody that would go to this extreme, but if it was someone from my company, here's a list of those who were laid off in the last year. Whoever it was seemed to know the layout. I would think it was somebody who worked here."

"We continue to go through the list. If you have any inkling or feeling about anybody, let me know and we'll conduct an interview."

Bernie rubbed his forehead. He could hear Marcie fidgeting near his office door. "Marcie, will you see the Lieutenant to the door? I believe his time is being wasted here."

As Jay turned away, Bernie said, "Let's keep this thing out of the papers…my company doesn't need any more problems."

"Yeah, our local media people check ambulance and police reports, but I'll do my best to keep it low-key."

6

Jay could do his best thinking when walking the sidewalks of Granite. Crime was rare in his adopted city and all of Green County for that matter. There was a time in small-town America when everyone knew the lives of everyone else. In most cases that old American tradition had changed. Most had moved away from clothesline gossip to computer companion. Granite was a bit of a throw-back. It isn't easy to hide criminal activity without someone seeing or knowing something. If a spray-and-run nutcase was going to do his business in Green County, then said nutcase would likely be found sooner than later. It had only been a day since Bernie was victimized and the consensus was that whoever did it probably was a one-hit wonder. If you talked to anybody on Main Street or in the local pub, they'd probably say *someone had a grudge,* and mission was accomplished. Unfortunately, that general belief changed after he left Bernie's home on May 2nd.

Peggy Lloyd had bought an old, run-down TV retail store ten years ago on a corner in Exeter. The Town was in the north-east section of Green County. Now she was owner and president of "Lloyd's Sound Systems." Her three hundred million dollar company is the largest employer in the county with five hundred employees. She had retail stores in four Midwestern states, but maintained her corporate office and principal factory where it all started.

They sold all the basics—audio systems, televisions, computers, and more. But Lloyd's bread and butter were high-end custom speakers. Peggy started manufacturing her own brand of speakers soon after she opened the first store. Today their showcase rooms provided such a varied array of tweeter, midrange, and woofer speakers that the sizes and qualities available were endless. It always amazed Peggy what her customers were willing to pay for their imagined designs.

She had been single all of her life and had accepted the extreme likelihood that things would remain that way. It had been a few months since her friend and tax advisor, Chloe Pilzner, set her up and shoved a surprise fortieth birthday party down her throat. It seemed everybody there had a significant other, or at least a whole other life outside of their careers. As rational as Peggy Lloyd was, the ever strong president of Lloyd's Sound Systems was starting to notice that her life sucked. She wondered why she didn't take note of the path she was destined to walk before that day. Was she that busy? Did her endless days of meetings, phone conversations, and plane rides have to swallow her entire existence? She'd made it through her birthday party by covering her thoughts of loneliness and perhaps vulnerability with her stoic mask of unquestioned leadership.

The comfort of her Lazy Boy in front of a warm fire did nothing to relieve her of the pain. Her breathing had become labored and her skin, clammy. It wasn't the start of a heart attack, or a blood clot, or any other physical ailment…that she knew. She didn't need a doctor, and it wasn't necessarily the big house that she had meticulously built to fit her needs that bothered her. It was the absence of that other person, that companion to come home to. She brought home a cat a couple of years ago. It looked like a Todd, so that's what she named it. There had been times that as Peggy left work on a Friday, an employee would pass by and ask the obligatory, "Busy weekend?" She would tell a half-truth and say, "Hanging out with Todd," never admitting that Todd was her lap buddy.

Peggy rinsed her face in the sink and stared at herself in the mirror. Her hair was a mix of brown and gray. She was beginning to show a hint of jowls. *I can't go on like this; I need to talk to somebody.* She picked up the phone.

"Chloe, can you come over? I know it's late...no, it isn't serious. I just want...need to talk."

She was going to tell Chloe everything. "*If anyone can help me, it's Chloe. She always knows the right thing to say and do,*" Peggy thought. She sat back and began to calm down...just a bit.

As she waited, the phone rang.

Hello, I'm looking for Peggy...Peggy Lloyd," the husky voice said.

"Can I help you?" Peggy looked at the caller I.D. and noticed it was a call from her plant.

"Sorry to call at this time of night Ms. Lloyd, I'm Telly Schaifer with U.S. Gas, and I was asked to check for a gas leak in showroom 'A' by your night janitor...ah...I think...Becher was his name."

"Yes, Mr. Schaifer, go on."

"Well, I went to check some other rooms, and...and, there's a body in one of the rooms, back in the corner by the window. I'm not sure...I don't think she's breathing. I called 911, but I thought you should know."

Peggy's attention to her personal needs vanished and was replaced with her leadership persona. It was a part of her that was always on call and could be counted on to take charge in seconds.

"I'll be right there."

Peggy left a quick note for Chloe and ran out the door.

She drove around the corner and parked in front of her company's office building. The shop had bricks added half-way up the front to give it the appearance of business offices, rather than the factory it had been. The actual manufacturing facility was now behind the offices and nearly covered the entire block. At first glance, it wasn't very anything memorable. However, after a customer toured her showcase rooms and the plant, they came away impressed.

She was surprised yet relieved to see that there were no emergency vehicles or police. *Best to check this out myself before things get out of hand, she thought.* This take-over feeling gave her an adrenaline rush and she sprinted from her car to the front door. Only a dim light lit the room in front of the reception desk. Clara, her receptionist was long gone, and the hallway leading to the speaker showrooms was dark.

"Pete...Mr. Schaifer...anybody here?" Peggy called out.

She smelled no hint of gas. She flipped on the hall light and could see the open door to showroom 'A'. She'd walked this hall hundreds, maybe thousands of times before, but this was different. *It's late, I don't feel very good, a possible gas leak, and someone may be hurt!* Peggy pushed open the door. *The man said gas, and a body.* The floor and shelves were filled with an array of woofer, midrange, and tweeter speaker systems, each meticulously set up with the perfect receiver and amplifier for the most accurate display of every audio range. She walked into the room, but still didn't smell any gas. The door closed quickly behind her.

The door made a soft "click" as it shut. There was the briefest moment of silence. Then, every receiver and every amplifier erupted to maximum capacity. Peggy reached to cover her ears, but realized that her eardrums had popped. Blood poured between her fingers. Speakers pounded all around her, screaming an unrecognizable beat. Peggy felt the floor rumble, the speaker cones bounce back and forth, stretched to their limit. She reached her bloody right hand to the door knob. It wouldn't turn. She couldn't stay erect and crumpled to the floor, her head between her knees. The pain was torturous. All the systems, thumping and dancing through the room, began to lose their tightness, and sounded as if they were going hoarse. Some of the speakers in the tall floor-to-ceiling systems began to push so hard that the cones tore loose from their baskets and mercifully buzzed or went silent. Peggy knew her speakers more than she knew her own employees. She knew each part and how they came together to make the best sound. The pain in her head improved slightly as each speaker began to blow out. Still, she tried to make herself small, hoping the pounding would stop. She thought of powering off all thirty units, but that would mean getting closer to each speaker and that didn't seem to be an option.

7

Pete Becher, the night custodian, was sweeping the floor of the driver production area. He heard the massive sound coming from the front office, and immediately knew something was wrong. Customers had been known to crank up the amps in the showrooms, but it was after hours and the sound was like nothing he'd ever heard. He reached the showcase door in less than ninety seconds, and found it locked. Through the small window, he could see someone crouched on the floor. Pete ran down the hall to the broom closet where the fuse box was located. He fumbled through brooms and boxes to find the string for the light. Finally seeing the fuse for showcase room A, he switched it off. The immense pounding mercifully ended. Dashing back, he fumbled with his keys and dropped them to the floor, instead kicking at the door with the heel of his shoe. The solid door would not budge. He picked up his keys, took a breath, and found the right one.

Crouching down, Pete held Peggy in his arms while calling 911 on his cell phone. He then realized that it was the company president cradled in his arms.

Peggy rocked in his arms and cried. She looked up to Pete and kept asking, "Why?" The word sounded off, somehow. She would say it too loud, then too soft. She didn't seem to possess the mechanism to moderate the tone. Pete didn't have an answer for her.

He asked her what happened, but she couldn't tell him. It dawned on him sickeningly, that she couldn't hear the question.

The County police arrived first, followed closely by the ambulance.

Peggy saw the paramedics talk to her when they first found her in the show room. They checked her over and decided a stretcher wouldn't be necessary. They bandaged her head. Peggy watched as a county officer sat down next to her in the ambulance and began talking to her. She could see out the window as the wind blew the tree leaves. The snow didn't accumulate much from yesterday's May surprise and most of it had already melted. Police were walking about. A man across the street stopped to watch for a while and then continued to clean the windows on a small appliance shop. To Peggy, it all happened in silence.

Chloe Pilzner arrived while Peggy was being examined. She called the plant when she got to Peggy's house, hoping to find out when she'd return, and was told about her condition by an officer. Sitting beside Chloe was Lieutenant Jay Barthus. He'd been called by the county to lend a hand. The county sheriff's department was looking into the similarities between Peggy's assault and that of Bernie Tennison. If there was a connection it meant one thing...the nutcase was still around. Jay had to agree that this probably was not accident. Two company owners in the same county getting hurt in a small county. What were the chances?

While officers closed off Lloyd's Sound Systems and sifted through it for any leads, Jay decided to stay in Peggy's hospital room.

"What do you have, Doc?" Jay asked.

"Huge speakers like that, bursting on at 160 decibels or more, can cause instant eardrum perforation. Peggy's inner ear, the cochlea, is likely permanently damaged. We'll need to do a set of exams and tests, but it doesn't look good as far as Peggy ever hearing again."

"Is there anybody I should call? Does she have a relative we can contact?"

"Her friend, Chloe Pilzner, has been calling. I think she mentioned a sister and a cousin."

Chloe had been listening quietly. Her face was red and blotchy. Her best friend, Peggy, laid in a deep sleep, out cold from a pain killer.

"Who would do this, Lieutenant? Peggy never hurt anyone. Everybody liked her. It doesn't make sense."

"How do you know it wasn't an accident?"

"She called me and asked if I would stop over. When I got there I found a note saying that she had to run over to the plant...something about a gas leak. Someone must have called her, detective. Maybe check for phone calls to her house. She wouldn't have run out so quickly unless it was an emergency. The speakers were turned up so loud that they damaged her ears and she apparently was locked inside her own showcase. That doesn't sound like an accident."

"We'll check the phone calls. If there's anything else you can think of don't hesitate to let me know."

A day later Jay sat at his desk updating his report on Peggy Lloyd. Next to him was Sergeant Jim Ruferd.

"Rufe, what makes this case like the Tennison case?"

Rufe scratched his pre-maturely balding head. "Well let's see. Both were severely injured. Both are owners of companies in the same county. Oh, and we don't have a spit of evidence or a clue as to who did this or even if it was done by the same person. Does that about sum it up?"

"That about sums it up, Rufe, except for one thing. They both lost one of their senses. Bernie Tennison lost his eye sight. Peggy Lloyd lost her hearing."

Jay Barthus stood up and grabbed his jacket. His big frame loomed over Rufe. It looked like a scene from David and Goliath, minus the slingshot.

Rufe glanced at his large buddy. "That makes sense, Jay!" he said with a visible smirk. "Two of them."

Jay ignored him. "That leaves three more…touch, smell, and taste. There's about fifteen miles between crime scenes and both attacks appeared to be well planned. Does that sound about right?"

"Oh…and they were both done after normal business hours," Rufe interjected. Rufe was thirty years old and only recently received a four year degree in police science. "I'm a late bloomer Jay, but my mother always told me, 'Jimmy, it takes you longer than a sloth to latch onto something, but once you do, you don't let go.' Sooner or later we'll get this guy, I'll bet my lucky Robin Yount jersey on it."

"We don't have a lot of practice with this kind of thing around here. You know, my mother said a few things herself. She'd say, 'Go to bed with optimism; the morning may well be your best ever.' Goodnight, Rufe."

Rufe stopped Jay just before he left.

"You can go with the five senses theory if you want, but it seems a little farfetched to me."

Jay stopped. "Think outside that four inch steel box once in a while, Rufe. You'd be surprised with what lurks out there."

8

Two more victims were attacked on consecutive days, May 3rd and 4th. The first was Kathryn Williams, owner of TJasoch Paper. With her husband semi-retired and her children grown and on their own, she had the time to cement her future with the company. After many years of inching her way up the paper industry management ladder, and moving the family from city to city, her move to the village of Adams became her planned retirement site. She was in the third year of her second five-year contract. In two years her retirement would be announced; except for belonging to a few corporate boards, her time for world travel was soon to begin in earnest.

Kathy's Monday began as usual. The chill in the air didn't surprise her, but it woke her up just the same. "Good morning," she said to everyone she passed on the walk to her office. Her glasses steamed up from the condensation and she could only make out the blurred images of her employees.

"A man from C.C. White Furniture came to check on your new desk, something about a flaw. I let him in," the front desk operator said as Kathy passed by.

"Thanks, Cassie."

As soon as she entered her well furnished digs, she dropped her suit case on the desk and reached for a tissue to clean her glasses. *When I get some time, I'm having laser surgery,* she thought. In the blur, she saw a figure moving toward her door.

"I'll close the door so we can talk."

As she returned her glasses to her face, she felt a prick on her upper arm.

Cassie watched the man from the furniture store leave. Later, she would recall the green baseball cap that matched his green overalls, his bearded face, a small tool box, and his short stature.

Fifty-eight year old Kathryn Williams remembered little of the man's visit. Employees found her leaning to the right on her black leather chair, a welt on her head, and her mouth gushing blood on the carpet. When the medics arrived they found the reason for the blood. Her tongue had been removed.

When the report came to Jay Barthus' office, the lieutenant was working on the geographic locations off the previous assaults. Each was located in the same county, but there didn't seem to be any connection, other than the senses theory. They were scattered all over the place and now with the addition of Kathryn Williams, ten miles northwest of Granite, he didn't see any way to anticipate the perpetrators next move.

Jay looked down at his desktop and fiddled with an envelope that had been dropped on the front seat of his personal car. It wasn't as though he was left with zero leads. Jay had a half-dozen potential suspects to investigate, but he knew deep down that they were probably dead ends. Most were just angry people who hated their neighbors. He glanced again at the envelope, moaned, and opened it.

A name, and nothing else, was printed in large capital letters. Though Jay found it intriguing, he placed it with the others and promised himself he would look up the name "Ted Paulson" at a later date.

Jay saw Rufe rush into the room. Rufe sat at his desk and opened a cool bottle of cherry juice. He was sweating and breathing hard.

Jay walked over to his partner.

"Are you okay? You look like you just finished getting whipped in a game of racquetball."

"Oh, yah...I'm fine. I was running a little late and sprinted up from the parking lot. Maybe next time we'll see who whips who in racquetball."

"Dream on, little buddy."

"So what's new?"

"Come into my office, I need someone to knock down some of my thoughts and I think you're up for it." They settled in and stood before Jay's big white board. "We're down to touch and smell, Rufe," Jay said.

"Wha...what?"

"The only two senses left are touch and smell." His diagram was a map of Green County and he'd marked the three locations of the victims. "The report says Kathryn Williams' tongue was cut out all the way back to the palatine tonsil. I guess that means the whole thing is gone."

Rufe fiddled with his hands. "I know what the report says."

To Jay, it seemed Rufe's thoughts were far away.

"I heard she's on oxygen because the surgery they did caused inflammation and blocked her airway. She'll be in the hospital for a couple of weeks. Then, I guess she'll be doing therapy. They need to help her eat, swallow, talk...all that good shit. She's written a few things down for me, but she is hurting something awful. She doesn't seem to show any anger over what happen. Maybe she's still in shock." Jay kicked a chair. "That's okay. I've got enough anger for the two of us."

Rufe averted Jay's eyes and said, "To bad, she and her family are great people."

Though Kathryn Williams could write answers to questions Jay asked her, they didn't gain anything more than the description they had earlier. No motive could be found, fingerprints were non-existent, and frustration levels were rising at a steady pace.

Now the media started to pounce. Less than a day after Kathryn Williams was attacked, Lieutenant Jay Barthus' relatively quiet world inched into new and undesirable territory.

Rufe seemed even more nervous than Jay. "I hope this thing blows over, Jay. Deana at the front desk said she got calls from Channel 2 in Madison, Channel 12 in Milwaukee, and two from Chicago. You gonna talk to them?"

"The captain is downtown giving a press conference right now. So far the media hasn't been causing us too much grief, but that could change in a hurry. Every officer in the County is on alert. I guess we better count our blessings that this guy hasn't killed anybody yet."

Jay glanced outside his second story window. Across the street was the Main Street Park. It was considered an old people's park—no swings, just benches and trees. The lack of kid-friendly equipment didn't stop the young ones from playing, however. Jay could see a few kids hiding behind trees and bushes and their lone hunter trying to find them. It made him happy to see kids playing outside instead of wearing out their thumbs on some mind-numbing video games.

Jay turned around and rubbed his temple. "Rufe, there seems to be an agreement on the force that our perp is someone local—someone with access to and knowledge of each business. The evidence department came up with a pretty big list; office furniture companies, hiring firms, shipping companies, supply companies, accounting firms, cleaning companies. It's going to take a while to sift through it. Based on the video, they believe the perpetrator to be about five foot eight and weighs in the neighborhood of a hundred and fifty. They couldn't tell if it was a man or a woman, but Kathryn Williams wrote on a piece of paper that she thought it was a man. In the meantime, all we can do is...damn...I'm beginning to hate this cell phone the captain gave me." The ring was loud and persistent. "It's like I'm tethered to this damn job, day or night."

This time the call was from the town of York. It rests on the upper northwest tip of Green County. Earl Jacquart, head of the two person police department called and told him of an assault on the owner and president of the food manufacturing plant, Ponto's Canning. Jay felt a cold sweat overtake him.

"It's Danielle, she's hurt."

9

The five mile drive to Ponto's Canning was a blur for Jay, but to Rufe it felt like his life was flashing before his eyes. Between the lights flaring, the siren screaming, and tires generally being used two at a time, Rufe closed his eyes and held on.

Jay knew the layout of the plant, but not nearly as well as he knew its owner, Danielle Ponto. He thought of his first encounter with Danielle. It was courtesy of a warning he dealt her for speeding, nearly seventeen years ago. At the time, the slim brunette was a recent graduate of Ohio State. She was taking a breather for the summer before entering the working world. Jay was in his third year as a patrol officer. He had pulled over plenty of curvy girls during those days, but never one that made his heart race like Danielle Ponto. He always tried to stick to the facts when dealing out tickets, but this was different. The hot sun smiled on Jay that day as it ran the temperature up and forced young women like Danielle to wear as little as possible. Her lips shimmered in the bright light and her dark sunglasses hid what he would discover later as beautiful, big brown eyes. Within five minutes he lost his *nothing but the facts* persona and changed a hefty speeding ticket into a warning. The warning came with her phone number and before they parted, he promised to call her as part of a public service. For the next two years Danielle and Jay were inseparable, and he was as happy as he'd ever been.

His public servant career in the sleepy town of Granite had begun to grow. He was invited to attend seminars in cities like Chicago and Los Angeles. He continued his police force education whenever possible and became known as an up-and-comer among his peers. He even thought of accepting a job offer in Chicago, but despite the salary increase, he decided that leaving Danielle would be too difficult. To him, Granite and Danielle became his north star.

Jay and Rufe reached Ponto's Canning in record time. Jay screeched to a halt as sand from the dirt road caused a localized dust storm.

"That's some driving, Jay," Rufe said, just happy to be alive.

A Blue Cross ambulance was parked outside the produce cooling building. Jay and Danielle didn't part ways because of lack of love, sex or money. It was because Danielle needed to find her way in life, or at least that was Jay's impression. Her business degree helped open a few doors and she quickly accepted the one with the best offer. After the initial excitement of a new position and her own paycheck, the day-to-day job left her bored and disappointed, however. She quit that job and agreed to work for her father at his canning business. In her teens she worked for her dad when she needed money. She made a promise to herself that after college her career would take her far from home. One of her biggest shock in life was that she began to like growing with her father's company. Her dad gave her time to learn the business from the bottom. When it came time for him to hand over the reins, she was excited to make her mark. Unfortunately for Jay, she spent less time with him and more time at Ponto's Canning. When they broke apart, it wasn't a screaming eruption, but more like a slow drift. To Jay it became a pride thing and he would not be the next one to call. For Danielle it was a shift of priorities and Jay was no longer number one on the list.

Jay recalled that every morning Danielle toured the entire plant, including the fields, and that the cooling area was near the end of her walk, right before the packaging department. *Does she repeat that tradition after all these years, he thought?*

The plant sold peas, carrots, green beans, and varied fruit all across the country. When Danielle took over, the employee count was at seventy. Now, the company employed two-hundred or more. She had done a good job, so good that Jay thought her size company might make her a target. He phoned her for the first time in years only a week ago to warn her about the crimes against business owners around the county.

10

That morning, a man with coveralls watched Danielle walk between the high shelves, glancing between her clip-board and the huge stock of produce. The man hid behind a crate of green beans. As Danielle approached, the man took three calculated steps toward her and hit her from behind with a billy-short club. He caught her as she fell and, upon seeing her face, gently propped her next to a two-foot high shelf. He paused for a moment and seemed hesitant, moving his head back-and-forth as a dog might when trying to understand something. He duck-taped her hands behind her back, occasionally getting his plastic gloves stuck on the tape, and then laid her down. His stocking hat covered most of his head, but what had shown of his face portrayed a nervous man who wasn't at all happy with what he was doing. He viewed his surroundings and began to tear at plastic wrap that covered some of the boxes. He returned to Danielle and sat her up against the shelf again. Placing the back of her head awkwardly on top of the shelf, he wrapped the plastic around her eyes and tied the ends tight to the steel mesh shelving. He tied another piece of plastic around her mouth. With her head now immobilized and face-up, he reached into his pocket and dripped the contents of a small bottle into both of Danielle's nostrils. As each drop fell, Danielle's face contorted as if she was given smelling salt. He could see she was beginning to come to.

Danielle woke with a large bump on her head that had her retching in pain. Her nostrils burned like nothing she'd ever felt before. She tried to raise her head, but found she couldn't. She attempted to scream, but that didn't work either with the plastic in her mouth. It was difficult to open her eyes, the plastic held them tight. As she strained, the image before her was nothing but a blur. After a minute, there was only silence. A worker on a forklift finally saw her trying to free herself and ran to her.

11

"She promised to be careful. I told her not to make the rounds alone," Jay mumbled to Rufe as they passed a load of workers outside the door. They were clustered about, talking in hushed tones.

Inside, Jay saw the Police Chief that had called him was talking to employees.

The warehouse was stacked with shelves twenty feet high. Boxes of produce were filled to capacity. A man with pitch black hair, and a mustache to match, shouted for somebody to close the door. He seemed more concerned over losing the cool temperature than the problem with the company's owner. Jay recognized him as one of the plant supervisors.

"Jay...over here!" Rufe yelled. They both ran in between shelving in the back of the room. Paramedics were on the floor working on Danielle.

"Danielle, are you okay?" Jay dropped to his knees and held her hand.

"Jay!" She squeezed his hand. "I've been better," Danielle said sounding as if she had a cold. "I guess I should have taken your advice."

"What happened?"

"She took a good hit to the noggin," said the paramedic. "Her head was tied down to this shelf, face up…weird, man. She had a real strong smell of peppermint up inside her nose. She said it hurt like hell, so we flushed her nostrils with water. We're going to need to take her to the hospital and get her checked out. This is pretty strange, man. When I called this one in, they thought I was on something."

Jay reached down and grabbed her hand. "Let's get you to the hospital."

Jay asked Rufe to drive the squad car back while he jumped into the ambulance with Danielle.

12

Marcus Wingate was tied to a large table. He woke confused and with a splitting headache.

At the corner of the table stood a short man in a dark gray sweatshirt.

Wingate quickly realized that, except for the stranger beside him, he was alone in his own building. He could taste blood dripping down from the side of his head. His hands were fastened to the steel table saw in front of him.

The short man's voice echoed in the empty room. "You know, life picks you by some strange and wonderful coincidence. So many humans never reach the momentous stage of birth and beyond. But you...you've been able to achieve much."

"What...why?"

"I know, life can be puzzling, Mr. Wingate. There are so many ways, so very many twists in the road."

The little man stepped closer.

The voice was maddeningly precise and articulate. "Death can be that way as well. It's a rare gift to know how and when your time is up. But you, Mr. Wingate, you have that advantage. You will die within fifteen minutes through severe blood loss. You will lose your hands at the wrist and it will happen right here on your very own table saw. That is the *what*...the *why* is complicated. Frankly, I have neither the time nor the patience to fill you in. However, be assured that your sacrifice is required. Know that tonight is not a senseless act, but a means to a greater end."

Wingate was terrified and struggled mightily to break free. It was useless.

"Nobody comes here this late at night. You have plenty of time. How can I defend my life if I don't know why it is ending?"

"Mr. Wingate, may I propose that you be satisfied with the standard *wrong place at the wrong time* explanation?"

"No!"

"Very well, I'll give you three minutes." He looked at his watch. "Starting now."

"Did I do something to deserve this?"

"I don't know what you may or may not have done in your life, but I do know I am not the one to answer that question. Go on, Mr. Wingate."

"Is there any way that I can convince you that you've made a big mistake? That is, you have the wrong man."

"No, I don't make mistakes. You have ninety seconds."

Wingate began to sweat and his relative calm was turning into complete and helpless panic. "What about money? Would money make you change your mind? I could give you..."

The short man reached for the table switches that would *begin* Mr. Wingate's *end* of life.

"I can tell you this," the little man said. "Had you not fired my son, you would not be in this situation. It's like I've been saying, life turns in so many different angles. I've taken the liberty to adjust the table blade to precisely fifty-five degrees. Five is such a perfect number, don't you think Mr. Wingate?

Wingate hung his head and looked defeated.

"Speaking of the number five, did you know that there are five stages of grief? I believe you hit on all of them. The first four are denial, anger, bargaining, and depression. I think it is time for the final stage."

Wingate looked up. "What's that?"

"Acceptance!"

The grinding of the saw blade began to race toward Mr. Wingate's wrists.

To omit many other analogies, in Architectonicall draughts, which art itself is founded upon fives, as having its subject, and most graceful pieces divided by this number. *Chapter 2 "The Garden of the Cyrus" by Thomas Brown*

13

The Green County Sheriff's Department was as dimly lit inside as the sky was outside. April in the northern Midwest was always a time when a man would reach for sunny spring weather, only to feel dampness and chill. By early May, the longing for mild weather was stronger with every sunrise. From the outside, the Sheriff's building itself had the look of something from an old detective movie. The steps leading into the large doors were rounded and plentiful. The brick complex had windows framed out with vertical bars set in. Though it portrayed itself as an early 1900's building, it was in fact only fifteen years old. The inside was a typical office with cubicles, desks, and computers.

Jay sat and wondered if the sun was ever going to appear. Above him was a poster of an officer watching a drunk fall out of his vehicle. The caption said, "Just how big were those two beers?" He wheeled his chair around and stared at the big white board in front of him. It was filled with questions that had no answers.

Two familiar voices broke him out of his thoughts. He looked out of his office window.

Coming toward him were Danielle, Rufe, and a medium built woman with short, curly blond hair. Jay pegged her age to be mid-to-late forties. The two women wore jeans and button-down shirts. Danielle's was bright blue, the blonde's orange. Jay wondered how long it had been since he had two fine-looking women coming to visit him at work…maybe never.

"You have your own room, furniture and everything," Danielle said. Her smile was a bit smug, he thought. Her nose was covered in a temporary bandage, but that didn't obscure her obvious beauty.

Jay grunted. "Yes, well, apparently the captain decided it would be better to keep me alone and caged."

Danielle glanced at Rufe. "Do you let him out or just throw food in and quickly close the door?"

Rufe shrugged. "We just try to ignore him."

Jay missed her abuse. "As I recall it wasn't the insults that made me break up with you; I think it may have been your inability to realize how good you had it."

"You broke up with me?"

Jay figured changing the subject might be the best direction. "Danielle, where are my manners. Please sit. They let you out of the hospital. How's your…ah…?" he pointing to his nose.

Danielle took a pile of paper off of the chair and sat down. "Doctors say I got lucky. I probably will get most of my sense of smell back. They said a little stronger concentration of that oil of peppermint and it could have been…well…bad."

"I'm sorry that this happened, Danielle. But, I'm glad you're going to be okay."

There was a pile of paper hiding his view and he needed to move it a bit. "Excuse the mess, I've been meaning to clean up. Time gets away from me sometimes." Jay's desk had very little free space.

"Rufe happened to be in the lobby as I was leaving the hospital. He asked if I would mind stopping at the department before I went home. I take it his motivation to bring me here was not entirely his own."

Rufe spoke up in his own defense. "I actually stopped to ask her a few questions." He glanced at Danielle and grinned. "Then I…we thought it might not be a bad idea to stop in and check out some suspect photos."

"I'm glad you decided to stop in, Danielle. I have to admit I did want to talk to you. Who's your friend?"

"Sara. She does our Human Resource work at the plant. She came to visit me at the hospital and was about to take me out for lunch when Rufe stopped by. Besides, this isn't going to take long, is it? I told both of you I didn't actually see who attacked me."

"Hey, isn't that the magic square?" She was looking at Jay's big white board filled with black dry erase marks.

Jay looked puzzled. "I'm not sure what you mean, Sara."

"A magic square!"

Jay had marked up the nearly square image of Green County. The county was arranged by nine somewhat evenly-divided sections. Jay had written the names of the four business owners who had recently been attacked on the squared image. Each victim was from a different section and Jay had them numbered one through four.

"A what?" Jay asked again.

"Can I draw something?" Sara asked.

Jay nodded.

Sara walked over to the white board and drew a separate 3x3 grid alongside the Green County square. "Remember, Danielle, it's like you showed me one time. It's the simplest of magic squares. It uses integers one through nine. Look, the top row is 4-9-2, second 3-5-7, and third 8-1-

6." She wrote the numbers on the grid. "In all directions, the sum is fifteen. Based on your first four numbers…that is victims, it seems to make perfect sense."

The smallish blond filled in Jays remaining county squares, five through nine.

Jay watched and wondered what this 'Sara' was doing marking up his white board. He also found it interesting that she had a Boston accent.

"See, the first square matches where the first attack happened on your county map. The number two square matches where the second attack occurred, and so on."

Jay looked at her grid and then at his rendition of Green County. "It does seem to fit. The first victim, Bernie Tennison was on the bottom center section of the county. The second attack happened at Peggy Lloyd's company, located at the north-east corner."

He checked the third victim, Kathy Williams, and of course, Danielle. It all fit.

"Well Sara, you may have hit on a possibility. At least it may be something to keep in mind."

Danielle and Rufe glanced at Sara as if she'd stolen their candy.

Sara backpedaled. "Oh, I…it doesn't matter. I, ah…like numbers. I guess numbers just stick in my head. When I see a group of numbers I like to unscramble them into some sort of pattern. It doesn't mean I'm right."

Jay leaned forward. "So by your logic, the next area would be…."

Danielle broke in. "The next victim may be in the center of the county, number five." She pointed.

"That's the town of Hortle, or near it," Jay said. "The only business I know of in Hortle is that door manufacturer. What's the name…Wingate…Wingate Doors? I heard they were having problems keeping the company going."

"I'm pretty sure they're okay. I saw Marcus Wingate at the Chamber meeting last month and he said things were picking up," Danielle said.

Rufe walked around the room with his hand to his chin. He appeared nervous. "Still, it doesn't really fit. The others employ at least two hundred people. I don't think he has any more than thirty."

"The sense of touch," Jay mumbled.

"What, Jay?" Danielle asked.

"The sense of touch. That's all that's left."

Danielle turned away. Jay's answer triggered something unpleasant in her memory, something she wanted to leave alone.

Jay saw her reaction. "It's nothing, Danielle. It's just a theory. This nutcase hasn't killed anybody yet and we need to make sure we catch him, soon."

"Before he does," Sara said.

Danielle's head jerked up and she gave Sara a curious look. "You know what? Maybe I'm just a little tired. You know how those nurses can be...waking you up in the middle of the night to see if you're getting enough rest." She trailed off, still looking in Sara's direction.

Jay followed Danielle's eyes. His suspicions were now locked and loaded. He stood up from his desk.

"Rufe, give Danielle a ride home. She can check out those suspect photos later."

He turned to Danielle. "I've got an officer stationed outside your home."

Danielle looked drained. She was tired from the day...tired of the secrets. "Do you think I need to be concerned, Jay? I really don't think this person is interested in finishing what he started. Besides, Sara and I were just going for lunch. Are you holding me hostage?"

"Danielle, it's necessary. First of all, we don't know who we're dealing with yet. Second, even if we did, we don't need to take any chances."

Danielle looked at the magic square on the board once again. "When were the other victims attacked?"

"Within the week."

"No, I mean, what were the dates?"

Jay opened the file on his desk. "Four consecutive days...May 1st, 2nd, 3rd, and 4th. Today is May 5th."

"Today's attack may be something special." Danielle said.

Jay watched her expression turn from fatigue to genuine fear.

"Jay, I think you need to call Marcus Wingate right now and warn him."

"Do you know something you're not telling me?"

"I know numbers. I trust numbers and they all point to Marcus Wingate."

Jay looked at the dates again. "Is his plant open on Saturdays?" He asked not really expecting an answer. "You're right, if this guy is as anal as he appears, he'll finish what he started."

Danielle held out the phone. "Call him, Jay."

As Jay dialed up Wingate Doors, Rufe asked Danielle to follow him to his desk. He spread pictures of suspects out in front of Danielle. "It might not hurt to look. You may not have seen him the other day when you were attacked, but maybe one of them will trigger something. These people have had a connection with some or all of the companies whose owners were attacked. A past employee, those who recently worked for them, some who were caught breaking into their warehouses...you name it."

Danielle looked up at Rufe incredulously and threw the mug shots down.

"Are you kidding me? Get those away from me."

Rufe picked up one of the pictures and put it in front of Danielle. It was one of a scruffy-looking Hispanic man. "What do you know about this one?"

She pushed it away. Just barely over a whisper she said, "Is this really necessary?" She glanced at Jay, who was still on the phone. "I told you, I didn't see who it was. But, you know as well as I that I don't need a picture to figure it out."

"This guy has a record so long I had to minimize it to fit on one sheet. He was fired from your place once your people found out he lied on his application. Same thing happened with some of the other companies, both in and out of Green County. You'd think he'd figure it out and move out of state, but not this bird. It's like he's tethered to our little piece of heaven here and won't be happy until we throw him back in jail. Jay figures this guy isn't smart enough to pull off what our perp did, but I...I don't know." Rufe pushed the picture of the Hispanic man in front Danielle, again.

"No, ah...I'm not sure." She started to get that uneasy feeling again, as if she lost something valuable and didn't want anybody to find out. She pushed her chair back and stood.

"Rufe, excuse me...I need to ask Jay something."

Rufe lowered his head and shook it slowly.

Danielle walked over to Jay's office. She closed the door and pulled the shade. Jay had just hung up his phone.

"He...he's an accountant."

"Who?"

"The man who attacked me, he's an accountant." She sat on an old cushioned chair in the far corner of the room. It reminded her of something in a black and white gumshoe flick from the 30's. She needed to talk to Jay, but for the moment felt more comfortable being across the room from him.

"I thought you didn't see him?"

"When things get busy, we hire account temps to pick up the slack. If they're good, we call them back. Ted Paulson is the one that we would ask for. He's kind of a quiet, little guy, but smart as a whip." Danielle said the last few words in a slow, concentrated whisper. It was as if she could smell something that triggered a distant memory.

"You're sure it was him?"

"I didn't lie, I didn't see him. But, I'm pretty sure it was Ted."

"You want me to check on this Ted?"

She looked out the door window at Rufe and then nodded.

"Okay then...anything else?"

"It might be best to keep this Ted Paulson thing to yourself."

"Do you mind elaborating? Danielle, I do this for a living. You're not telling me everything you know."

"Yes, I mind. What about Wingate?"

"No answer at the Wingate home and all I get at the plant is a recording. I think I'll take a ride."

"Why don't we go together? His business is on the way to my place. Besides, maybe I can help. I think I've earned it," Danielle said, pointing at her nose.

Jay was about to dismiss the request and send Rufe out with her, but she had a point. That was the problem with her, she always had a point. Even, when they had been an item, he could never say no to her, and now it seemed like he still couldn't. Those big, dark eyes made most men forget what they were saying or doing. It wasn't like Jay to go against his better judgment. Jay watched her get up to get her coat and wondered why he didn't try harder when they were together.

Danielle opened the office door and looked back at Jay. "What's it going to be?"

Jay thought about her request. *There really is nothing to stop her from going on her own, unless I put her under house arrest. She wouldn't be a happy camper if I cut off her wings. When in doubt, compromise.*

"You'll stay in the back of the squad and lock the doors. That's the best I can do. If you see anything suspicious, honk the horn."

Danielle gave her friend Sara a hug. "Can you drive yourself home, Sara?"

Sara whispered, "Are you sure you want to do this?"

"I'll call you later."

Rufe, looking incredulous, voiced his opinion. "Jay, you're not seriously thinking about bringing Danielle to Wingate's place, are you? Don't you think…?"

"No, apparently I don't think."

Rufe watched Danielle at the door. He gathered up his mug shots and shoved them into his desk drawer. He wanted to say more. He wanted to change the path they were following, but fell into place like he always did. His eyes seemed to say something that was not being repeated through his mouth.

Jay got his car keys and whispered to Danielle, "We'll get on this Ted Paulson right away, Danielle…as soon as I get back from Wingate's."

Danielle whispered back, pressing her lips to his ear. "Let's not make a big thing out of it. Nobody else needs to know about it."

Jay had a lot of questions rolling around in his head but understood that Danielle had her own way of dealing with things. Besides, he knew her personality and if she was hiding something, she damn well had a good reason.

14

It was after closing when Jay, Rufe, and Danielle arrived at the entrance of Wingate Doors. The office building was detached from the wood plant. Only Jay was tall enough to see through the transom of the door. He could see a man cleaning the lobby floors as they arrived.

Jay tapped on the window, but the janitor didn't notice. Finally, after Jay pounded on the door did the man look up from his duties. He dropped his mop and looked out a corner window. When he saw the squad car in front he ran to the door.

"Lieutenant Jay Barthus," Jay said, making sure the janitor saw his badge. "I'm looking for Marcus Wingate."

"Sorry sir, he's not in his office," the young man said nervously. Jay could see he was dealing with a slow but enthusiastic kid. "I was just in there. His briefcase and coat are gone. I think he left for home." He paused to think a while. "Some nights, he walks through the wood plant before he goes home. If his car is still parked out back, that'll probably be where he is."

"Thanks…ah…Robert," Jay said, pointing at the red cursive name embroidered on his overalls. "Do you have the plant keys?"

"Do you think you can show us the wood plant, Robert?"

"Sure can, Sir!"

"Do you think you can call me, Jay"

"You bet I can, Sir…Jay."

They walked quickly to the plant. Danielle watched from the car. The sun began to drop out of sight.

As they approached the factory door, Robert could hear one of the plant's table saws buzzing. "That's odd. Nobody's supposed to be working the tables tonight."

Robert looked toward the back parking lot and pointed. "Mr. Wingate's car is in the back. It's the white Buick."

Robert turned the door knob to the wood plant and was slightly surprised that it was unlocked. Jay, Rufe, and Robert walked past the wood plant supervisor's small office.

Jay poked his head in the room and could see a messy desk with paper and three-ring binders covering the top. From there it was up a few steps and through to the entrance of the main floor. The winding sound of the table saw seemed to increase with every step.

"You'd better show us to the saw room Robert," Jay said urgently. He was sweating a little.

Behind Jay, Rufe kept notes on a small pad, using any bit of lighting he could find. With each step the smell of freshly cut wood became stronger. As they walked through the glue press area, Rufe felt a tug from behind. Between the dim lighting and that constant buzz of the saw, Rufe's heart skipped a beat. He looked behind and saw Danielle.

"You scared the shit out of me. What the hell are you doing here?"

"Sorry about that, Rufe. I honked my horn but nobody came." Her eyes were casing the place as if everything needed to memorize for a test. "So what's going on?"

"You're going back in the car, that's what! You better just turn around before Jay see's you."

"I thought I better come and tell you that a car drove off behind the plant. I heard it, but I couldn't see it very well. It's getting pretty dark."

Jay glanced back. When he saw Danielle, he shook his head. He didn't have time to deal with her. The sound of the table saw drew all his attention. They passed a conveyer that held jagged rectangular wood pieces. Beyond that was a wood press and further yet a large blower.

"The tables are just around the corner, Jay," Robert said.

The room was large and held four table saws. Each table was big enough to hold and cut most any size door. A string dangled from a light just above each table. Only one light was glowing. Despite the huge overhead intake fans, the smell of sawdust and burned wood lingered from the day shift. The third table saw from the entrance was running and its operator did not look capable of stopping the blade from spinning. While Robert and Danielle turned away, Jay and Rufe approached the table.

"How do you turn this thing off?" Jay shouted to Robert over the blade's constant buzz.

Robert turned back to the table, trying hard not to look at the bloody mass in front of it. He was more than the nightly cleanup crew. He did occasional maintenance, and he knew enough about the machinery to get by.

Robert sounded like he was about to vomit. "There are two switches for these tables. It takes two people to turn it on, but either switch can turn it off," Robert said. He reached under the table, just above the knee of the body of his dead boss, and stopped the saw.

In the silence the room became a concentrated nightmare. The body sat, bent over, its arms held in place by a guard-rail that was meant to clamp down on pre-finished doors. Its hands were severed at the wrist. Jay was mesmerized by massive amount of blood that spilled...everywhere. The dead man's head was down, about an inch from the tabletop. Jay moved it, slightly, to see the face. A couple streaks of blood were dried to his cheek as if his head was hit hard with an object. His skin was almost gray and the expression was one that Jay would remember for the rest of his life. His eyes were wide open with a stare of death's surprise.

"Robert, is this Marcus Wingate?" Jay asked.

Robert was visibly shaken to the core, but managed to answer. "Yes...that's Mr. Wingate. What...who would do this?"

"Robert, go back to the office building. I'm calling for backup. There'll be some officers here in a little while. Why don't you help them out and put some lights on outside and a few in here?

The young man turned to walk away, but glanced back as if to verify that what he saw was true.

"Oh, Robert...it would be best if you didn't mention what you saw here to anyone outside of the Sheriff's Department just yet...okay?" It was more like an order than a request.

Robert nodded and disappeared around the corner.

Jay called the Hortle Police Department, Captain Laura Juul of their own Green County Sheriff's Department, and the Wisconsin State Patrol. He would leave it up to Captain Juul to decide if she would want to inform the FBI.

Rufe, meanwhile, phoned for an ambulance and an investigation team.

Danielle moved back and watched from a dark corner as Jay and Rufe began to examine the room. Her mind was filled with emotion and unanswered questions. She was afraid, angry, and confused, but guilt became the strongest agitation to dismiss. *I should have done something sooner. Why did I wait so long?*

Robert switched the overhead florescent lighting exposing the reality that was in front of them.

For a moment, Jay had forgotten that Danielle was with them. Now he saw her staring at Marcus Wingate's grotesque body as if it was an unfinished puzzle. Jay walked to her and put his large hands over hers.

He turned to his partner. "Take her out of here, Rufe. Make sure someone is stationed at her place." Jay lowered his head. "Then go to Marcus' home. Someone needs to tell his wife."

"Will do, Jay." Rufe didn't say anything about the car Danielle had heard leaving the back lot.

An officer arrived to escort Danielle out of the building just as the ambulance arrived. Jay followed as Danielle was walked out. She turned and said, "You were right you know. His sense of touch was removed."

Jay nodded his head and walked with her to the squad car. "Mind if I stop by tonight? I just want to make sure everything's secure."

"I know you still have to pursue the guy, but tonight he attacked the fifth and last of the senses. Do you think he's finished?"

"That's a nice thought, Danielle, but first things first. We need to catch whoever is doing this. We need to catch him and put a stop to this madness."

"Remember what I told you about Ted Paulson."

"Do you think this Ted is capable of murder?"

"I don't know, but I think he's worth checking."

A van with *Channel 5 News* written on the side pulled in alongside Jay. Danielle climbed inside the squad car. Jay closed the door and rested his arms on the window ledge.

"The media's been reasonably kind, but I think that's going to change real soon."

"See you later, Jay. Remember to smile. Nobody likes a grumpy cop on the ten-o-clock news," Danielle said as the officer drove down the dark driveway.

This type of newsworthy story was an unusual occurrence in a small Midwest town. Milwaukee and Chicago had their share of terror, but not here in Green County. The heartland didn't produce the Ed Geins and the Jeffrey Dahmers very often. Up until now, the media hadn't really put together what was happening, nor had they gotten any confirmation from the various departments. Lieutenant Jay Barthus understood that, dealing with a murder, the circus was about to begin and he would be forced to go down a road he'd never traveled before.

A tall, thin, red-haired newsman and stumpy cameraman exited the van. They rapidly placed a tripod holding a bright light just outside the office building. Jay walked toward them. He didn't know how they'd gotten wind of what was going on or how much they knew, but boundaries had to be set, and he was going to set them.

"This is as far as it goes, boys," he said to the skinny one. "You can ask questions, but don't expect much. Five minutes, and then you pack up and leave. We're blocking the driveway coming into Wingate's as soon as you're gone. Understood?"

The newsmen scanned the area, and noted the ambulance and squad cars slowing to a stop at the wood plant. The news crew of two had been driving back to the newsroom after doing a story about a Town of Sylvester farmer with a chicken that had three legs. They'd seen a couple of squad cars with their lights on and decided the action couldn't be any more lame then the chicken story. Neither one of them had the faintest idea what was going on here but it looked promising.

"No problem, officer. Can we start by having your name?"

Jay looked at the owner of the deep voice and found it hard to believe it was coming from the freckled young man who looked like he may have just passed his tempts. He held out his hand. "Lieutenant Jay Barthus."

"I'm Pete Chandler. Can you tell us what you know so far, Officer?" The freshman reporter had no idea if he was on to something or not.

"A body was found in the factory at approximately 7:45 tonight."

Pete looked at his cameraman. His startled glance did not go unnoticed by Jay.

"You followed a squad and took a shot, didn't you?" Jay asked. "Damn it."

"My boss told me to try it once in a while. As long as I'm here, how about giving me the name that goes with that body?""That's all we have for now, Pete." Jay was mad at himself for spilling. "You're going to need to pack up now boys. I can't stop you from using the little bit you have, but can you hold off until 10 o'clock? Don't do any of those *breaking news* bits, okay?"

"I can't promise you, but I'll do what I can."

Jay figured that meant *kiss my ass.*

15

Officer Roger Engels drove Danielle straight home, then did a sweep of her home's interior. "I'll be right outside if you need anything."

"Are you sure you wouldn't prefer to stay inside?" Danielle asked.

Ignoring the question, Officer Engels said, "Everything looks fine inside. I've got to make sure it stays that way." He locked and closed the door behind him.

Danielle had a good idea what 'the magic square' at the station meant. Whenever she thought of Ted Paulson, her stomach twisted. It reminded her of when she'd broken her leg skiing at the age of 17. The doctor who'd pinned her back together seemed nice enough, but possessed a quirky, strange sense of humor. He became very attentive to her needs while in the hospital and even insisted he'd wheel her to the waiting car upon her release. Weeks later, she began to get obscene and almost violent phone messages. Her service didn't have caller ID at that time. But she'd known something didn't feel right. The voice sounded muffled, but calculated. The police suggested she lay the phone down and let the unknown pervert talk to himself until he was blue in the face. Soon the calls stopped, *probably out of frustration from the caller's inability to get a reaction*, she thought. Though the voice was disguised, Danielle felt she noticed certain nuances. She would bet the farm that the foul-mouthed pervert was the very doctor that inserted hardware into her lower right leg. She told her mother about her thoughts on the doctor, but without any real proof the matter dropped.

Many years later, that same feeling came over her. It wasn't the doctor this time, but the familiar voice of the accountant, Theodore Paulson. She had heard that voice many times at the office. Then, one day she received a call concerning an invitation.

"We are a secret society, a society of old heritage and traditions, as well as new thoughts and ideas," the voice explained. We concern ourselves with a certain lifestyle…a lifestyle that we think might be to your liking. We study the Pythagoras teachings, logical history, symbolism, and religion. We, as our own entity, find that the number *five* is our center. It is built into our lives in every aspect and every path we take."

At that time, Danielle became intrigued.

The voice on the phone continued. "We are aware of your interest in numerology. Our society explores the relationship between numbers and living things. Our society is called, *The Five*."

Danielle thought it a bit intrusive that they had dug into her past and discovered her fascination with numerology. The study of numbers was a major part of her studies in college. That, however, didn't sway her need to accept their invitation.

They eventually met in a dark tavern. Danielle expected the person in the corner would be the accountant. That was not the case. A much younger man waited for her. However, the voice did sound vaguely familiar.

She recalled the meeting as being very enlightening. Danielle wondered why this secret group wanted her. The young version of Ted Paulson was much more animated and excited about having her join and learn about *The Five* in comparison to the voice on the phone. "I'm going to need more time, and perhaps, a little more information before making such a decision," she told him.

The young man seemed to take offense to her delay. He left the bar saying, "We'll be in touch."

A week later, Danielle received another call from the secret society. She accepted the invitation to join *The Five*. From that point on, her life would never be the same. She was wrong about Ted Paulson, however. He soon became a good friend and someone who coached her in many of the teachings of the society.

16

Jay left the Wingate murder scene around midnight. He arrived at the home of his ex-girlfriend a half-hour later.

Danielle heard the mumble of a short conversation outside her front door. She looked out her living room window. Clearly, Jay was in the process of sending Officer Engels home.

She opened the door. "Jay, you look beat. Why don't you call the officer back and get some sleep. I'll be fine."

Jay felt protective, responsible, a little overwhelmed, perhaps overmatched, and yes…tired. But, truth be told, if given a choice between his moderate two-story in Granite or spending the night on watch with Danielle, he'd choose Danielle every time.

"Taken a shine to Roger, have you?"

"He's young enough to be my…younger brother. Besides, he chose his car over me, and just sat in front of the house," she said walking toward the kitchen. "Tell you what, come on in and sit down. I'll fix us a little snack and we can catch up. Maybe you can tell me how you were able to survive all these years without me."

"Roger was just following on-duty protocol. I, on the other hand, am off-duty and can follow my own instincts," he said, giving her a sidelong glance.

"Still got that charm thing going for you, huh? What's it been Jay, about fourteen, maybe fifteen years?"

"You know, Danielle, you look good for someone within an arm's length of forty."

"Well, clearly you still know how to throw those seductive words at the ladies."

"Some things you just don't lose."

"You look good on television. Ever think about a career in front of the camera?"

"Let me guess, that little prick from Channel 5 broadcasted his hot story on the news faster than a greyhound in the park."

"It's been on all night. I wouldn't worry about it. You didn't come off as too much of an ass." Danielle looked pleased with herself.

As she worked her magic with toasted cheese sandwiches, Jay watched her every move. When they'd dated, she wouldn't have been seen without her full complement of makeup, dress, and rock-solid hairdo. Tonight, her casual appearance, and that bandage on her nose amused him. The uptight girl he once knew now seemed comfortable with herself. She sported tangled hair, yoga sweatpants, and a freshly washed face without any hint of makeup. Despite her new dress-down style, Jay couldn't help but see the stunningly beautiful, smart, and, at times, brash woman he remembered. For the moment, fifteen years, give or take, disappeared. If she'd gained any weight it was in the right places, as far as he was concerned. The Danielle in front of him on this night wasn't the nervous, quick-tempered ball of fire from years past. Despite her recent attack and the horrendous scene at Wingate Doors, she seemed confident and calm—almost strangely calm.

"I thought of calling...often...just to see how you were doing. But, as time went on, I just felt, you know, people move on," Danielle said, cutting her grilled cheese in half.

"I know what you mean."

Jay had noticed during his investigation at her canning plant that she wasn't wearing a wedding ring. He glanced at her hand again, just in case. "So, how have you been able to stop the men of Green County from dragging you to the altar?"

"I've had a couple of close calls, but you know how I hate to settle."

"Ouch, that one stung a bit. Just give me a minute and I'll come back with a zinger."

"Since you brought up the subject, how have you fared with the ladies?"

"No close calls to speak of. For a while I was leading the league in hits and RBI's. Eventually, I took myself out of the lineup."

"Why?" Danielle asked, handing him a plate. She sat at her dining table.

"I figured...ahh...never mind."

Changing the subject quickly, he asked, "Did Roger do a check inside your home before he left?"

"Yes, he did. Ummm...Jay, I have something on my mind and I need to tell you about it."

"Don't you think you're moving a bit fast?"

"Mind out of the gutter. This is serious."

"Sorry."

"It may be nothing, but that accountant...you know...the one I told you about."

"Go on."

"There's something about Ted Paulson that's not right. Toward the end, just before I decided to stop using his services, I would catch him staring at me. He would turn his head when I looked up, but I knew it just the same. He was always brilliant when it came to numbers. Years earlier, before his son died, we talked a lot about numerology, and how certain natural occurrences through history can be tied to a process of numbers. That magic square on your whiteboard would mean a great deal to a guy like Ted Paulson. After his son was gone, his whole demeanor seemed to change, and after a while, I got kind of freaked out. I told the temp agency never to send him again."

"Besides the fact that he's creepy, and knows numbers, what makes you think he needs to be looked at?"

Danielle had no intention to go deeper into this than she already had. "Isn't a hunch good enough? Who else do you have on your list to check out?"

"I can't get a search warrant on a hunch. What about his son? What happened with him?"

"I don't know...Ted never talked about it. I heard Wayne killed himself."

After finishing their snack and cleaning the dishes, they talked until finally giving way to a yawning contest.

Danielle got up and retrieved some blankets and a pillow from a closet. "Tell you what, you can sleep on the couch. You can protect me from all the bad guys of Green County from there."

"You'll let me know if they climb the outside wall and come into your bedroom, won't you?"

"I can take the first couple, but any more than that...I'll call out."

17

As he slept on the made up couch, Jay had a vivid dream. It wasn't a nightmare where the cop struggles with the criminal, but it made him sweat just the same. He dreamt of Danielle. He felt her closeness as she stood silently between the kitchen and his makeshift bedroom. Jay watched her naked body ascend the stairs. In his dream, he followed her to the bedroom. Just as they were about to make love, the wind blew through the window, and with it came leaves. Hundreds of them flew into the room, covering the floor, the bed, and finally Danielle. Jay reached out to find her under layers of colorless foliage. When he woke, he found himself on all fours next to the couch. He stood up and noticed that the disappointing end to the dream hadn't affected the result that came with the sexual vision, as his boxer shorts pointed outward proudly. He sat down and chuckled to himself. He looked toward the stairs and for a brief moment wondered how Danielle would react if he were to knock on her bedroom door. He pulled the covers over himself and sighed before once again falling asleep.

Jay didn't know whether it was the morning sunshine that beamed through the thin bay window curtains or the smell of fresh brewed coffee that brought him to his feet. The machine in the kitchen was percolating, but its owner was nowhere to be seen. He walked to the stairs and could hear the faint sound of running water. *I'm sure she's fine, but I wouldn't be doing my job if I didn't at least check it out,* Jay thought, smiling to himself.

Jay ran the stairs, two at a time. As he strolled through her bedroom, he noticed the bathroom door was open a couple of inches. He pushed the door open and was about to say, "Good morning" when he noticed her wrist and hand resting on the tub rim. Her hand wasn't moving. "Danielle," he shouted as he madly pushed open the shower curtain.

Danielle screamed, thoroughly startled out of the trance brought on by the comforting hot bath. It was complete with lilac bath crystals that she laid out only moments ago, while completely relaxed in her own world of music. She threw her headphones off. "Jay, what's wrong? What happened?"

Jay sat on the toilet seat. He could feel his heart pumping loudly. "I saw your hand and...I don't know...I thought you were...damn, you have a piercing scream." He took a deep breath.

Danielle began to laugh.

"What do you find so darned humorous?"

"I was just picturing Rufus finding our lifeless bodies, dead of heart attacks. My naked body in the tub, and you sprawled out on the bathroom floor with your boxers. That would have added a pretty weird twist to the case you're working on, don't you think?"

Jay thought about what Danielle said and laughed as well. Turning toward her, he could see her slouched in the sudsy bath water. His eyes were drawn to her breast. He tried to look away, but couldn't.

"I believe your job is to protect, not explore," Danielle said, covering her top with a washcloth.

Jay snapped out of it and walked toward the door. "I was just canvassing the area…looks fine, very fine." As he left the room, he got a call on his cell. "Danielle, I've got to go. There'll be squads going by or stopping frequently today. We've already got somebody watching your accountant's place. Are you going to be all right?"

"Don't worry about me. Just be careful. You're not dealing with your average guy here."

"I think I know what I'm doing." Jay looked back and gave Danielle an exaggerated wink. "I saved you from a deadly bubble bath, didn't I?"

"Yes, you are my hero." she said in a monotone voice. "See you tonight?"

"I think you can count on it."

Rufus was waiting for Jay in his squad car. "I checked on Ted Paulson's son, like you asked."

"What did you find?"

Rufus opened his notebook. "His name was Wayne. He was a quiet guy. After high school, he got an associate's degree in computer science and, get this, he used to work for Marcus Wingate."

"Wow, Wingate Doors. What happened there?"

"Nothing much. He and another guy were considered the entire IT department. The lady I talked to in personnel this morning said he was employed with them for about four years. He didn't get paid much, but he seemed to like the people and the job. When sales fell, he got caught up in the lay-offs. The H. R. folks told him that he should go for his bachelor's degree and maybe they'd hire him back when things got better."

"How did he die?"

"Suicide. He was found hanging in his closet."

"Wow! How old?"

"It says here…twenty-five."

"Never married?"

"Nope."

Jay scratched his head. "Check out the other companies whose owners were victimized and see if Wayne Paulson attempted to get employment there. If so, this could be the motive we've been looking for."

It didn't take long for Rufe to dig up the information that Jay expected. "The other four companies checked out. They all had résumés from Wayne Paulsen in their files, but none of them had hired him.

It wasn't much, but it was enough to get a judge to sign a search warrant on the Theodore Paulsen residence at 309 South Maple Street, in the town of Sylvester.

Jay and Rufe pulled into the driveway and rang the doorbell. There was no answer, and the door was locked. The only information they had on Theodore was that he was now working on his own. As an accountant, he could be working from home or temporarily at a business owner's office. The house had two steep gables, the type that would make any roofer want to quit his job. The 1950's vintage home had a small single-car attached garage. The handle on the outside of the garage door indicated that it was not updated with an automatic garage door opener. Jay tried the handle and was able to pull the door up. Sunlight now shone through, and Rufe found a door to the left of the garage that led to the house. Once they'd moved past the basement door, they entered a hallway between the kitchen and the meager living room. The accountant's home included an office and a bathroom on the first floor. Upstairs there were two small bedrooms with slanted ceilings. Jay could see the home was tidy, as if everything had been placed in a precisely designated area.

Rufe ascended the stairs and searched the larger bedroom of the two. "It smells like old people," he said to himself. The light through the window was enough to see everything he needed to see. He noticed a small stack of books on a nightstand. Rufe noticed that nearly all of them were concerned with numerology. Though Rufe knew the old man lived here alone, he noticed the bed was made up and two pillows rested near the headboard. In the shadow between the pillows, he saw something that didn't quite fit. He reached over to see what it was. Rufe jumped about a foot in the air and nearly pissed his pants as a cat yowled and careened out from under the covers.

Jay ran up to the room from the kitchen and saw the feline running down the stairs opposite him. He grinned at Rufe.

"Shut up." Rufe said.

Jay went to the far bedroom and found it locked. With a bump of his shoulder, the hollow wooden door opened easily with only slight damage. Jay immediately took in the smell of dirty socks, mixed with a rank odor that triggered a bad memory. In his early policing career, he'd spent a summer partnering in Chicago. The two patrol officers got a call asking that they go to a wooded area behind an old city high school. It was up to Jay and his partner to check out a report. Later, it was confirmed that the body had been there for a couple of months before the snow had melted. The memory of certain scents never leaves a person. That repulsive odor was there in the room, though faintly.

Jay walked across the room and pulled on the blind strings to fill the room with sunlight. The bedroom definitely had the feel of a place that hadn't been touched since the death of its former occupant, Wayne Paulson. Underwear and the like were thrown about and on top of the unkempt bed. A small desk held a computer monitor, an array of papers and post-it notes. Jay didn't see a computer base anywhere in the room. He turned to the closet, and found the odor to be at its strongest there. It was empty on one side, but filled with clothes and shoes on the other. Jay had looked over the case report earlier and agreed with the suicide ruling, based on the information given. Wayne Paulson had been found hanging inside his closet. To Jay, it smelled as if Wayne was buried in it.

"Rufe, get in here and take some pictures."

Back downstairs, the accountant's office was just that— an accountant's office. Inside were a computer desk, bookshelves with accounting material, and a small television on top of a metal filing cabinet. Jay turned away and glanced at the papers strewn about Ted's desk. Some of the notepapers repeated the same sentence: *That all brothers of the order should observe strict loyalty and secrecy.* Jay kept one of the notes and made a mental post-it to confiscate the computer before they left.

From there, Jay and Rufe descended to the basement. Jay flipped the light switch, revealing two doors at the bottom of the stairs. On the wall to the left were hooks holding several coats and jackets. Jay opened the door to the right. He flipped a switch on the wall and saw a dull room full of paint pails, a washer and dryer, a multitude of boxes, and an unkempt workbench. Jay motioned for Rufe to take more pictures.

Upon entering the other room they both stood and took in the sight before them.

Jay said, "Some people collect stamps, others mount fish or deer antlers on their walls. It looks like Ted Paulson made a shrine to *the* number *five.*"

There were pentagrams, quincunx patterns, painted roses with five petals, and the five-circle Olympic emblem. As they looked further, countless other symbols and quotes became visible. Homage to the number five stretched from the ceiling to the covered walls.

Jay walked forward. As he stepped, he realized his shoes made a strange clinking noise. They looked down to see the white carpeting covered with nickels. Jay flipped another wall-switch and the back of the room lit up. On the wall to his right was a life-size painting of a rich-looking Roman from many centuries ago. On the bottom, it said, "Pontius." Jay looked at Rufe and scratched his head.

Rufe snapped more pictures.

In the back, Jay's attention turned to a large wooden door with thick metal strips. It did not have a handle, but a lever that needed to be pulled up in order to unlock it. Jay unlatched it and pulled hard. The door opened and a light went on automatically, illuminating a pentagonal room. Jay's eyes focused on another white carpet that had five circles in the middle, each bigger than the next. The center ring was yellow, followed by green, blue, red, and gold. Written on the yellow center, the word *earth* seemed to reach out like a hologram. Each circle was labeled with a symbolic meaning. The green circle read "water," the blue "air," the red "fire," and the gold "psyche." The ceiling held nine squares, and Jay recognized immediately that it was the magic square that Danielle schooled him on at the Sheriff's Department. Above the magic square were the words "Ruler of the Soul."

"Keep taking pictures, Rufe. I don't know what it all means, but anything this weird has to mean something." Jay's voice sounded as if a small echo followed each word in this strange and oversized basement. The room was damp and Jay noticed that the dehumidifier in the corner was unplugged. "I think we have enough here to at least pick this guy up and ask him a few questions."

On the far wall, a thick glass case stood on top of a small wooden shelf. Inside the case, a golden key rested on a small pedestal.

"Rufe, is that a...whaddaya call it...pentasomething...at the base of that key?"

Rufe peered in close to the glass and squinted. He had been having some problems seeing up close lately, but was too stubborn to have it checked out. *I'm too young for this, he thought. It's downright embarrassing.*

"It's called a bow, not a base, and it's in the shape of a pentagram...another symbol featuring the number five. The key blade looks like the rotary type first used by the Romans."

Jay always wondered where Rufe came up with this stuff, but he didn't bother to double check his partner's facts anymore. Rufe always seemed to be right when it came to odd tidbits.

"There's a keyhole here in the wall," Jay said, while Rufe started to look for a way to get at the key.

"Short of blowing it up, I'm not seeing a way to open this thing."

Jay put his hand to his jaw and started to think about possibilities.

Just then, Jay's cell rang out.

Rufe could hear a familiar but muffled voice. The officer said, "She's leaving, should we follow?"

"You mean Danielle?"

"Yeah."

"Sure, but don't make it obvious...and keep me informed. Hey...and pick up that accountant guy, Theodore Paulson."

"On what charge?"

"I just want to ask him a few questions," Jay said.

18

Theodore Paulson fit the mold of a quiet, reserved accountant. His wife, Mary, had been dead for almost two decades. She'd insisted that Teddy not insert "She battled courageously…" in the paper upon her death.

"I had no choice in the matter," Ted whispered to himself. "That is what she always said. Why is it that people feel the need to express their courageous fight with cancer in the paper? They do as the doctor tells them, and many times, it's not enough. Nothing courageous about it."

Ted nodded his head and mumbled, "Yep, that's what she always said." He drew a quincunx symbol in the sand below him with a dried-up stick.

He was sitting on a bench in the park, kiddy-corner from his house. He'd watched the officers enter his home. It wasn't a surprise to Ted. It seemed nothing came as a surprise to him anymore. He and Mary hadn't been able to have kids of their own, so they'd occasionally taken in foster children. The last one was Wayne. When Mary died, he'd decided to adopt Wayne, and the two had become inseparable.

Ted wasn't the athletic type. Going into the backyard with his son to play catch wasn't even a consideration. The lack of family sports activities didn't hurt Wayne at home, but it did cause mistreatment during school gym classes. The boy was uncoordinated and awkward in his attempts at any sport, and the more he tried, the more his fellow classmates ridiculed him. Those incidents' only made him closer to his father. Wayne had found solace in his interests and hobbies, namely numerology and the beliefs of Pythagoras and other philosophers. But life's indignities tend to catch up with troubled young men. The bad memories begin to pile on top of one another. Each new hurt can bring a young life to its breaking point.

Ted was close to his son in every aspect except one: he couldn't feel Wayne's pain. There were times, when Wayne was at an age that most of his peers had left home and married, he had turned inside himself and left their home for a day or two. Ted didn't ask him about where he'd gone. He figured Wayne would tell him when the time was right, but that time never came. To Ted, his son's death had accomplices, and they would not escape unpunished.

Ted reached for the book next to him on the bench. The hardcover book was old and dingy, as if it had been read a thousand times. The title on the cover was faded and no longer legible. On the spine the title "The Prose of Sir Thomas Browne" barely showed itself. Ted picked it up and turned to one of his favorite writings, "The Garden of the Cyrus," from the 17th century author. He let the words engulf his thoughts on the mystical mathematics of God in nature. This was his sweet spot. He felt comfortable engulfed in the world of numbers.

When the officers were finished invading his home, Theodore Paulsen stood up and headed for his car. Before leaving the park he sent out a short text message from his cell phone. Ted had matters under control, things just needed to be tidied up a bit.

His sixty-five-year-old face looked haggard and tired, but his eyes were focused. The CD in his car stereo played one of his favorites, "The Marriage of Figaro," by Mozart. Ted's life had the outward appearance of someone well-to-do. He enjoyed the things that current society perceived as important to the rich. He golfed, listened to symphony music, went to plays, and enjoyed a good bottle of wine. "All within my means, he thought to himself." But, the utmost part of being Theodore Paulson is his position as head of the state chapter of a secret club…a brotherhood with a history, a long history.

Ted didn't immediately go home. He drove clear to the southeast corner of Green County and stopped in front of an old bus stop.

"Were you followed, Danielle?" Ted asked.

"Maybe…I don't know."

"No matter," Ted said with little concern. "You're a bright girl, Danielle. There are consequences in any action. Your decisions, as they currently stand right now, hold more weight than most. Do you understand what I'm saying Danielle?"

Danielle thought about what the accountant said and decided to cut to the chase. "It was you, wasn't it? You were the one who attacked me at the plant. You stopped, didn't you? You could have taken my sense of smell away if you wanted to, but you stopped. Why?"

Ted looked at her, and for a brief moment, his face portrayed a man who truly cared for the woman in front of him. Did she, briefly, turn his thoughts back to a time when all was right between them? He would not answer her. "You are friendly with someone from the Sheriff's Department. I'm quite certain that this person's future would be much brighter if you were to play out this thing in the direction it needs to go. I will be cleared of all charges and everything will fall into its precise pattern. Am I making myself clear?"

Danielle was in a corner. She wondered if Ted had a gun, but knew it didn't really matter. Even if she overpowered him, she was aware that he belonged to something beyond a secret club. He also had something of hers, something that was precious and could not be compromised. It would be up to her to make things right. But with all the cards stacked against her, it would be extremely difficult, if not impossible. She, perhaps, knew as much about Ted as he did her. His local chapter followed the same beliefs that the ancients held to. Their capabilities were a serious matter…this much she knew.

"Yes, Ted, I understand what you're saying."

"We have to follow through, Danielle," he said, avoiding her eyes.

Danielle left. Ted waited a few minutes and stood to leave, as well. He was not surprised to see police officers approaching. As they put his hands behind his back and applied handcuffs, he watched Danielle pass by in her car with a stern, knowing look. He was read his rights and immediately brought in for questioning concerning the recent attacks and, of course, the death of Marcus Wingate.

Danielle wondered if it was a mistake to have him picked up. In the back of her mind, she knew she had started something that could not be undone without more people getting hurt.

19

The interrogation room at the Green County Sheriff's Department was not like those you see on television. The usual dreary, dull, rectangular accommodations with the one-way mirror that Ted expected were actually a well lit boardroom, complete with a couch. Jay stood in the corner of the room, having a discussion on his cell phone. Ted sat in the middle right-hand chair next to his lawyer, Phil Garnett. The astute-looking Garnett was conveniently in town and had driven to the aid of Ted upon his call. Garrett was as round as an oversized exercise ball. He stood a full foot less than Jay, but twice the weight. His black reading glasses looked helpless and tiny as they sat engulfed by his enormous head. Most of his business concerned itself with Madison to the North, and Chicago to the South, but not today. Rufe sat at the end of the 8-man table and waited for Jay to start the conversation.

Jay motioned for Rufe to come to him and whispered, "I just got off the phone with Danielle. She said her take on our little fellow here may have been just a wrong feeling. Now that she has had time to think about it, he may just be a harmless odd duck."

"Are we still going to question him?" Rufe asked.

"We have to. I have a crew checking out his car, and I don't want to let him out until they're done. Besides, it's not very farfetched to think that someone may have gotten to Danielle, although she wouldn't admit it."

Jay introduced himself to Paulson and his lawyer. They both shook his hand, and although Ted and his lawyer already knew more about the tall officer than his own mother, they kept appearances up.

"Do you know why you're here, Mr. Paulson?"

"Please, call me Ted. To answer your question, yes, they told me upon my arrest. They said you had questions about some of our illustrious industrial leaders."

"Okay, Ted it is. Can you tell me where you were and what you did on May 5th?"

Ted's lawyer was about to say something and Ted just blinked at him.

"Well, let's see…last Saturday. I got up early, as usual. Did some exercises. Fellows my age need to keep the old joints loose."

"Can't blame you for that…go on."

"I had a quick breakfast and started working on income taxes for those folks who had to postpone their filing date. I don't think I have to tell you how busy it is for us accountants this time of year."

"I can imagine. Did you work on tax paperwork all day?"

"I went out to Charlie's Restaurant for lunch, worked until 5:30, made a light supper, watched some television, did some light reading, and went to bed about 10:00P.M."

"Is there anybody who can verify what you did that day?"

"Well, I live alone, but I suppose my computer would have times and dates of use. You can check with Charlie's as far as lunch goes."

"We'll do just that, Ted. As a matter of fact, we got a search warrant for your home and used it already. We'll have your computer back to you by tomorrow, I promise."

"I'm a little fucking confused, Lieutenant. I thought that the magistrate would need something in the way of *probable cause* before issuing a legal search," lawyer Phil said.

"Our Green County Court Judge wouldn't have issued the warrant if he didn't think there was probable cause," Jay answered.

"I want a copy of the affidavit," the chubby lawyer insisted.

Jay sat his towering frame on the shiny oak table and made sure his words were heard loud and clear.

"You probably think this small-town sheriff's department will be a push-over for a big time lawyer, but I know a few things about how to conduct a murder investigation," Jay said, with force.

The fat man removed a handkerchief from his front-left suit pocket and wiped the sweat from his enormous face. "I don't give a flying fuck if you're Serpico or Barney Fife, I want the affidavit."

"Such language, Phil...do you eat with that mouth?" Ted scolded his lawyer, as if he was correcting a first grader. "Please, go on Lieutenant. Tell us about the warrant."

"The warrant is sealed."

"What do you mean sealed?" Garnett asked, with a little less exuberance.

"Like I said, sealed, as in *People v. Hobbs*. You're a big city boy, Garnett. You know where this is going don't you?"

The lawyer stood up as quickly as his girth would let him.

"I think we're done here, Ted. Unless they plan on arresting you, we'll be on our way."

Jay stood and smiled at the two men.

"No. No arrest, we're just asking a few questions, checking out leads. We'll be in touch, though, Ted, I'm sure of that."

Ted Paulson stood and folded his arms. He smiled as happily as a grandfather pushing his granddaughter on a park swing. Even the dark shadows under his eyes seemed to wrinkle up into a joyous grin.

"Don't make promises you can't keep, Lieutenant."

"I'll make this one a priority, Ted."

Ted Paulson and his lawyer walked out of the sheriff's building confident that they would not be coming back. Jay decided he'd make it his mission to make sure they were wrong.

"*People v. Hobbs,* did you pull that out of your ass, Jay?" Rufe asked, admiring his superior's wit.

"Have a little faith, Rufe. I was a little afraid that if Danielle was right about our little Ted here, she might be in some trouble. So I asked my judge buddy how we could make sure her name was protected from our suspect and his lawyer. He...ah...showed me the way."

"Danielle's phone call before our little meeting sealed the deal."

"What do you mean?"

Jay put on a light jacket. "She was trying to convince me to drop Ted Paulson as a suspect. He got to Danielle, and I need to find out what he said to her."

"You want company?"

"No thanks, Rufe. Besides, you have all that paperwork to fill out on our meeting with Paulson today. The captain will be asking for it."

"Oh yah...can't forget to do the paperwork. Thanks Jay," Rufe said sarcastically.

Jay drove his personal car rather than his squad, and pulled into Danielle's driveway. She was planting rose bushes near the west side of her home.

"I'm surprised the ground isn't still frozen," Jay said getting out of his car.

"It was a long, cold winter, wasn't it?"

"I'd like to talk in the house?"

"Sounds serious," Danielle said as she stood up. She wore cotton garden gloves that looked a mess.

Her face was marked with mud and Jay tried to rub it off with his hand, but only made it worse.

"I'll wash up inside. I'm glad you took your personal car," she said.

Danielle dropped her gloves on the ground and followed Jay to the front. As she closed the door, she looked back to see if anyone was watching. This did not go unnoticed by Jay. Danielle raised her finger to her lips, gesturing to Jay to keep quiet. She walked through her home, grabbed a washcloth, and then continued to a door that led to the backyard. After twenty more paces, they sat down on a couple of lawn chairs that circled a fire pit.

Cleaning off her gardening, she said, "Jay, there is a lot more going on here, in Green County, than it appears."

"Paulson got to you. He pressured you to look away, didn't he?"

Danielle thought carefully about what Jay had asked.

"Yes."

"What does he have on you?"

"He has you, Jay. He threatened to hurt you if I didn't get you off his back. I think he can do it, Jay. I think he has the means to get to anybody."

Jay leaned over. Resting his elbows to his knees, he put his fingers on his forehead and rubbed it, as if he was trying to force some answers out of his brain. Just then the aluminum chair buckled under his weight and collapsed to the ground. Despite the gravity of the moment, Danielle could not hold back the laughter.

"How...how...many is that now...six or seven?"

Jay just rolled to his side and held his head in his hand. "I'm thinking seven," Jay answered, referring to how many of Danielle's chairs he'd broken over the years. "Did you ever think of, perhaps, investing in lawn chairs that can actually hold some weight?

Danielle reached down to give the big man a hoist up, but Jay pulled her down to his level.

"Do you really think I'm going to let that little jerk get the best of me?" Her face was now an inch from his, as she lay comfortably on top of him. His arms were locked around her.

"That little jerk has connections. Are you going to let me up?"

"What kind of connections?" Jay said, ignoring her question.

"Let me go or you get nothing."

"Kiss me first."

"What?"

"You heard me. Kiss me and you're free."

Danielle licked her lips ever so slowly. She looked into his eyes and edged closer to him. Jay loosened the grip on his captive just enough to allow her to knee his billiards into the side pocket. His arms opened as if his balls were the button on an elevator. Danielle jumped up from the ground and watched intently as Jay coiled into the fetal position.

"I didn't say *knee my testicles* and you're free," Jay grimaced. "A simple kiss would have worked."

Danielle sat on a lawn chair. "I like spontaneous kisses, not the forced kind."

Jay rolled over, with effort, and sat on the grass. He wasn't about to attempt another lawn chair.

"You didn't answer my question about Ted's connections."

"I don't know. Not for sure."

"Is this another one of your feelings?"

"Yes…with an added touch of research." Danielle got down and sat on the grass next to Jay. "You need to promise me that you will be very careful."

"I'm always careful."

"I mean very careful, Jay. When you leave here, you need to look around, and if you see anything suspicious, call for backup. You need to check everything before you go somewhere or make a decision."

"Go on." Jay said, taking in what she said while trying to extract what she knew.

"I think Ted is a member, or possibly the leader of a small group that follows the teachings of Pythagoras. It is an ancient society with their own beliefs on history, symbolism, religion, and as you've seen…the power and magic of the number *five*."

"How dangerous can a small group of number-worshippers be?"

"I don't want to speculate on how big they are or how dangerous. They could be everywhere and be very well-connected. If so, you will want to be careful with…you know…who you talk to." She put her hand on his face. "I do know that they are very secretive and take care of their own."

"Kind of like the mafia with brains instead of guns."

"I guess you could say that."

"You know, I'm not the only one that may be in danger now. If they are well-connected, they know you didn't follow Ted's demands. I'm putting you under our protection again. In the meantime, if you should have contact with Ted again, tell him you think the Sheriff's Department is looking in another direction. That should keep his mind off of us for a while."

"And if he doesn't believe me?"

"We'll keep as low a profile as we can. I just need some time to get more information on all of this."

Jay stood up, followed by Danielle.

Danielle looked around her yard, as if checking for spies. "Lean down. I need to tell you something."

Jay bent over, and for his reward, was given a nice, long kiss.

"Nothing like a spontaneous, unforced kiss," Danielle said, walking toward her backdoor.

"When you're right, you're right," Jay said with a grin.

20

Martha Wycoff had spent the morning delivering food to elderly people who were unable to get out themselves. She had been a volunteer for a number of different programs since her husband Earl, passed away some time ago. Martha pulled into her driveway just before noon.

"I don't know where the time goes," she said to her cat. Martha's oldest daughter, Laurie, had asked her if she wouldn't mind taking care of her cat *temporarily*, while she looked for an apartment that took pets. Laurie claimed she'd found the feline in the woods, but that was a lie. After her father died, she'd felt her mother needed some companionship. For the first few days, the cat was into everything—so much so that Martha decided to call her "Really." Every time she saw the little menace on top of the refrigerator or in the dirt with her plants, she'd said, "Really." Now, seven years later, Martha loved her companion.

Really walked around his bowl of food and made a pitiful excuse for a meow. The bowl was empty and she wasn't going to put up with it. Within seconds, her little white paws reached up to knead Martha's leg.

"I know…I forgot to feed you before I left this morning," Martha said. "I had a lot of things on my mind. You won't starve."

Martha dropped a cup of kitten chow into Really's bowl. She picked up a pack of Belair cigarettes and tapped on the bottom. Retrieving a smoke, she lit up, sat on her couch, and began to flip through television channels.

Martha was a retired school teacher, but she hadn't changed her fashion statement much in the last thirty or forty years. She still wore her hair up and sported pointy Browline eyeglasses, the same ones that had been big in the 1950's. She placed her half-finished cigarette on her vintage picnic ashtray with the red-checkered beanbag bottom and got comfortable for her afternoon nap.

When Martha Wycoff woke, she was surrounded by fire. She tried desperately to get off the couch and crawl to safety, but was soon overtaken by the smoke. Within seconds the fire engulfed her living room curtains, walls, and the very couch she lay on.

21

Danielle came home from work exhausted. She kicked off her shoes and plopped down on the comfortable leather recliner in her office. It had been five days since Marcus Wingate had been found murdered in his wood plant, and as far as she was concerned, no news was good news. She had been getting daily progress reports from Jay on the case, while being discreetly watched by Jay's fellow officers during various times of the day and night. For the moment, things had quieted down.

She heard a thud at the front door and figured her evening paper had arrived. Dragging her sorry ass out of the chair, she got the paper from the front porch, and poured herself a glass of Riesling before sitting down again. The sunshine beamed through the small opening between her curtains, presenting plenty of light for a quick look through the Monroe Times. After skimming the front page news, tossing the sports and ads aside, she glanced at the community section and then turned to the obituaries. She didn't do it out of a taste of morbidity. Being a business owner, she had a lot of acquaintances, clients, and employees. Should one pass away, Danielle needed to acknowledge the loss. When it came to family and friends, however, her mother covered that, spreading the news well in advance of the local newspaper.

Eight Green County citizens had passed away recently, along with two previous county dwellers that had moved away after retirement. Danielle didn't see anything unusual about the entire lot; one from cancer, two "after a long illness," three were older than dirt, one from a tractor accident, and one at home. She didn't recognize any of them.

Danielle was about to fold the paper when she glanced again at the front page of the community section. On the bottom corner was a picture of a small red house, badly damaged as firemen attempted to contain a fire. The caption below read: *A fire took down this home in the early afternoon yesterday. The victim lived alone and it appeared the flame may have been started by a lit cigarette. Further investigation is pending, but at this time, it appears as though it was an accident.*

A cold sweat poured over her as she turned the pages back to the obituaries section. The picture of the deceased that she now concentrated on didn't ring a bell the first time she'd passed over it, but putting it together with the name, she realized she did know this person. It read: "Martha (Holt) Wycoff, age 67, died Wednesday, May 10th, at home." She glanced down further and there it was. "Martha taught 5th grade at St. Elisabeth School in Adams for 30 years."

"Mrs. Wycoff...my 5th grade teacher. She was one of my favorites," Danielle thought. She found herself thinking back to a carefree time—a time when grownups did all the worrying and ten year old little girls were busy being...well...little girls. Then, as was her habit of late, she tried to connect what was happening in her own life with what she had just read. Died on the 10th...5th grade teacher...my 5th grade teacher.

Coincidence...has to be nothing but coincidence. Danielle picked up her glass of wine and headed upstairs for a bath. She ran the hot water and soon steam set itself onto the mirror. She bent over the sink and wrote the impression of the magic square. *The murder of Marcus Wingate was the fifth attack and happened in the very center of the county, corresponding with the magic square's number five. Number six on the square is in the bottom right corner...the very area of the county where my former teacher lost her life.* Danielle quickly wiped the image from the mirror with her towel, as if trying to erase it from her mind.

Quincunxes in heaven above;quincunxes in the earth below; quincunxes in deity;quincunxes in the mind of man;quincunxes in bones, in optic nerves, in roots of trees, in leaves, in petals, in everything. *Samual Taylor Coleridge on Sir Thomas Browne's "The Garden of Cyrus."*

22

The Community House of Granite was a low-budget YMCA. Jay and Rufe had just finished two hours of sweaty racquetball and were seated on the wooden bench in front of their respective lockers. It wasn't exactly a Sunday afternoon ritual, but they did get together one or two afternoons a month. The strategies used between the two men always remained the same...Jay tried to bounce it over Rufe's head, while Rufe would attempt to dribble the ball low to the ground.

"You have improved greatly, young wizard of the ball court," Jay said.

"You will not hold your lofty title much longer, oh great master," Rufe retorted.

Jay wiped his face with a towel and placed it around his neck. "Working tonight?"

"Per your request, the captain has us set up in the bedroom of a house across from Paulson's place. She figured it would be less suspicious if we did that rather than sit in our squad car. Thanks for the extra work." Rufe said sarcastically.

"You are very welcome. I actually have been wondering if my request needs to be adjusted. A watched pot never boils. Maybe we should bring him in and charge him for the murder of Marcus Wingate."

"Do you really think we have enough on him?" Rufe asked.

Jay thought about it for a minute. "No...we probably don't, but I really hate this guy. For an accountant he sure acts like pompous ass."

Pompous ass or not, we don't really have anything worthwhile."

"We will."

Over the next couple days, Jay had been working hard on the Ted Paulson case. Between that and all of his other duties, he was able to spend precious little time with Danielle. When he did call her, she rarely answered. Even so, Jay found her quiet and somewhat distant during their conversations. He wondered if it was him or the pressure of knowing her life could be in danger. Jay wanted to see her in the worst way. He wanted to help her, protect her, but most of all...he wanted to be with her. Sitting in his office wasn't getting him anywhere with Danielle and the Paulson case wasn't moving the way he had hoped.

"Where you going?" Rufe asked, as he watched Jay head for the door.

"Danielle's place, she rarely returns my calls. The few times she has she sounds funny, as if it's hard for her to breathe. She insists she's all right, but something is going on. I want to find out what it is."

"Need some help?" Rufe asked, reaching for his jacket, even though the temperature was a comfortable sixty-five degrees.

"No, I've got it."

Jay stopped before walking out the door. "I talked to the District Attorney yesterday. Surprisingly, he thought we might have enough to hold Paulson in jail for murder. He wanted me to wait until tomorrow while he put some things together, but I have a feeling we should pick him up now. I don't know how long we can hold him, but a day or two is better than nothing. Take care of it, would you, Rufe?"

"I'll get right on it, Jay."

Jay didn't waste any time and used his lights and siren privileges liberally. If Theodore Paulson had done something to harm Danielle, sneaking around and trying to show him that the department would kneel to his threats was not how to conduct police business, he'd decided. He was going to Danielle's home making as much noise as he could and to hell with the accountant.

23

Danielle did not respond to the doorbell or Jay's repeated knocks. He reached for the key that she kept hidden in a magnetic key box under the gas grill around the corner and let himself in. Looking through the window the living room appeared dark, but with her car in the driveway he thought she must be home.

He opened the door and poked his head inside before entering. "Danielle, it's Jay, is everything all right? I've been trying to reach you," he said, working his way through the kitchen.

He opened the door to the left. Jay remembered the room as a bedroom made into a den or office. It was dark, with just a faint bead of sunshine showing itself through a slight opening under the window blinds. There, in the corner, sitting on an old rocking chair with a scarlet cloth seat, was Danielle.

He drew the blinds open and was surprised to see his beautiful Danielle looking anything but, as she rocked slowly. Her legs were crossed, up close to her body and covered by a blanket. The dark circles around her eyes, as well as the pale tone of her skin, made her look like somebody else—not the bright, confident woman he knew.

"You shouldn't be here, you know. People tend to get hurt who know me. You'd better go away, Jay. You'd better go far away, Danielle said in a quiet voice."

Jay glanced across the room. In front of a small couch was a short wooden table with papers scattered about. Books were on the floor, the pages were marked with a yellow highlighter in certain areas. Danielle was a noted neat freak, and the messy table did not fit her usual mode.

He knelt down by Danielle and put his hands on her shoulders, trying to rub the tension out. "What happened, Danielle? What's going on? Did he hurt you? Did that little bastard hurt you?"

"He's hurting everybody but me. It's all there, on the table. After we found Marcus Wingate's body at the door factory, they...he killed my old grade school teacher. He then murdered my grandfather and my little cousin, Amy. Today it will be somebody else. It could be you, Jay. I'm not sure."

Jay looked around the room and wondered if what she was saying could be true. If so, he thought, she must know so much more than what she stated earlier.

"You may be right, but staying here in the dark won't do you or anyone close to you any good. Show me what you have. We'll work together on this."

Danielle didn't want to fight any more. She felt alone and outnumbered, but somehow Jay's presence started a faint spark that needed to be ignited. That small flame began to push her back to who she really was.

"I don't know. I don't want anybody else getting hurt."

"Danielle, I've never known you to give up on anything. Your sister Rita told me that when you were in your teens you were hiking with her when she fell and broke a bone in her foot. She said you carried her for miles to your car and found help. And when your mother got sick, you stood strong and helped your father get through it."

"But...this...this is different."

Jay smiled to himself and thought back ten years. "When your parents grew older, you took on the responsibility of an entire company. You could have taken an easier path. You could have married a tall, extremely handsome cop and started your own family, but you couldn't turn away from your father and all the people who relied on his company for their paycheck. Danielle, I was mad as hell with you back then, but yet, I understood, and...I admired you at the same time."

Jay picked her up from the chair and hugged her tight. "We'll stop this guy, along with anybody else that's involved. I promise you that."

Danielle bent her head back and looked up at Jay. "I wonder if that tall, handsome cop is still around. I sure would like to make it up to him."

Jay kissed her. The scent of her body took him back in time to a safe and happy place. It was as if a recurring dream continually brought him closer to the treasure he had been seeking, and those forces have finally won him the prize. But, just as in the dream, reality set in.

Danielle broke from Jay's embrace. "Sara, Sara Miller!" She yelled out the name as if it brought everything into focus.

"What's wrong?"

"I think she may be in trouble."

Danielle hurried over to the papers she had strewn on the table. "I'll start from the top."

They both sat down. The table was a menagerie of newspaper clippings and diagrams.

"Sara was right about the magic square. After Marcus Wingate's murder, the pattern of the square continued. Marcus was murdered in the middle of Green County. He was the 5th victim and all of the previous victims were attacked on consecutive days, May 1 through May 5."

Jay's cell phone vibrated. Jay saw Rufe's name on the caller ID and answered it, walking out in the hall.

Jay looked more puzzled than worried as he ended the call.

"What is it?"

"It was Rufe. Before I came out to your place I asked him to pick up Ted Paulson. He said old Ted was nowhere to be found. We'd been watching him every day and on the day that I decided to pick him up, he disappeared. Doesn't make sense."

Danielle's eyes dropped.

Jay's first thought after telling her about Ted being on the loose was that she looked *scared stiff*. It was an old phrase, but it fit her perfectly. Jay, on the other hand, could not help but feel there was some sort of leak at the department. When he was finished here, he was going to make it a point to find out how Ted Paulson tends to stay two steps ahead of him.

"Go ahead, Danielle. You were saying?"

Danielle was indeed *scared stiff*, but she pushed on.

"It would have been reasonable to think that Ted would stop victimizing after what happened to Marcus Wingate. After all, he was the one who actually fired Ted's son. In his sick mind, that contributed to Wayne's suicide."

"That appears true. The department hasn't heard of any unusual attacks since the Wingate murder."

"That's just it. He's filling his magic square under the radar, and he's doing it to punish me for helping you with the investigation."

"How?"

"On May 11th, my fifth grade teacher died in a house fire. The date followed the pattern of the previous victims, and the area follows that of the magic square. She was the 6th victim and number six on the square is located in the south-eastern corner of the county."

Danielle pushed Martha Wycoff's obituary column toward Jay.

"There wasn't anything suspicious about this. If I remember correctly, she was a heavy smoker and simply fell asleep."

Danielle retrieved the article from Jay. "I don't think it was that simple, but at the time I chalked it up to coincidence."

"What made you change your mind?"

"On May 12th, my cousin Johnny died."

Jay picked up the clipping from the table. "John Silton, the little boy that drowned in a pool?"

"I went to the funeral. His mother, Heather and I have known each other all of our lives. We would always get caught up on things during holiday visits. I almost didn't go to the funeral and when I arrived I wished I hadn't. It was unbelievably sad, Jay." She shrugged and changed the direction of the conversation. "I thought there was a chance that Johnny's drowning didn't have anything to do with me or Ted Paulson. His home was not in the middle-eastern part of the county, so it didn't fit the magic square's number seven. But, as I sat in the back of the funeral parlor, an older gentleman began talking to me."

Jay knew where this was going.

"He was crying and his voice cracked. He kept wiping his eyes with his handkerchief. He talked about how bad he felt. He said he lived a few miles away from Johnny with his daughter and her husband. Little Johnny and his grandson, Shane, would take turns going to one another's home to swim. The grandfather was left in charge of watching the kids when they were swimming. That day his daughter and son-in-law were off to work. Johnny's friend Shane hurt himself and the grandfather went in the house to bandage the boy's knee. When he returned, he found Johnny lying face down in the three-foot side of the pool. I asked him the address. When I went home, I checked to see if the address fit the square. I think you know the answer." Danielle looked helpless.

Jay put his hand on Danielle's knee. "We had to investigate it. I remember the look on the old man's face when I was asking him questions. I wanted to make the hurt go away, but there was nothing anybody could have done. I told him that it was an accident that couldn't be helped. I've seen this before. It'll take some time for the old guy to ease up on himself."

"Jay, I felt as if I pushed Johnny into the pool and held him under the water myself. I don't know how I can ever look at Heather in the face again."

"You can't say for sure that Paulson had anything to do with this."

Danielle pressed further. "On May 13th my grandfather Herbert Yates died."

"I didn't know."

"He was on my mother's side and I don't think you ever met him. He was eighty-five years old. He suffered from many of the things you'd expect from someone of his age, but nothing life-threatening. My uncle, Porter, found him alone on his garage floor, under his white Oldsmobile. They claim it was carbon monoxide. He lived in the south-west corner of the county, another perfect match with the magic square."

Jay understood that it was possible for all the things Danielle believed to have happened on the very spot that the magic square diagrammed. It also could have been just coincidence. Still, though there was currently a lack of proof that the accountant was involved at all. Jay knew one thing for sure, if Ted Paulson was the guy, he couldn't have done it alone. Ted was being watched day and night.

"Today is May 14 and there is only one spot left open on the magic square, the number nine. Is there something you need to tell me?"

"I was just getting to that. You're right, only one number remains. Since something has happened in Green County every day since my old school teacher died, today should be no different. Number nine, the top-middle square is in the north-central part of the county. The only town to speak of in that area is New Glarus. That is just a couple of miles east of my company."

Danielle fought off the need to cry, scream, collapse, or break something. She didn't know what emotion hurt more—anger, guilt, or sadness.

"So what does your company have to do with this?"

She looked up with red, drained eyes. "Sara Miller...Sara Miller, remember her from payroll? She stopped at your office just before we found Marcus Wingate's body. I think Ted may have seen me with her...probably watching the department or something. A person from our personnel department called me around noon today. Sara hasn't been in her office all day. They called her husband and he said she left the house the same time he did, about 8:00 this morning. No one has seen or heard from her since. Jay, her home is in New Glarus."

"I'll have people look for her right now. What is her address? What kind of car does she drive?"

"There's more Jay, much more. I delayed telling the department about this. I don't know...I thought maybe if I looked myself, or got help from work. I told Sara's husband that I would call the police, but I didn't. I was afraid of what might be next. I finally called, but I wasted an hour of precious time...time that might have helped in finding her."

"What do you mean? I was at the department all day. I didn't get or hear of a missing woman report."

"I called the sheriff's department about 1:00 PM. They told me they'd get right on it."

"That's odd...no one said a word to me."

Jay stood and went for his cell phone, but Danielle put her hand on his.

"Wait, Jay there's something else. I don't know why the department didn't tell you about my call, but I think there is another pattern being followed, and it might help find Sara."

Jay put down the phone. His mind was now buzzing with strange information that didn't fit in with anything he'd learned from his past courses or seminars. This had officially become bizarre and for the first time he was feeling out of his league. What else did his ex know about the strange world of Theodore Paulson?

"You'd better sit down, Jay. This may take a while." Danielle took a deep breath. "There is a society of sorts that Ted Paulson belongs. This society has a lot in common with the Pythagoreans."

"Excuse my ignorance—the what?"

"Pythagoras was one of the first known great teachers of ancient Greece. The Pythagoreans were his brotherhood. They carried number worship to its extreme and based their philosophy and way of life on it. Among other things, they believed there to be five essences: fire, water, air, earth, and something they called "quinta essential," or the fifth essence. The fifth essence is the *all embracing divinity*. It encompasses all—life, death, protection and justice. At first, it was the pattern to which I thought Paulson was following. But this society uses other traditions from other cultures, as long as they fit into some sort of numerological pattern. In this case...I think Ted may be following The Five *Cardinal Points*.

"I'm not sure I'm following you. Can you draw me a picture?"

"The Five Cardinal Points translates into a set of principle directions—South, North, West, East, and Center. Each corresponds with a color, a season, and an element. The elements of the Cardinal Points are actually similar to those of

Pythagoras elements but with a couple differences. The Cardinal elements are fire, water, metal, wood, and, as with the Pythagoreans, essence or the center. Don't you see—the society follows some or all of the teachings of Pythagoras. They branch off to other cultural teaching when it fits into their plans and goals. To Pythagoreans, the number five was a living being, the spiritual intelligent embodiment of all that is principled and justifiable."

"Is that a bad thing?"

"It doesn't have to be. Like any group, some members or branches can become extreme in their beliefs." Danielle looked over mounds of books and paperwork strewn about the room. "Jay, I'm good with numbers. I've been doing nonstop research into all matters that pertained to numbers and ancient philosophies. Before you broke me out of the paralyzed state I was in, research was the only thing that kept me sane. I was obsessed with finding out what Paulson's next move was before it happened."

Jay understood that fright can freeze the strongest of people. But he sensed that Danielle was working hard to leave her fears behind.

"Are they just local? Do they have some sort of rule book or declaration?"

"He likely is following the old way, from around 515 BC." Danielle handed him a print-out.

1. That at its deepest level, reality is mathematical in nature.
2. That philosophy can be used for spiritual purification.
3. That the soul can rise to union with the divine.
4. That certain symbols have mystical significance.
5. That all brothers of the order observe strict loyalty and secrecy.

Jay looked again at the list. "The last one...number five, I've seen that somewhere before."

"Where?"

"I think it was at Ted Paulson's place."

Jay heard the theme song from an old sitcom, but he couldn't recall the name of the show. He looked at Danielle and said, "Really!"

"It's my cell. I must have left it in the kitchen."

She ran out.

Jay was about to find her when she ran past him into the office.

"Anything important?" Jay asked.

"No...just a small fire to put out at work...nothing major." She took a breath and continued. "Jay, I don't think we have enough time to go over everything right now. The earth is the fourth element. I think Sara Miller was abducted and may be buried somewhere in New Glarus. Since May 11th, when Martha Wycoff died in the house fire, someone has been giving me little clues. I think we both know who is playing this game of life and death with me."

Jay's usual calm and collected manner was transforming into anger and frustration. Danielle noticed, but continued with what she knew.

"Until today, the clues meant nothing to me, because they appeared well after the victims were dead. But this one...this one is different...it gives me hope that Sara is still alive."

Danielle bent down, retrieved a book from her unkempt pile, and showed it to Jay.

"I found this outside my back door this morning."

Jay looked at the book. The title was "The Garden of the Cyrus" by Thomas Browne.

"It's Browne's vision on how art, nature, and the universe interconnect with the number five or patterns of five. Under chapter three I found this highlighted:

But not to look so high as heaven or the single quincunx…Observable rudiments there are hereof in subterraneous concretions, and bodies in the Earth.

"There are thirty-five cemeteries in Green County, but only one in New Glarus, it's called Evergreen Cemetery. It's only a hunch, but I think we'd better go there."

Jay needed to be up to speed. Following ancient patterns was not his forte, but it sure seemed to be Danielle's. When they were together she had never shown this side of her. He desperately wanted to know what had happened during those fifteen years. "Can you quickly tell me how The Five Cardinal Points fit in a pattern?"

Danielle wanted to hurry out the door, but she understood Jay's need to know.

"In Dynastic Chinese, the principle direction of "South" corresponds to the color *red* and the element of *Fire*. My old teacher died in a red house that caught on fire. Her house was located in the southeast corner of Green County. My little cousin was next. His death corresponded with the North Cardinal Point. The North Point is linked to *black* and *water*."

"I understand the water, but where does the color black come into the picture?"

"At the funeral they told me that he always wore his little black scuba diving suit. That day was no exception. Grandfather was…"

Jay looked down at the print out Danielle had concerning The Five Cardinal Points.

"Okay, I'm seeing what you mean. Your grandfather indicates West…white…and metal. But Sara Miller, where does she fall into the pattern? East, the color green, and the element of wood doesn't help much, does it?"

"If my hunch is right, they have her at the Evergreen Cemetery. The location is right, and the element of wood could be by trees or worse...a coffin. Let's hope we figure it out when we get there."

Jay reached for his jacket as they both headed for the door. "As good a guess as any...I'll call for back-up."

Danielle stopped abruptly, and Jay nearly ran her over.

"I don't think that's a good idea, Jay. We don't know if we'll find anything. I could be completely wrong. Besides, I don't want to make a big thing out of this. If they have Sara, I don't want them to decide to hurt her when they see a bunch of cops swarming the place. But, it's your choice."

Jay thought about it briefly. Finally he walked her to his car.

"Okay, we'll keep it between ourselves...for now."

24

When they reached the cemetery, the mid-afternoon sun was hidden by dark clouds. Evergreen cemetery was located just east of St. James Catholic Church. The sacred building, erected circa 1870, stood high on a hill. Jay raised his eyes to the church. The shuttered brick house of God appeared to stand in authority as if those whom once occupied it looked over the cemetery with reverence. There were several entrances into the cemetery. Jay had never been to this place before, but his impression was that this place was old and worn down. In fact, it appeared almost forgotten. Although the cemetery itself was not gated, at the far end he saw a gated area.

Danielle pointed. "Drive all the way to the back, over toward the east. There must be something that fits the clues."

Jay approached the gated family plot. Danielle motioned for him to pull over. The temperature was still comfortable, but the loss of the sun behind the clouds was beginning to send a slight chill into Danielle's bones. She shivered, and wished she had something covering her sleeveless arms. Jay put his arm around her as they walked toward the gated tombs.

"Look, those gravestones. Isn't that...?"

Danielle looked down at the gravestones situated just before the gate. They were flat to the ground and grass had grown over much of the inscriptions. "You're right, there are five of them set in the form of a single quincunx."

Jay knelt at the four squared stones plus the one in the middle. "Nothing looks disturbed. Maybe we should keep looking."

Danielle opened the book she had brought with her – The Prose of Sir Thomas Browne, and read the highlighted part again. "It says, *not to look so high as the Heaven or the single quincunx*. I think it means we should look beyond." She took a step toward the gated plot.

Jay took a few steps and gazed over the impressive family resting place before him. Between two large stone crosses was a granite wall, complete with carved columns and a rounded top. The walls and gates were covered with an overgrowth of green vines in full bloom, though mid-May seemed too early for such lushness. In large lettering, the etched words began with, "The burial grounds of W. Dunlap Van Handle Sr." From the top to the bottom of the wall was a family history that included dates of birth, dates of death, and even a reference about each family member. It ended in the mid-1950's.

What caught Danielle's eye was the date listed near the bottom for William Van Handle Jr. 1905 – 1955. "Let's go, Jay!" She said.

Jay pushed the unlocked gate open. The hinge squeaked and the pitch screeched higher and higher. Beside the large mausoleum that appeared to house W Dunlap Van Handle Sr. and his immediate family, there were many tombstones resting within the gates. Danielle separated from Jay and wandered behind the mausoleum.

"Jay, it's here," Danielle yelled.

Jay ran over and found Danielle kneeling over the tombstone of William Van Handle. He bent down next to her before a freshly dug grave.

"You think they buried her. You think they buried her here, don't you?" Jay said, knowing the answer. He started digging with his hands, wishing he knew if the bastards put her six feet down or just under the surface. A few inches down, his hands hit wood. At a frantic pace he pushed the dirt aside. The site revealed a wooden casket. Jay found the lid was not nailed shut. He opened it easily. It was empty.

Suddenly a voice startled Jay. "Oh, the thought did occur to me, but we decided she would be more valuable as a sort of… trade-off."

Jay knew the tone of that voice. When he turned, Ted Paulson stood in front of two tough-looking fellows who held a crying and spent Sara Miller. She had a white cloth tied over her mouth.

Off to the side, under the eaves of the mausoleum, Danielle held her head down as if she had just given Jesus to the Romans. When she lifted her eyes to Jay's, she could see betrayal on his face.

Jay knew what had happened. He'd been set up. His ex had brought him to this place as a trade for Sara. It may have been done under duress, but it stung just the same.

"Thank you, Danielle! Ah…the one that got away. The trouble you are causing knows no bounds. It's important to make things right and well, there you have it."

Danielle looked at Ted with contempt.

Ted put his hand out. "I'll take your car keys, lieutenant."

Jay stood defiantly until the beefy one with the goatee pointed his revolver toward him. The other one patted him down and removed the gun from inside his jacket, along with a knife from his sock.

Ted handed Jay's keys over to one of the goon's. "Take the women to their homes. The officer's SUV will be adequate transportation. No lights or playing with the gadgets, mind you. We don't want to cause a stir. Then bring the officers auto to where we discussed. Is that understood?"

The man with the long sideburns nodded and began to proceed with his instructions. As Danielle and Sara filed into the SUV, Ted had one more bit of advice.

"It would be best for all concerned if you block my existence from your mind. Come up with a good story for your disappearance, Sara. A lot depends on it." Ted made the last statement in a forceful, demanding way. "Tonight could prove to be quite interesting. Fasten your seatbelts."

25

Ted's bodyguard handcuffed Jay, with his arms to the front and pushed him into the backseat of a striking blue SUV with dark tinted windows.

Jay looked down at the handcuffs. They appeared to be the same issue the sheriff's department used. Jay didn't see the point in discussing that with Ted Paulson.

Ted felt he'd been forced to take matters into his own hands. *As usual, I have to do everything myself,* he thought. He pulled himself up and into the back seat with Jay. His small build afforded him plenty of room to fold his legs and melt into the corner. He looked Jay over as if he never met him before. That was the nature of Ted's personality. He saw no need to memorize a face or a person's personality unless it directly affected him. Ted Paulson used his intellect as a collection of useful knowledge for those things that mattered in *his* life. Everything else was noise, and that noise was to be dealt with quickly, and then discarded.

"You are a rather large person, aren't you?"

Jay made no attempt to answer.

"Start driving, Carl," Ted ordered his goateed bodyguard.

The thick window between the front and back seat closed and made it obvious to Jay that the driver could not hear their conversation.

"It is said that a rainbow has seven colors, lieutenant. In order they are; red, orange, yellow, green, blue, indigo, and violet. I like blue."

"The fifth color of a rainbow. You seem awfully fixated on the number five, Paulson. Why do you suppose that is?"

"Has that defiant bitch, Danielle been discussing my life with you? No need to answer, I'm quite aware of your conversations." Ted paused to make sure he was composed and in a steady state before continuing. "She's rather brilliant in her way. She knows a lot more than she lets on, you know."

Jay had been hoping this little trip wasn't going to include confessions from the little accountant. He knew that such a conversation could only mean one thing—Ted would see to it that he would not live to see another day.

"It had to be done, you know," Ted said.

"What had to be done?"

Ted smiled with an expression that Jay took as *"Don't play stupid with me, you big dumb cop."*

"The people that got hurt, they don't understand the mind of a young man. They sit in their offices and make hiring decisions like emperors. Think of all the people they refuse to hire for one reason or another. They don't even bother to call them. In the meantime, the prospective employee waits and jumps whenever the phone rings. When it ends up being Aunt Martha on the other end, the life slowly gets sucked out of them. Were you ever in that situation, Lieutenant?"

Let him vent, Jay thought. When the time is right....

Ted looked back at Jay. "Don't bother to try escaping. The driver in your squad car will not hesitate to hurt his passengers if he doesn't hear from me at ten-minute intervals. It's all part of the plan."

Jay wondered if this nutcase could read minds.

"Paulson, these people you hurt, like Bernie Tennison...he didn't deserve that. He didn't even know your son. The same could be said for Peggy Lloyd and all the rest. Isn't it enough that they have to worry about their own families and their employees? How can you expect them to take care of those who don't get hired as well?"

"In life, Lieutenant, someone always has to pay the bill. Well...the buck stops at the owner's doorstep. Had they taken the time to better evaluate my son, perhaps the outcome would have been different. Don't get me wrong, lieutenant, I don't say that they need to hire everybody that walks through their doors, just be kind to them. Let them know why. Perhaps tell them how they can make themselves more desirable for the next one. But these people didn't bother to help my Wayne. They never called him back. Correct policies were not put in place. No, what happened to them was required. There wasn't any other way...no other way."

Jay looked at Ted incredulously. *What the hell, I'm on my way out anyway,* he thought. "You stupid little titmouse, how is hurting and killing business owners going to make people hire differently? That's like trying to fix your neighbor's TV by throwing yours out the window. It doesn't make sense."

"Lieutenant, I...we weren't trying to fix anything, at least not all at once. It's about the correct measure of revenge, plain and simple. You change things one small step at a time. Revenge is an eye-for-an-eye process. It can be achieved in many different ways." Ted smiled to himself and muttered, "Nose-for-a-nose, ear-for-an-ear...if they learn something, that's all the better."

Just as quickly as the smile came to his face, it disappeared. He knocked on the window and motioned to his driver to stop the car.

The car was driven to the side of the country road and Carl the bodyguard pulled Jay out.

Ted glanced out of his window and watched his protector pummel Jay with several blows to the stomach and head.

"Put him back into the car, Carl."

As they drove off once more, Ted continued their discussion.

"You see, Lieutenant, there is a payment to be made for all infractions. You verbally insulted me and we physically assaulted you. Done and done…payment in full."

Battered and bruised, Jay conceded that the short-shit had won the battle, but the war itself was still in question.

"I feel compelled to tell you a few things, Lieutenant. Your future looks rather short at this point, but you merit some semblance of explanation."

"Is there any particular reason why you feel the need to tell me about your dirty little secrets, Paulson? It's not like I'll be joining this cult of yours." Jay's right cheekbone was beginning to swell.

"Ah…but that's just it, clarification. I seek clarification, for you…for me. It's important to understand how people think. By clarifying something that is not yet in focus, and studying the reaction, one can learn a great deal about human behavior." He took a pause as they passed a large farm stocked with milking cows. "First of all, we're not a cult. I believe you have the right to understand why your life will not last as long as you may have hoped. Before I begin, tell me what you believe to be true concerning myself and the occurrences that seem to have struck your little county."

Jay sat quiet. He did not feel the need to encourage the little bastard—until Ted pointed a gun at his head.

"Five people were attacked; each victim had one of their five senses damaged. One was killed. All five were pillars of the community and leaders who owned their own business. The attacks seemed to follow a pattern concerning which section of the county would be hit next. The pattern used was the magic square; each number corresponded to the approximate area that the next victim was to be attacked. How am I doing?"

Ted showed no sign of emotion. Jay, on the other hand, thought he would much rather choke the life out of Ted Paulson than continue their little talk.

Ted sensed it was time to fill in the rest. "Let me finish for you. Despite an incredible lack of evidence, Danielle became instrumental in attaching my name to these crimes."

Jay moved in his seat and winced as his bruised ribs let him know that it was going to take some healing before the pain would dissipate. "Let's just say that it had become very apparent that an accountant with self-esteem issues was responsible for what was going on in Green County."

"Again with the name calling. We'll let it go this time."

Jay was grateful for that.

"You started looking into my background and found the issue with my son, Wayne. You came to the conclusion that I needed to pay back those companies that didn't hire him after he'd been laid off. After the fifth victim, the department began to think that maybe things would go back to normal. You thought the quiet would give you more time to find evidence and eventually arrest me. Unfortunately, Danielle wouldn't keep her mouth shut. She forced my hand. Besides, the magic square needed to be fulfilled. Nice and tidy, that's the way I like it, nice and tidy."

Jay noticed the accountant rubbing his hands and his voice reaching a higher octave. *It's a big "if" but, if I ever get out of this alive, it may help to know more about who may be involved besides Ted Paulson.*

"You said it's not a cult, what is it?"

"It's a way of life, Lieutenant. *You...we* don't have enough time to go into specifics, but living a life through the teachings of ancient truths is a good base. We believe that the base, however, allows for constant updating and improvement to fit the times that we exist in."

"Who's we?"

"Well...it's nice to know Danielle didn't let too much slip during your little conversations. I'm not surprised, but it doesn't hurt to double check."

Danielle just moved up another notch on Jay's betrayal scale.

"As far as whom we are, I prefer to keep our conversation on *why we are.* Although many of our laws of life and teachings go back as far as Pythagoras, more than twenty-five hundred years ago, we first became organized May 5th, 1950. We are a culmination of great teachers, philosophers, numerologists, prophets, alchemists, and others who understand the essence of nature."

"Why so much importance on the number five?"

"The Pythagoreans called the number five 'nature'. They saw it as a kind of mathematical perfection. It is the number of marriage, feminine being the sum of the first even number *two*, and masculine the first odd number *three*. The Upanishad, Hindu scripture say that, "Whatever exists is fivefold." Dynastic Chinese were early sources of the magic square and The Five Cardinal Points. Some of the ancients said that *five* is the *human soul*. To Christians, the number five is prominent everywhere. There are the five wounds of Christ, Pentecost or the fiftieth day. The Roman Catholic Church has

The Five Joyful Mysteries, The Five Sorrowful Mysteries, and The Five Glorious Mysteries. There are symbols such as the pentacle and all of its mystical meanings. Nature gives you the five petaled rose. You have five fingers and five toes, five senses, five basic tastes ....the list goes on. The importance of the number five is not the number itself, however, but the whole of what five represents in all of our lives. I could go on, Lieutenant."

"I think you've made your point."

The SUV slowed and pulled into a long paved driveway that curved through a thickly wooded area. Finally, they stopped in front of a stately mansion. Ted Paulson got out of the vehicle and motioned for his man to remove Jay, who was still handcuffed.

"Ah...we've arrived at our destination." Ted raised both arms as if he were Moses. "I give you Amalthea!"

The magnificent professorial mansion appeared to be ancient, but to be sure, it was not. Jay recalled the construction notice in the newspaper though he had never seen the finished product.

"You didn't build this place on an accountant's salary." Jay stood out from the car and took in the sight on top of the mansion. "Who are you people?"

The amber stone mansion stood five stories high. On the top was a grand Georgian clock tower.

Ted Paulson had the look of a proud Papa.

"You are admiring our clock tower. The fourth story merely holds the room needed for the swing of the rather large pendulum. It's a Three Train Turret Clock and is accurate to within about 15 seconds a week. Not bad for a design from 1890. About once a month I go up and make any adjustments needed."

Ted took out his handkerchief and patted his sweaty forehead.

"Just above the clock hands is our pentagonal bell house with louvered openings."

It appeared to Jay that the clock was in working order. It had just struck four o'clock PM and its mechanics rushed out a strong, yet elegant ring. With each well-toned ring, Jay wondered if he would live to hear the next chronological performance.

Whether Jay wanted to know the particulars or not, Ted wanted him to know. "The name Amalthea comes from the fifth largest moon of Jupiter, and Jupiter is the fifth planet from the sun. Every room in Amalthea has five walls...as does the building itself."

"You'll see that the lawn is well groomed. As you know, we had rather cold conditions brought on by a nasty winter. That frigid weather seemed to push itself sickeningly into our spring season. But I think we beat Mother Nature."

Jay took in everything around him. He thought about times in his past when he had been up against it. At those moments, he saw things with more clarity than ever before. Jay was now in that zone. Though he was never one to give up the ship, life looked bleak and reality was forcing him to calculate the probability of survival. So he took it all in—from the gold-leaf weather vane on the roof to the clear water that ran down a winding stream in the back of Amalthea, his five senses seemed to be at their strongest.

He could hear the cool stream. The smell of blossoming flowers and fresh dirt was intense. His eyes were transfixed to the West, where apple trees and morning glories surrounded paths with small benches that fit perfectly along and into the deep woods. *How could that be?* Jay thought. It is too early for flowers to have bloomed.

Some men and woman walked slowly along the path, or were sitting at benches. They seemed to be in their own worlds, thinking deeply and paying no attention to anything outside their own space.

Ted returned to the back seat of the SUV and opened his briefcase. He removed a type of headphone. He instructed his hired-hand to remain outside Amalthea and placed the earpiece over the man's head.

Ted Paulson stood with Jay, overlooking the large house. Speaking softly, but louder than a whisper, he said, "The United States is not a quiet country, Lieutenant. We prefer to be in areas where thinking comes easily and noisy distractions are not an issue. We have one chapter in each of the fifty states. Each chapter has five charter members...five and no more."

"Two hundred and fifty!"

"You are quick with the numbers, aren't you?" the little bastard said sarcastically.

Jay didn't have any problem ignoring the accountant's comment. He was busy looking at the home of the Wisconsin chapter of five lunatics. Its overall shape appeared to have five sides, just like Paulson had said. The entrance was nothing short of spectacular. The two large wooden doors were carved with five circles, each circle representing an ancient element. The symbols of water, fire, air, and earth were easily recognized within the circles. The fifth and middle circle was divided by the two doors. Its symbol was confusing for Jay, though he remembered Danielle saying it was the center or essence of life. Above the door a pentagram rested inside a half-circle. The symbol was carved with the point up.

"We are not religious zealots or devil worshipers, Lieutenant. We don't have an agenda that includes world domination. We keep within our realm, and only deviate outside of it when it involves protection or adjusting a wrong."

Jay looked at him as if he were spewing venom. "You've been making a lot of...adjustments, haven't you?"

Ted dismissed Jay's last editorial.

"Our chapters are not located in big cities and this is intentional. That would go against everything that we adhere to and believe in. No…we need the quiet…a place that allows for member growth, both physically and mentally. Humans are adapting to the crudeness and poisonous fumes of city life, but not well. We are a people who need nature."

Ted led Jay down a wooded path, his right hand in the pocket of his suit-coat firmly holding on to a .38-caliber.

"We bring our *auditors*, as well as *The Five*, to these places of perfect nature, in order to discover their natural tendencies and abilities."

"Auditors?"

"Some are those that aspire to become one of *The Five*. Of course, most don't achieve that level. It takes daily dedication and learned knowledge. As well, there would need to be an opening for such a thing to happen. Most auditors are completely happy to be here and take in what they can."

Jay stopped and looked down at Paulson.

"The lieutenant is wondering why there wouldn't be strife among those auditors that seek advancement and do not attain it."

Jay felt his mind being read again.

"As with so many things, history has a unique way of providing answers. Some small ancient societies had great rules to live by. They kept their numbers low and taught their people well. But in the areas of security and defense of their own, they were deficient. That, at times, led to their downfall. Let's just say we have taken great pains in protecting our own. We have very little, if any, complaints from within. It's those from the outside that keep us ever vigilant."

The path went on and the auditors remained oblivious to their presence.

"Everything has a purpose, lieutenant. Here, we try our best to keep consistent with the perfection of the number *five*. You can see the apple trees are in abundance; the gynoecium or apple core contains five carpels arranged in a five-pointed star. The greenhouse we just passed is for raising star fruit trees, typically sub-tropical in climate needs. They produce a fruit with five-fold symmetry. The beautiful morning glories and other pentagonal-shaped or five-petaled flowers have no problem blooming early, with our help."

Ted had made a couple of calls to the driver who was to drop off Danielle and Sara. During the last, Jay heard Ted say, "Very good, come back to the compound." That had been some time ago, and Jay had started wondering whether it would be safe to charge the little man without causing harm to the ex-hostages.

"Just to our left, you can smell and see our colorful garden. Not all of our plants are in concert with the number five. We have bush honeysuckle, declined trillium, purple pitcher plants, pink lady-slippers, and many more. You may have noticed many of our trees have a reddish mushroom growth at the trunk. They are the granoderma lucidum. As with many of our plants, we grow them to study their medicinal value. That bracket fungus has been found to lower blood pressure, cholesterol, and blood sugar. More tests need to be done, but it is promising," Ted said. He stopped and shook his head. "That seems like an odd thing to say when the Chinese have been using it as medicine for over 2,000 years."

The path broke into a fork. Ted pulled the revolver out of his pocket and motioned for Jay to take the path to the right.

Ted Paulson pointed the gun, "Over there Lieutenant, behind the smokehouse."

Jay backed up behind a small brick cabin. He didn't see anything unusual at first. Aside from a few apple trees and the well manicured lawn, everything looked natural. Then he saw the deep, rectangular hole in the ground. He bent down on one knee and immediately understood that he was beside what very well may be his final resting place.

"So, Ted, this is it? This is where you've decided to leave the body? I hope you took precautions. Sheriff's Departments don't take a missing lieutenant very lightly." Jay reached behind as if using the ground to help himself up. He quickly scooped up some sand, dug up from the grave, and hid it inside his right hand.

"Oh, don't worry, Lieutenant. Your decision to leave the department is already in the beginning stages. No need to bother yourself with trivial matters. Congratulations are in order. You are the final installment of the magic square."

Paulson pointed his gun at Jay's head.

Just as Jay directed his handful of sand toward Paulson, a shot rang out. Jay ducked and swirled to the ground. He wondered if he had been shot, but he didn't feel anything. A second later, he looked back at Ted. The accountant stood straight for just an instant—and then fell forward into the fresh grave. Jay saw blood pouring from the left side of his forehead. He was relieved to note that the ninth and final section of the magic square had just been fulfilled by someone other than himself.

26

Captain Laura Juul had given Rufe an order. She'd told him that a position for a Lieutenant in a southern state had opened up. The position was to be filled by Lieutenant Jay Barthus. Though Jay didn't yet know he had accepted this position, it was Jim Ruferd's task to make him take the job. Rufe was given two choices—either his partner would be sent to another state or Rufe would be fired. Rufe admired and cared for Jay very much. He had an idea why those with power wanted his partner out of the local scene, but he didn't have to like it. Lieutenant Jay Barthus' immediate release from duty was already accepted by the Department. All the papers were in order. It was regrettable to lose a good man, but it was out of Rufe's hands. Rufe was prepared to tell anyone who questioned the departure that Jay would stop by and say his goodbyes as soon as possible. Rufe was not alone in this little cover-up…not by a long shot.

Rufe would do as the Captain required, but not until he made a trip out to the countryside. His other life had matters that needed attending to, and his other life was the one that really mattered to him. He'd understood from the beginning that in order to reach certain goals, one had to do difficult tasks and make hard decisions. He hadn't known then if he'd have the stomach for it, but when the time came he'd surprised them all, even himself. He wanted Jay to be removed from the situation until cooler heads prevailed. And after all, the new position came with a hefty raise. Jay could start over. No harm would come to him. *What could be wrong with that?* The captain had told Rufe he was to make this happen quickly. Rufe was sure everything would turn out fine. As soon as he came back, he'd find Jay and take care of things.

27

Jay scooped up the gun that the fallen accountant had dropped and darted behind the smoke house. He didn't notice until now, but Ted's weapon was a rare breed. Jay had certainly seen a Colt Detective .38 Special before, but never one with a gold cylinder and inlays.

The sun was beginning to disappear and Jay's attention to his surroundings was temporarily misdirected by the putrid smell escaping the smokehouse. The fragrance of rotted fish was not Jay's favorite.

The sound of leaves rustling in the woods had Jay pointing the golden gun in that direction. A tree seemed to use its branches to throw a rifle out, near the grave. It looked a lot like Jay's own short-barreled riot shotgun—the very one he kept inside his police vehicle.

"It's me...Danielle." Danielle walked out from behind a large ash tree that sprouted as many as ten smaller trunks protruding skyward from its main base.

Jay hesitated and slowly moved out from the protection of the small smokehouse, his gun still pointed at Danielle. *After all,* he thought, *she could have another gun. She might have meant to shoot me, but missed and hit Ted. But then, why not just let Ted do the job?*

"We don't have much time, Jay. Either you trust me and you live, or you don't and you die. Which is it?"

"I'm not sure you understand who is currently carrying a gun?"

"I'm not saying I'll kill you. What I'm saying is someone else will kill you." She looked back at Amalthea. "Please, Jay. We have very little time to waste."

Jay believed her, and in those beautiful eyes he could see something he remembered from a long time ago. Her strength and her caring had not been evident before. He decided to go for the trust...with a side of caution.

"What's the plan?"

"First we bury Ted. Then we run like hell."

Danielle grabbed a shovel while Jay pushed dirt into the hole from the pile beside it. The body was barely covered when they heard the sound of men and woman approaching from the path in the woods.

Danielle dropped her shovel and motioned for Jay to follow her in the opposite direction. A fence surrounded the forty acre compound. Danielle ran as if she knew every inch of the heavily- wooded tract. The trees were thick, and maneuvering around them was more difficult for Jay than for the much leaner Danielle. His bruised ribs didn't help.

It was a relentless dash through the natural obstacle course, and it didn't take Jay long to regret the less-than-healthy diet he'd been courting for the last decade. People always joked about police and their donut laden appetite, but for Jay it rang true. He might not have reached the beer-belly proportions of many of his fellow officers yet, but every year it seemed as if his gut got bigger and his heart raced faster.

When they reached a fence leading to the road, Jay saw his officers SUV parked and waiting. He didn't bother to ask her how she was able to get the vehicle there so quickly. Jay put his hands to his knees and gasped for air. His face was red and blanketed with sweat that ran down his forehead and into his eyes.

As Danielle was about to climb over the chain-link-fence, Jay, despite his obvious fatigue, grabbed her from behind and pushed her back against a tree.

"We...don't...leave until you tell me what's going on."

Danielle gathered herself and, with her back to Jay, swung her right leg high through the air. The sudden half-circle was an instinctive move that connected her foot with Jay's jaw.

Jay's head pounded in a short lived streak of pain. As Danielle swung around to deliver another blow, Jay's forearm blocked it at the knee and sent her tumbling to the ground. He quickly pounced on top of her and held her down.

"Where did you learn how to...? Never mind, I think I know." Jay felt his jaw while holding Danielle to the ground with his other hand.

Sweat dropped from Jay's head and landed on Danielle's face. "Gross...can't this wait until we're gone? They can't be very far behind us."

There were so many things that had happened in her life in the last decade. Jay felt he deserved to know the truth.

"Start from the beginning, and let's do something different this time...stick to the truth."

"I'll tell you while we drive. It's not something that can be said in a minute. Now get off of me you big...."

Jay stood up and cautiously gave Danielle a hand. "You're probably right, but I want to know everything down to the last detail."

Danielle nodded as she and Jay climbed the fence and took the SUV on the road.

Danielle looked over at Jay as he drove down Highway Q. Her mind was racing. She understood that by killing Ted

Paulson, she was more than just a breakaway member of a sect. She was now *the enemy*, and that scared the shit out of her.

"Where are we going?"

Though Jay hadn't grown up in Wisconsin, he knew Green County about as well as anybody. He'd seen glimpses of Amalthea from the road before, but had never bothered to inquire about it. He hadn't been up in these parts for a while, but still recalled bits and pieces of the backwoods. "I know a place, besides...I'll be asking the questions."

"Shoot," Danielle said before realizing her choice of words.

"Start around the time we broke up and go forward from there. I want to know how deep you were in this thing, from beginning to end."

Danielle took a deep breath. She felt like she was about to take a step off a high cliff and was taking Jay with her. She decided to start with the biggest secret first.

"You...we have a child."

"What?"

"We have a girl. She's going to be fifteen...tomorrow."

Jay slowed down to a crawl. "Okay, I wasn't expecting that."

"I wasn't expecting to tell you."

Jay took a breath and sped up a little. "You were pregnant when we split?" Jay thought about asking the obvious question—*Why didn't you tell me?*—but the answer was just as obvious. They'd broken up, in part, because Jay wasn't very big on starting a family.

"Those early days, after Phoebe was born, were tough. After her first six months I went back to work. It was so lonely. I thought about telling you so many times, but I couldn't force my baby on you."

"Her name is Phoebe?"

"Well...that's another story. I'll get to that."

"Where is she?"

"She's...fine. They would never let anything happen to her."

"Who's they?"

"That's what I'm getting to. You see, about the time Phoebe was a year old, I heard from Ted. He presented me with a path for my life. It was just me and Phoebe. I needed something else. I needed something that had direction, meaning, goals...and *The Five* became that something. I was always good with numbers. I began to quickly ascend *The Five Steps* it takes to become one of the chosen five."

"You were one of them?"

"Yes...oh yes, in a big way. Technically, my seat is empty now, but...not for long."

"What do you mean?"

Danielle was full of secrets...secrets that, over the years, had become her own. Her life was based on knowledge of all things learned, history, and goals that only belong to her second family, *The Five*. Revealing some of the particulars to Jay felt like not only a betrayal, but a sense of deep fear. It was a fear of not only those who might be forced to dispense punishment for her betrayal, but the frightening revelation of the truth about herself.

"Jay, I'll need to tell you things about *The Five* that I never thought I would reveal to anybody on the outside. At this point, I don't see any other way."

Jay engulfed her hand in his. "I can't be of any help if you don't confide in me completely."

"We are incorporated across the country as Pednat."

"What's Pednat?"

"Pednat, Inc. is a word scramble. It stands for Pentad, the Pythagorean term for the number five. It also stands for life, power and invulnerability. We use the symbol of the pentad as a sign to recognize each other, just as the Pythagoreans did."

"I suppose you have it tattooed somewhere on your...body." Jay looked her over. "Can I see it?"

"No." She showed the tiniest semblance of a smile. She continued, "It's on an entry key card. Gee whiz, Jay it's not like we tattoo or brand people with a hot iron."

"Sorry, sometimes I watch too much TV."

Jay thought perhaps on some warm summer day in the distant future, provided he had a future, he would sit down and learn more about all the terms Danielle was throwing at him. For now, he merely tried to keep up.

"After being accepted to The Five, a member begins as a *novice* and, from there, they advance to a *minor*. Together, the novices and minors are called our auditors. If they are found to possess the characteristics required, they can reach the *circle of the major*. Just beyond the *circle* and below *The Elite Five* are *The Five Tables*. By that time, they are well past the basics and are learning advanced body and mind exercises. You just witnessed an instinctive move I never would have attempted fifteen years ago. Your daughter entered *The Five Tables* when she was just thirteen. She is one of our twenty-five brightest. It is unprecedented. At her young age she has advanced so fast and with so much knowledge and strength that she will surely be picked for *The Elite Five*, that is, the five members who rule the state chapter. The five that run the entire organization are called *The Pentium Five*. Where and who they are has always been a deeply kept secret."

Jay's anger was now showing. He was told that not only does he have a daughter he'd never met, but she is knee deep in a secret murderous society's inner circle.

It wasn't difficult for Danielle to sense his anguish.

"Jay, *The Five* was your replacement. They became Phoebe's father and I not only condoned this, I pushed and encouraged it." Danielle could scarcely say the last couple of words.

"What happened, Danielle? Your little society must have been doing well for quite some time. Until now they've kept under the radar. I've never heard of them. Why did they decide to do the things they did? Why hurt people?"

"It was Ted! Each of the chosen five has a leader of sorts. Though each of *The Five* is equal, there has to be a point man, someone to go to with questions. Ted was the connection between our state sect and the *Pentium Five*. Ted was our contact to them and he couldn't or wouldn't let the other four know how or when he communicated with them."

"Where's my daught...where's Phoebe?

"She wasn't always Phoebe. I named her Emily when she was born. About ten years ago her name was changed in honor of one who had once served as a long standing member of *The Five*. At our funerals, it is tradition for those who belong to *The Five* to throw five pebbles on top of the casket as it lay in the ground. Phoebe asked if she could do the honors. Your five-year-old daughter threw only four pebbles. We urged her to throw the fifth, and when she finally did, it landed in the middle of the four other pebbles and scattered them. The four outside pebbles landed in a perfect square, making a quincunx pattern. "Little Phoebe" is known as a cardinal number that is the sum of four and one. When this was witnessed by all in attendance, it was agreed that the signs were too strong to ignore. I concurred, and her name was permanently changed."

Though Jay found the story of his daughter's name fascinating, his mind was on her whereabouts. "Where is she?"

"She's at Amalthea...or at least that's where I last saw her."

"Then we need to go back. We need to get her out of there."

Danielle was exasperated and tired and the tone of her voice made it evident. "Don't you think I would have if I'd been able to? I've thought of picking her up and flying to another country, or changing our names and identities, but there is more to it than that."

Jay took a hard right onto an old dirt road. It was nearly impossible to see in the darkness of the night, and he'd almost missed the turn. As the SUV passed through the overgrowth of trees, he could hear the cracking of dead branches under the tires. He stopped in front of a dilapidated farm house with a large front porch.

Danielle searched the SUV for a flashlight and found one in the glove department.

Jay opened his window and drew in some fresh air. "Well, something went right today. I didn't know if this old place would still be here. A few years ago we had to evict a family from this broken down old house. It was dangerous just to walk around inside the place."

Before Jay left the SUV, Danielle put her hand on his and said, "Phoebe turns fifteen tomorrow. I'm worried about her. You're right, we need to make sure she's safe."

"We'll find her. We'll make sure she's all right." It was a promise that Jay meant to keep.

For a farmhouse the place was extremely small. Jay remembered it as having a kitchen and one bedroom. The outhouse was in the back, but even years ago when he'd removed the occupants it had looked like a mild wind would take it down.

Jay stepped slowly toward the front door, vigilant of the weak floorboards. When he reached it, he was surprised to find it still locked. In an attempt to show Danielle that he could kick with power as well, he booted the door just to the left of the handle. Instead of the door breaking open, as Jay anticipated, his foot went through the rotted wood and his leg became lodged in the hole he had made.

Danielle, meanwhile, stepped inside one of the several broken windows and opened the door from the inside. Jay was still attached to the other side and cursed as she helped to remove him from his predicament.

When Jay had recovered from his encounter with the door, they settled into two wooden chairs with a beat up kitchen table between them. Jay tested his chair before sitting, he didn't want another incident.

"Who are *The Five*? Do I know them?"

"The chosen five from each state are traditionally called *The Noble Five*. There was myself, and of course, Ted. I replaced Ted's son Wayne a couple of years ago. Phil Garnett, a lawyer from Chicago, is another, though he spends most of his time here in Green County."

"I've met him…kind of a big fat ass?"

"Yeah, that's him, but practically a genius in the study of law and numbers."

"Who else?"

"The other two might kind of surprise you. As if my life isn't in jeopardy enough, this bit of information will put the finishing touches on my cement boots."

"Well?"

"Your partner, Jim Ruferd—as well as your captain, Laura Juul."

Jay sat stunned. His partner for the last five years had a double life of sorts. It took a moment for him to get his head around what Danielle had said.

"So that's why he's been acting strange lately. Little things were beginning to show themselves. I didn't quite know what it was, but something wasn't right. I thought it was something else."

"What?"

"He always got quiet when I would kid him about a girlfriend or his personal life. I thought he was maybe, you know...gay. I thought he was struggling with the coming out thing."

"You always were intuitive about those sorts of things."

"Wow! Sarcasm, who would have thought?"

"Believe me, he's not gay."

"You're joking. You and Rufe...together, I don't believe it."

"Good, because it never happened. I'm talking about other members. He's quite the girl magnet around Amalthea."

Jay's thoughts turned to his boss. "What about Captain Juul? She was captain of the department before I was hired. She could have taken me off this case. If she didn't like me poking around, why didn't she get somebody else on it?"

"You got the first call. Everybody needed to go through the motions, not look suspicious."

"I'll be dammed. How long has Laura been part of *the dark side?*"

Calling a group of people she'd invested years into *"the dark side"* did not sit well with Danielle.

"I'm not going to tell you again. It was one rusty nail among those that shine."

"Sorry! But if the rest of *The Noble Five* are such wonderful people, why are we afraid for our lives, as well as our daughter's?"

"To answer your first question, Laura's been one of *The Noble Five* for over twenty years. All together, including her early training, she's been with the sect for thirty years. That's longer than Ted. To answer your second, good people sometimes get led down the wrong path by someone they believe in. That's what happened to Phoebe and that is what happened with the other *five.*"

This was an enormous amount of new information for Jay to take in. His past life and all that went with it seemed to be drifting into another dimension. He knew his place on earth, and though not everything was smooth sailing, there was purpose, ritual, tradition, and a comfortable routine. Now it had all changed. What had seemed normal before is not. He only knew that he needed to make things right. For now, however, he had more questions and confusion than he had answers.

"So right now, Rufe, the Captain, and the rest think I'm dead."

"If they are in bed with Ted on this, then yes, they probably think Ted shot you and dropped you in the grave out back. But, if Ted was on his own, they may be checking out that grave as we speak. They'll find Ted's body."

"Why was Rufe helping me find out who was responsible for the mutilation of our company owners? Why wouldn't he have tried to steer me away from Ted Paulson?"

"It was all part of the plan."

"Tell me about the *plan*?"

"All members of *The Noble Five* were ordered to report to a special room. It only fits five people. Ted had put a plan together and presented it to us for a majority vote. His plan was to avenge the suicide of his son, Wayne. He showed us the list of those companies that didn't hire Wayne and didn't have the courtesy to even give him a rejection notice. Ted felt it all contributed to Wayne's demise. He showed us the master book of five. It spelled out that members of *The Five* who are hurt by outsiders are to be avenged. He reminded us of our oath when we agreed to become one of *The Noble Five*. His plan was drawn out as it happened. Rather than wait and find out if someone like you would put some clues together and link them to the sect, Ted decided to push the matter. He knew he would be brought up on charges, and he knew the case against him would be dropped due to lack of evidence. I'm afraid the pull he had in the long branch of the law, goes much farther than just Rufe, and Captain Juul."

"I take it you were the clog in his plan?"

"The vote was three to two in favor of Ted's plan. Rufe and I voted against it, but we understood that majority ruled. We knew that a majority meant that we had to follow along with the plan precisely as it was written."

"You couldn't do it."

"I wouldn't do it. I felt that Ted had gone over the deep end on this. We were meant to learn how to use numbers to achieve a perfect harmony between matter, body, mind, soul, and spirit. The specific steps of revenge, as written, did not specifically mention the types of torture that ensued. It could have been interpreted in many different ways. Before the vote, he made it sound like we would exact our revenge by hurting them financially or by finding something in their background that could cause embarrassment and humiliation. I didn't trust Ted. After the first act of violence on Bernie Tennison, I was out. It didn't set things back into a balanced state, as Ted had tried to persuade the others. We argued over it incessantly, until I realized Ted was going to hold his ground. I finally decided it was time to turn away from this family that I had grown to love."

Jay took a deep breath. It felt as if he hadn't taken in a solid volume of air in days, and it felt good. He was beginning to understand what Danielle had been going through and wondered when the last time it was that she let good clean air fill her lungs.

"I take it *The Noble Five* were not in favor of your decision to leave."

"Nobody had ever tried it before. Once you were chosen, and you accepted, you were in it for life. I thought of it as the mafia without the violence. Ted's immediate reaction was one of defiance. Since there is no precedence, there can be no acceptance. He eventually contacted the *Pentium Five.* When Ted presented us with their answer, I had no way to know for sure if he was making it up or following orders."

"What did they decide?"

"I could leave under certain conditions. I would be monitored for the rest of my life. It would have been as if I were under house arrest or had to check in with a parole officer."

"Was that it?"

"Not even close. The decision to leave with my daughter would be left to Phoebe. She would be allowed to make the decision as to whether she wanted to leave with me or stay with *The Five.*" Danielle took a deep breath. "She chose the sect."

"She what?"

"If I'd done this earlier, it would have been different. After so many years...she's entrenched in it. Her entire being is *The Five*. I've never told her why I decided to leave. It was forbidden to discuss meeting details with anyone other than *The Noble Five.*"

Jay didn't see the point in asking her why she didn't just grab her and run. This wasn't just a matter of five people in each state. He now knew that each sect included hundreds of members, most of which were professionals in their field. However, nothing was mentioned about leaving the country.

"What about Europe? The Fives members are only in the states, isn't that right?"

"I've been afraid to go down that path. I knew it wasn't likely I could arrange an escape to another country without Ted finding out. If he could kill and maim his victims in the name of *The Five*, he could do the same to me. Over the years, Phoebe had become a granddaughter of sorts to Ted. There was a time he would have done anything he could to make sure she continued her life with *The Five* and eventually became a member of the Noble Five. But in the last year he'd changed; he could snap and hurt her."

"So you decided that the only way out was to kill Ted."

"He had to be stopped. He had you and it was me that put you in this situation," She paused. Only half of her face could be seen as the three-quarters moon shined through one of the few windows that were not broken.

"That's two people I've killed today." Jay noticed that Danielle was continually wringing her hands as if she was trying to push the death off of her fingers.

Jay thought for a moment. "The SUV driver."

"I...I asked him to drop us off by the plant...out of the way...behind the packaging building. Sara was crying and was understandably confused. She was having a hard time moving her legs because she'd been tied to a chair all day. I persuaded the driver to help her to a picnic table that rested under a large oak tree. I knew what Ted was about to do to you. I needed the SUV, and I needed it fast. I thought of Phoebe and my stomach ached, wondering if he might decide to hurt her as well. As the driver bent over to help Sara, I took his gun from his coat pocket and pointed it toward him. He picked up Sara and held her in front of him. He said he was going to break her neck if I didn't give him the gun. I shot him, Jay."

Jay grabbed her and hugged her tight. "You didn't have a choice, Danielle. What else could you do?"

"I shot him in the neck. It sprayed all over. I can still see the blood on Sara's face. The horror she must have felt. I told her to call the police and I left. I assume Captain Juul cleaned up the mess."

"I'm sorry you had to go through that, Danielle. I wish I could take it all away."

"Jay, I've killed a member of the *Noble Five*. They have Phoebe. I don't know what they will decide to do with her."

Jay held her. She smelled of fresh pine with a scent of light perfume. He could see her pain and those eyes, those beautiful eyes, were moist. He kissed her as if the kiss could make the hurt go away. A part of him wanted her right then and there, but he knew their ordeal was not near over and it was time to meet his daughter.

Jay held her close and whispered. "We have a daughter to find. We need to protect her, whether she wants our help or not."

Danielle turned her back to Jay. "I know…Phoebe is the most important person in my life. I wish you could have seen what it was like. Until Ted became unhinged, it was a place of beauty and magic. She's been oblivious to what has been happening. From the outside, because of one man, it will appear that *The Five* are some sort of ugly cult. The very publicity that they shun will haunt them, and the good that was always a part of their nature will be lost. I'm still not sure if taking Phoebe from *The Five* will help her. Ted Paulson is dead. Maybe he's taken the poison of the sect with him."

Danielle knew that events sometimes transpired to a point at which there appeared to be no way to make things right. Whether it was God or the human spirit, life would always present a small window of hope if she looked hard enough. She was looking now for that tiny opening. She stood up and moved to the window that was sending moonbeams into the dilapidated old kitchen.

"It'll be light in a few hours, but I don't think we can wait. We need to go back to Amalthea. We'll convince the others that Ted's death was not only needed, but was the only way for *The Five* to correct many wrongs."

"It's not that easy, Danielle. They all played a part in the crimes that Green County endured in the last couple of weeks. There's a debt to be paid."

"I think it may have been Rufe that attacked me at the plant, Jay. Don't you see? He was forced to do his part. When it came time for him to take away my sense of smell, he held back. He could have followed through and finished the job, but he couldn't. Everybody was a pawn to Ted. Ted's the only one that truly deserved to be punished for what happened."

"What about the cover-up? What about the *Noble Five*...Rufe, Phil Garnett, and Captain Juul? They all hid the truth."

Danielle stood up, grabbed the car keys from the kitchen table and walked toward the door. "I understand they need to pay a price for following that madman, but right now we need to find Phoebe. I don't think there is much of a choice here."

She could see he was struggling, but time was not on their side.

"We had better get back to Amalthea before they make a decision that doesn't go our way. What's it going to be?"

Jay placed his pistol just inside the front of his belt. The gold Colt revolver went in the inside cover of his jacket. He then retrieved the rifle.

"Let's go! You drive," he grunted.

28

Except for the headlights, the visibility was now totally black. The trees on both sides of the road were tall and left no trace of a moon. If not for their daughter, they would be driving in the opposite direction.

"I've never seen her. I don't know what Phoebe looks like. I would have noticed pictures on the walls or framed on your desk," Jay said. "I don't remember seeing any trace of her in your home."

"I boxed them up the day you provided me with protection. I tend to take care of things on my own."

"Yes…and how is that working out for you?"

"Smart ass!"

Danielle reached back with one hand and unclasped her necklace, handing it to Jay.

"Open the locket."

Inside was a small picture of Danielle with a young girl. Phoebe had dark hair, lighter than her mother's, and longer.

"Her smile looks like yours. She's tall. I wonder where she got that trait." Jay scratched his head. "She's beautiful, Danielle. I was envisioning a young girl with my mug, and it wasn't pretty."

"Phoebe is smart, pretty, and, yes…tall, but something more. I guess…headstrong is the word. Sometimes she can be downright stubborn. They've held her from me, but my guess is she hasn't been doing a lot of protesting. I don't know what Ted told her about me, but she seems to idolize that little creep. If she ever found out I killed him…well, I don't think she'd take it very well."

Jay watched Danielle drive the many hooks, turns, and bends the road before them offered. The trip back to Amalthea seemed to be taking longer than did their escape from it. "When did you last speak to Phoebe?"

Danielle didn't have to think back far. "It was a few days ago. Phoebe called me, and I remember feeling as though someone was listening to our conversation. She was happy that day. Some of *The Five* asked her if she would prefer to continue being home schooled, rather than waste her time and talents at Lincoln High School. In Phoebe's mind the answer was obvious. It wasn't a question of if she would be schooled at Amalthea…it was *when*."

"Didn't she question your recent absence from her life?"

Danielle didn't think of her life with her daughter in those terms. Jay's question bothered her, and yet, intrigued her. When your daughter's adopted father is an accumulation of many, her life is divided up in different directions and time is less a consequence than a so-called *normal life*. Phoebe often left home to run clinics for younger children or to be a student in the life process that is the way of *The Five*.

"I expect that any questions she may have had about my whereabouts were answered to her satisfaction."

"What was the last thing she said to you?"

"Actually," she said looking at her phone. "She just sent me a text."

"What does it say?"

"It's a sort of riddle. She's always trying to stump me. It says, "*It may be too late by the time you arrive, I'd try Pentateuch 555.*"

"What is that supposed to mean?"

"I don't know."

If they were going to attempt to remove Phoebe from Amalthea, it was Jay's nature to understand Phoebe's mind set. Many times the last words spoken are the most meaningful.

29

It had been a couple of hours since the sun went down. On a normal weeknight Amalthea would be dark and empty, save for an occasional security light. Danielle knew that at this time of night the only human remaining on the compound would be their night watchman/handyman, Harry Conwell. This wasn't a typical night, however. They didn't park the SUV in the same place as it had been earlier. Rambling through the woods when it was still light out had been hard enough, but trying to do the same at night made little sense. Jay left the rifle behind, but took Ted Paulson's pistol. They parked off the road less than a half-mile away, jumped the fence and walked toward the back of the mansion.

Danielle stood behind a tree about fifty feet from the old smokehouse and said, "It's lit up as bright as my Uncle Jack's house during Christmas."

The tall lights shone over the compound, casting shadows from the trees.

They walked closer to the grave that had held the body of Ted Paulson a few hours earlier. Jay wondered if perhaps they had stumbled into a different, but similar, realm. He could see the smokehouse, but the ground nearby looked neat and tidy. There were no shovels, no piles of dirt, and, most striking, no grave.

"They covered it. My grave...the grave, it's filled and covered with turf. Did they assume it was me or did they check out the body first?" Jay almost sounded offended by the unceremonious way they'd covered his remains.

Danielle looked around as if she was scanning for clues to an unanswerable question. "I don't know what their next move is, but it won't take long for them to realize Ted is gone."

"Is there someplace that we can get a look at them? If they've huddled together discussing their options, maybe they have Phoebe with them."

"If they're still here—and I can't imagine where else they would be—then I'd bet on the Pentahedron Room."

Danielle knew from Jay's look that he needed an explanation.

"It's a three sided room, like a triangle. Counting the ceiling and floor, it then has five sides. They call it a polyhedron with five faces. That is...it has three squares on the side and two triangles, top and bottom."

"Okay?"

"It's a type of emergency room. A place where ideas, thoughts, and decisions are made when one has little time to ponder alternatives. Nobody leaves the Pentahedron Room until a decision is made. If the door is left open, we might be able to see them from an outside window. I don't think we'll be able to hear them from out here, however. There aren't any windows in the room itself."

They ran one at a time toward the back of Amalthea. The scattered trees were just thick enough to hide the shadows brought on by the heavily lighted compound. From there, they crawled to the bushes that surrounded the building. Danielle reached the targeted window before Jay. She could see the lobby. Jay inched in next to her.

"That set of five circles in the middle of the lobby—I saw that same pattern at Ted's private home."

"It's a symbol of The Five essences. It's similar to the Cardinal Points that Ted was using. The symbols in the lobby are representative of the Pythagoreans," Danielle whispered. She scanned the room. To her right, she could see the door into the Pentahedron Room.

"There, to the right. The door is slightly open. It's a little dim, but I can see Laura and Phil. There are no chairs in that room. You make decisions more quickly if you are forced to stand."

They remained silent, hoping for more movement from within the oddly angled room. Jay watched Phil, who seemed to be doing most of the talking. From his vantage point, he could make out hand gesturing from someone near the door. It was probably Rufe, since only three of *The Five* were left. Ted was dead, and Danielle had left them. Jay wanted desperately to see his daughter. Feeling that those in the room were at blame as well as Ted, he wanted to spread his hands around Phil's thick neck and choke the life out of him. Then they heard footsteps.

Danielle put her finger to her lips, and Jay reached for his pistol. Three figures wearing dark clothing and wielding rather heavy firepower, walked past them. They'd come from the same direction as Danielle and Jay had moments earlier. As soon as the three gunmen passed, Jay signaled Danielle to go back into the woods. But as they got to their knees, they turned to see one gunman behind Jay and another reached down, pulling Danielle up, his forearm now tightly around her neck. The man behind Jay bent down and relieved him of his pistol.

"We have them," one of the men relayed into a device on his wrist.

The device responded with, "Bring them down."

30

A short walk to a back door brought the two captives down a narrow stairs and into the northwest side of the lobby. To the right was the Pentahedron Room. Jay glanced inside, but it appeared empty.

"Shoes off," one of the gunman ordered.

Danielle already had hers off. Jay had been envisioning his soiled shoes dragging nicely across the pristine white carpeting, but the gun at his back changed his mind.

They were marched to the left of the lobby and down a well lit hallway to a large oak door with a multitude of translations of the words "The Five" written on it. The only version that Jay understood was the English one. The room, however, was very familiar to Danielle.

The room seemed to be as perfect a circle as humanly possible. In its center was a pentagonal table with five chairs placed around it. Artifacts of all types laced the walls. There were swords, armor, aged books, cased letters, and a veritable treasure of paintings. Jay and Danielle sat in the two empty chairs. Jim Ruferd, Phil Garnett, and Laura Juul were the occupants of the other three. One gunman stayed just inside the door, his ears covered with headphones, while two others guarded the outside.

Rufe's expression was one of resignation and guilt. He'd tried to convince himself that he had very little to feel guilty about, but it pained him to see his partner being held at gunpoint.

Phil Garnett, the heavy-set lawyer, and Laura Juul, Jay's department captain, were wearing business attire that went well with their authoritative demeanor.

Jay sat quietly, but if looks could kill, the three that sat across the table would've already been in the obituaries and buried.

Danielle broke the silence. "Where's Phoebe?"

Phil wiped sweat from his forehead. "Before we get into the details of your daughter's whereabouts, we have a few questions of our own." He stood, revealing pants that, in some neighborhoods, young men would consider shorts. He leaned over and looked Danielle in the eye. "Are you out of your fucking mind? You shoot Ted, and then have the balls to come back here making demands."

Captain Juul pulled the fat man down. "Take it easy Phil. What's done is done. What matters is…what happens next."

As Phil moved uncomfortably in his chair, Danielle briefly recalled Ted's illustration of the new chairs that he'd ordered only a year ago. They were better described as thrones. Ted explained that *The Five* should have something to signify the hard work and dedication it had taken to achieve such a status. Each throne was made of Honduras mahogany, and the hand-tacked dark leather cushion was of the highest quality. Carved into the right-hand spindle was a male figure inscribed inside a pentagram, while the left held that of a female. Together they hold the symbol of the divine nature of mankind.

In the end of each arm-rest is a quincunx pattern. The four corner dots, as well as the center, are gold-leafed.

Rufe transfixed his eyes on Laura Juul, but his words were directed at Jay and Danielle.

"Jay...Danielle, we want to...that is...we've made arrangements that we think will ensure a reasonable outcome."

Jay couldn't hold it in anymore. "A reasonable outcome...assault, murder, kidnapping...what do you expect the endgame to be? Rufe, Laura, fat boy, you're all so entrenched in this it would take an earthquake to bury it."

Phil Garnett smiled despite the nickname Jay had used to address him.

"Speaking of burying something, I believe you two did just that, didn't you? Theodore Paulson is the guy you're looking for. No one else was involved, just Ted." The paunchy lawyer leaned back, looking satisfied with himself. Still, sweat poured down his temples and stains left an oval shaped shadow the size of a football around his armpits. "Of course one of you, or both, shot and killed the man. Shot and killed an unarmed man, the way I see it. It would appear you took police matters into your own hands."

Jay looked, incredulous, at the three conspirators.

Danielle, on the other hand, was not surprised. She knew each of them and what they were capable of. She knew Rufe much better than Jay did, despite Jay's five years as his partner. She'd gone through many of the same processes, procedures, trials, failures, and successes that her three contemporaries had.

She glanced at her three ex-partners and saw them in a new light. Why hadn't she noticed before it was too late? All three were members at a young age. To them the life within *The Five* was like being Caucasian. You just were and there wasn't anything else to be said about it. Rufe had been a member of the Colorado version of Pednat Incorporated for years before moving to Wisconsin. He'd been thirteen when his mom and dad got him involved.

Laura Juul had been about the same age, living in California, when she joined. Phil Garnett was so young he couldn't remember a time he hadn't been a member.

Danielle stood, causing the armed men to point their weapons. She looked at one of them with a knowing smile.

"What am I going to do, Joseph, make a run for it?"

Joseph didn't comment or change the direction of his rifle barrel.

Danielle took a deep breath and probed the room, as if the walls held clues to a puzzle. "We were in the Pentahedron Room, remember? It was early March. Ted went on and on about doing what was right. He was hell-bent on revenge for the death of his son and wanted our support. We voted…and majority won. The plan was carried out. All company owners were to lose one of their senses, thereby making the memory of his son, Wayne, whole again. I, and to be fair, Rufe, were both against it. I couldn't do it and I wanted out. It was then that Ted must have decided I was to be one of the victims." She glanced at Rufe. "What happened after that? Why did you go along with Ted's scheme to hurt my friends and relatives?"

They looked at her as though puzzled.

"The Cardinal Points, my teacher, my little cousin…you killed them." She pointed at the large brown leather book in the far corner of the room, the glass case covering it as it lay on top of a grand oak pedestal. "There's nothing in that book that states "kill a deserter's friends and family.""

The big lawyer stood up once again and asked his two comrades to follow him outside of the room.

Jay and Danielle could hear the muffled sound of discussion, but could not make out what was being said.

Moments later, they returned to their seats.

Laura Juul, her brown eyes staring into Danielle's set of greens said, "Danielle...and we mean this as honestly and sincerely as we possibly can, we don't have a clue as to what you are talking about."

Jay sat back. "Bullshit!"

Danielle studied the three across from her.

"I think they mean it, Jay." She was still standing. She turned and covered her face with her right hand. "That bastard did it himself. He did it on his own."

Rufe looked as if he'd swallowed a wasp. "After I saw what happened to Marcus Wingate, I called a special meeting. It did not include Ted. We decided to have nothing to do with Ted until we got further instruction from the *Pentium Five.*"

Rufe, who had been looking down at his hands, gazed up at Laura and Phil. "Ted carried on as if nothing had happened. But something had definitely changed. Tell us about the Cardinal Points."

Danielle could see, perhaps, a chance to get them to fight with her, instead of against.

"Ted planned to finish out the magic square. Now that his son's suicide had been avenged, he turned his attention towards me. He not only hated me for leaving, I believe he thought he could get rid of me and replace my position with my Phoebe. As is Ted's way, he started to mess with my mind and leave his little clues."

Phil grumbled, "Everything's a game to that man."

"It started when I read that my old grade school teacher, Martha Wycoff, died in a fire."

"Fire correlates with red and south," Laura interjected.

"Correct...she died in her red house in southern Green County. There were four other occurrences. My grandfather, my little cousin, and Sara Miller were all his victims. Ted laid out clues for me to see. I was able to put together all of them…except Jay. He wanted me to bring Jay to him for a trade with Sara Miller."

The room fell silent until Rufe stood. As he spoke the tension that seemed to have a stranglehold on him, lifted but did not disappear.

"He's not dead."

Jay could see the confident officer he had known for years finally returning.

"Who…who's not dead?" Danielle barely got the words out of her mouth.

"Ted…he didn't die, he's alive. We heard a shot, and put the compound on alert. We ran to the back, and saw the hole. Something was moving in the dirt."

It was Laura's turn to speak. "We pulled him out from the hole and brought him inside. His face was covered with blood and dirt. I can understand why you thought he might have been dead. After we cleaned him up it was evident that the bullet hit him near the right temple. It was more than just a flesh wound, but we couldn't tell the extent of the damage."

The rotund lawyer leaned back. "We bandaged him up, and we were making arrangements to bring him to St. Vincent's Hospital when he stood and refused to go. He said he was feeling fine and needed some time alone to think."

Phil pointed upward. "He's been upstairs ever since."

Danielle was a little more than shocked. "Where's Phoebe?"

"She's fine. She insisted upon helping Ted—feeding him, cleaning him up, getting him a change of clothes," Rufe said. "They're in the cenacle. Ted insisted on that room."

Jay stood and gave Rufe a look that would have made a pit bull cower away. "You let that madman alone with Phoebe?"

Jay's hatred for Ted Paulson was much more intense than he ever had for any other human being, including that of

Raymond Golan. About five years earlier, Jay had gotten a call about a possible domestic dispute. When he'd arrived, he found Raymond's girlfriend huddled under the basement stairs. Her knees were curled up to her chest and she tilted her head, like a curious puppy. After coaxing her out, Jay found her right eye protruding through the socket and a large open cut beneath it. Blood dripped down the side of her face. There were other bumps and bruises, including a dislocated shoulder. But what struck Jay, and what had become permanently ingrained in his memory, was the look on Raymond Golan's face as they carried his "squeeze" out to the waiting ambulance. The curled lip, the toothpick dangling from his mouth…he was telling Jay that he didn't give a shit. He'd hit her that night just like he had done many nights before, and he would do it again. She would come back to him or he would find her, but the cycle of abuse would continue one way or the other. If Jay was a betting man, he'd have bet all he had that the girl would be waiting for him when he got out of jail. He wanted Raymond to run, or take a swing at him—anything that would give him an excuse to hurt the man five times worse than the man hurt his girlfriend. What was worse was that Raymond knew. He knew that Jay would beat him into a coma if given the chance, so he played just inside the boundaries. Because he had, that was where it had to end. Jay had fought the urge to beat him senseless and, in doing so, he won. He kept his job and was able to fight the next battle. Raymond spent time in jail and that was the best Jay could hope for.

   With Ted Paulson, Jay's ability to keep his cool had left the building. This time it was all too personal. This time self-preservation meant little. It was a daughter he'd never met and Danielle that mattered. He ran to the door where the guard held his ground. Jay was about to dismantle the guard when Phil Garnett waved him off. Jay ran out of the room and up the stairs with Danielle not far behind.

31

When Jay reached the top floor, he looked down a long hallway with two doors on his left and three to the right. He had no idea which to choose.

Danielle, on the other hand, knew exactly which room Rufe had been referring to.

"Every room in Amalthea has something distinctive and meaningful about it. The cenacle is no exception."

She sped past Jay to the middle door on the right.

The door was open, but just a crack. Danielle reached for the light-switch. The central chandelier illuminated a well-appointed room with a gothic vaulted ceiling where borders reached the center. Jay was not surprised to count five borders.

They madly searched the sleeping area, dining nook, and bathroom. There was no one to be found. Jay only found bloody bandages in the bathroom sink.

Danielle leaned against a book shelf just off of the dining area. "I'm not liking this." She looked over at Jay, who was searching for anything that might help them consider their next move.

"This room is used as a kind of overnight apartment. We put people here that might be visiting." She glanced over at

Jay to see if he was listening. "It's called the cenacle room because the cenacle is considered the room of the Last Supper." Danielle emphasized those final two words.

Jay let her words sink in, despite the growing anger and anxiety that set up shop inside his stomach.

"I don't mind if that madman gets crucified, but what about Phoebe? Did she go with him willingly, or did he force her?"

Danielle heard the rambling of Rufe and Laura Juul just outside the door. Phil Garnett was still lumbering up the last few steps of the stairs.

"I don't know the answer to that, Jay."

"I'm sorry, Danielle," Rufe said, having noted Ted and Phoebe's absence. "We'll have security do a check around the compound."

Jay briefly wondered if Rufe knew he was Phoebe's father. He quickly decided that he didn't give a shit one way or the other. "I need to find the bastard, Rufe. When did you last see them?"

Rufe looked at his watch. "Couldn't have been more than an hour ago."

Rufe left while Danielle and Jay continued to scan the apartment for any hint of where they might have gone.

Jay rubbed his forehead and walked toward Danielle.

"Wasn't it about forty-five minutes ago when Phoebe left you the text message?"

She took out her cell-phone again and read the message out loud. "It may be too late by the time you arrive, I'd try Pentateuch 555."

"Let me see that." Phil Garnett pushed past Laura and walked across the room to Danielle. He was breathing hard.

Danielle watched the lawyer and wondered what made him the way he was. She always knew Phil as a person who wasn't one to think about anybody's feelings. He said what he felt needed to be said without worrying about any outside effects. Some small part inside of him was missing, and after so many years, it was never going to find its way to the surface.

"If Phoebe is with Ted, it's because he either promised her something, threatened her in some way, or she's unconscious. Either way I don't think we have a lot of time. Ted's thinking is completely out of whack, but he's proficient and quite precise in whatever path he takes." The fat man sat down and wiped sweat from his forehead with a handkerchief. His big white hankie could have passed for a small bed sheet. It had become a part of him since his weight reached and surpassed the three-hundred-pound level.

Jay stood over the lawyer and handed him Danielle's phone. "Does this text mean anything to you?"

Phil glanced at it. "It means Ted has turned this into his own little game. Riddles and rhymes may be something that Phoebe enjoys, but Ted…well…he's a different animal. It may have been sent from Phoebe's phone, but she's not the one who sent it. This is Ted's." Phil glanced at the text again and gestured to Danielle. "Hand me that Hebrew Bible over there, the Biblia Hebraica."

On the top shelf of a small bookcase in the living room held a Holy Bible with gold lettering over black leather. Danielle had seen the old book before and noted that it was of a 1716 vintage with Hebrew text. It contained a Latin preface with margin notes. The book was truly a bible for the scholars.

Phil paged to the table of contents and looked over the Old Testament. Though the words appeared very fuzzy to him without his reading glasses, he could make out the larger print. Phil was quite sure that he was the only one in the room, perhaps within the state, that could read the written word of the Hebrew language.

"Here it is. Pentateuch is the first five books of the Hebrew Scriptures...the Old Testament. Pentateuch 555 could mean the 5th book, the 5th chapter, and the 5th verse."

While Phil was searching for his reading glasses to read the smaller print verse, Danielle took control of the bible.

"*Deuteronomy* is the fifth book of the Pentateuch." She pointed down. "There's the fifth chapter." She began to write the translation of the fifth verse.

Jay was happy to see the combined look of surprise and jealousy on Phil's face as Danielle finished jotting down her interpretation.

It read: *I stood between the Lord and you at that time, to declare unto you the word of the Lord; for ye were afraid because of the fire, and went not up the mountain.*

Phil looked over her work, raised an eyebrow, and grumbled something inaudible.

Laura Juul stood just inside the hallway door and absorbed all that had and was transpiring. She felt her life with *The Five* unraveling. *The Five* was her safe life...the half that kept her sane and allowed her to use her highly intelligent mind for something other than police work. Unlike Jay, college had been more of a breeze for Laura. She retained what she read and did it quickly. She'd been the one that most people couldn't stand, because it appeared as though she never worked for her outstanding grade point average.

She'd chosen criminology for her major, but numerology was her passion. In her senior year at Notre Dame, she had been introduced to a Professor Emeritus by the name of Vincent Gikland. The long-retired professor of mathematics and science had heard about the young Laura's intellect and interest in numbers. Professor Gikland had become Laura's first contact with *The Five*. His influence had been immeasurable to her, and he had led her to the path she chose. Laura had never married. She'd come close a few times, but her men could not get past certain particulars that were her own. Over the years, she'd developed her own ways of doing things, and she wouldn't let others enter those parts of that life. Not having a man in the house, much less a bunch of kids, had never been a big problem for Laura...she liked her independence. With retirement from the Sheriff's department a little over a year away, her plan was to travel and visit all fifty sects of *The Five*. It would be the start of her campaign to endear herself to the *Pentium Five*. She'd set a life goal to learn with the best. In the back of her mind she had always held onto the slight possibility of one day becoming one of the *Pentium Five*. She'd never told anyone of those plans.

32

Ted Paulson was keeping a close eye on Phoebe Ponto. Standing next to her, he found it funny that she was now several inches taller than him.

Ted was having a difficult time keeping control of his intellectual faculties. Ever since his brush with death, his head hadn't been right. He drifted from one memory to the next with only momentary lapses into the present.

Phoebe understood what was expected of her. Do what Ted Paulson wants and your mother lives. She didn't doubt for a second that Paulson was capable of following through on his threats. She officially became fifteen years old after midnight, and being held captive was not how she'd anticipated celebrating.

Ted looked at the tall brunette, and their history together came flashing back. He always noted that Phoebe did not have the Sicilian look of her mother, but that didn't stop her from channeling that side of her heritage. She often wore a brightly colored Coppola when feeling happy, changing to a dull, gray one when not. The old Coppola was given to her by her grandfather, who wore the flat hat as so many did on his homeland island of Sicily. Phoebe knew how to have fun and when to be serious. She also was a student of self-control and self-preservation.

The teachings of *The Five* became more difficult as members progressed. The further along members developed, the more cryptic the process became. Riddles were used as a measuring tool for many members. This method filtered out those that were not at the level needed to achieve the knowledge and harmony available to the few that possessed the needed abilities.

Phoebe took each step as a challenge, as well as something to look forward to. Ted had been the principal teacher in many of Phoebe's sessions, and she'd learned much from him.

Phoebe understood that something had changed in Ted's life. So much so that he had failed to consider the end game. How many times were she and the other young members told to make decisions based on the whole and not just the front half? But yet, here was a master of the inputs and outputs of knowledge following his own path without consideration of others or the future.

"In the morning…it all happens in the morning," Ted said as he sat at his makeshift desk. He was madly going over a multitude of numerical equations. In between each wild stroke of his pencil he wringed his hands together like two slimy night crawlers clinging together in the wet grass.

Phoebe watched and, just above a whisper, asked, "Are you referring to my birthday?"

Ted, having forgotten about Phoebe's big day, recovered quickly.

"Yes…yes…fifteen is quite a milestone in one's life." And that was it. There was no time to be distracted with trivial annoyances. He needed to stay on task or his mind would take an array of short vacations, and that wouldn't do. Time was slipping away and there was much to do.

"You know, Phoebe, your mother and the rest...they think my little clues and riddles are just silly learning tools. They will soon find that they have real meaning...real substance. They think I leave the words behind because I'm old and want to outsmart them. But they will understand that such riddles should always have...." Ted grimaced for a moment. The pain in his head, brought on by Danielle's rifle shot, pierced him like being stabbed by an eight inch letter opener.

He nearly lost the path of his thought, but somehow found his way back. "Yes...the words have meaning, but they also have substance." He smiled to himself. "It is the substance that they fail to see."

33

Captain Laura Juul walked over toward Jay, Danielle, and Phil. She understood that the uneasiness between Jay and her was one-sided. For years she worked with Jay, whether it was working a case or as a mentor and boss. Through mental strength exercises and other abilities that she'd learned during her long life with *The Five*, she knew how to quickly put emotions aside—the type of emotions that might interfere with the next thing. In this case, the next thing was to find Ted and Phoebe before something bad happened.

When first talking with a possible adversary, Laura learned how to diffuse any animosity, before a discussion takes place. To approach Jay and Danielle, she needed to call on that ability.

"Danielle, do you realize who attacked you at your canning plant?"

Danielle looked directly into Laura's eyes. "At first I thought it had to be Ted. But, I think it might have been Rufe."

"You're right, Danielle. We told Ted that we would take care of your punishment ourselves. Rufe volunteered, but only to save you, not hurt you. If we would have allowed Ted to do his dirty work...well...it wouldn't have turned out very well for you. In order to understand Ted, we have to think like Ted. We need to be one with his state of mind."

Jay was not like the others. He hadn't learned how to set aside his impatient tendencies and any other emotions he had or could feel. The working relationship he had with Rufe and Laura would forever be changed. There would never be a comfortable tie between them again.

"If that means we need to think like a loon, I certainly believe you and Rufe can pull that off."

Laura understood Jay's anger, and pressed on. She read out loud," I stood between the LORD and you at that time, to declare unto you the word of the LORD; for ye were afraid because of the fire, and went not up into the mountain." She flipped the bangs of her short red hair away from her eyes and sat down.

Danielle smiled as if she'd just found a part of a large five-hundred-piece puzzle that everyone swore must have been missing when they bought it. "Laura, the *Pentium Five*."

Laura looked back at the words. "Yes…Ted was like our Moses. He communicated the words of the *Pentium Five* to the rest of us."

Danielle continued. "But we wouldn't play his game. We didn't follow his need for revenge. Being afraid of the fire is Ted's way of saying that our own morals kept us from what needed to be done. We couldn't blindly follow a path led by a madman who justified what he was doing by making up new rules as he went. We assumed he was getting the green light from the *Pentium Five*, but I doubt that now."

Laura continued to delve into Ted's mind. "For Ted, the fire was like an impenetrable wall. He thought that we were weak, and did not have what it took to get through the wall…a wall that he himself built. Therefore, it was up to him to perform all punishments. But as he completed one task, it led to another."

She paused and reacted as if a realization was now hitting too close to home.

"He may now find that not only did he have to punish Danielle, but the rest of *the five* may need his version of discipline as well."

Danielle bounced a #2 pencil against her temple. "Ted was always going somewhere…like a cottage or something. For a couple of years he talked about his little place in the woods. Does anybody know where it was?"

Phil shuffled. "I don't think he ever told anybody where it was. I was beginning to think the place was just in his head."

Rufe walked in the room while Danielle and Laura were dissecting the words from Deuteronomy.

"Any luck finding Phoebe?" Jay asked, knowing the answer.

"We know Ted's car is gone. That's about it."

Phil Garnett suddenly grunted out, "Shit, what an idiot," he said to himself, pointing to the old bible. "It's right here. The name given to the fifth chapter is *The Covenant at Horeb.*"

Danielle understood immediately, but she wasn't the only one. They all said it simultaneously.

"Mount Horeb!"

Jay knew the village well. He'd hiked the area many times. "The village is only fifteen miles north."

He grabbed his jacket and started to rush out of the room.

Danielle grabbed his arm.

"The verse talked about not going up the mountain. There are at least ten mounts, peaks, and tall rock formations in the area. Which one were you planning on checking?"

"All of them if I have to."

Deuteronomy 5,5: I stood between the LORD and you at that time, to declare unto you the word of the LORD; for ye were afraid because of the fire, and went not up the mountain.

34

For Jay, the last few days were becoming a blur. He was running on instinct and frustration. Finding his way on instinct was second nature to him, but the frustration grew inside due to the handicap he carried. He was surrounded by brainiacs who knew more about Ted's world than he could ever know. This was a distinct disadvantage, and he would have to learn how to use their knowledge as a set of tools. Going solo was not going to be an option and it ticked him off.

He stepped back into the room. Pushing a window drape to the side, he attempted to look out, but the view was clouded with condensation. His hand swiped across the glass like a squeegee to reveal that a grounds keeper had retrieved the SUV that Jay and Danielle parked just outside the compound. It was now mid-May and after an especially frigid winter, spring was finally warming up the Midwest ground. Jay looked at the clock on the wall and nodded to Danielle.

"There may be an advantage in getting to Mount Horeb in the dark."

Rufe reacted as he always did…a step ahead.

"Take the SUV in front. We'll be right behind you."

When they reached the highway heading north, things began to feel like they were falling into place for Danielle. Sure, she'd have liked nothing better than to have Phoebe at her side, but since that was currently impossible, she'd take what she could get. The thought of working to find Phoebe with Jay and her colleagues from *The Five* gave her a sense of comfort. She and Jay were in the front car, while Rufe, Laura Juul, and Phil Garnett drove behind. They were on her side. It was the little army of five against Ted. She had been right to defy him. It had taken the others a while, but they'd finally seen the light. She had nearly all of her family back and they would help her complete things. Danielle didn't like it when parts of her life didn't equal a solid number. But sometimes, the pursuit of the whole was just as meaningful as actually reaching the whole.

They took a country road rather than the state highway. The country road was a straighter shot, and it was more likely that Ted also would have used this route. During the day, this would be a very hilly and scenic route. At night, it was like a rollercoaster ride in the dark. It would take a little over twenty minutes to get to the center of Mount Horeb, but none of the five knew exactly where Ted was. As they reached the edge of town, however, they saw a fire burning on a hillside.

Jay slowed the car and pointed. "Up there...what do you think?"

Above them and to the west Jay could see flames, but little else. Danielle's nod was all he needed to find the first right turn and head for the blaze. He wasn't certain if the fire meant Phoebe was there, but it was all they had.

Danielle repeated what they read under *Deuteronomy*.

"For ye were afraid because of the fire."

As they drove through sloped and sometimes thickly wooded landscapes, the bright visual occasionally disappeared, leaving a very nervous Jay straining to find his target. Rufe stayed steadily behind Jay. They all hoped they were not wasting precious time.

A long few minutes had gone by before Danielle saw a flicker of light through the tips of the trees.

"I just saw it! Just to the south. Take another right."

Jay's tires screeched as he saw the turn at that very moment. They were on East Creek Road and, though the right turn got them closer to the flames, the road ended about a half-mile from their destination. Jay parked at the dead end and Rufe stopped quickly alongside him. Jay got out of the SUV and surveyed the area. The darkness was just beginning to lighten and, from his vantage point, finding a road to the fire didn't appear to be an option.

"We'll have to run from here."

Phil Garnett extracted himself from the back side of Rufe's car. He didn't like hearing the word *run*, but knew it was inevitable.

Phil rubbed his chin. "Just beyond the fire up there…can you see it? It looks like a bunch of tall rock formations. Is anyone familiar with this area?"

Jay took a good look. "I think that may be Donald Rock Pillar. I tried to climb it once. Too steep, it's over 900 feet."

Phil took his handkerchief and wiped his forehead. "If this fire is Ted's doing, we'd better get up there."

The grass was wet with dew and tree roots tripped them up—but still they ran. Each had their own reasons. Jay, more than anything, was focused on Ted. He wanted Ted to die and everything else would fall into place.

Danielle wanted Phoebe. Nothing else mattered but her daughter. She needed to find a new beginning with Phoebe, and until she was safe, none of the other pegs would fit.

Phil Garnett felt the guilt of a lawyer who knew his client was guilty but did his job and made sure he wouldn't see the inside of a jail cell. For a guy that didn't appear to have a conscience, this surprised even himself.

Laura Juul simply wanted to find meaning in the last twenty-five years of her life. She wasn't about to let Ted Paulson ruin what she'd helped to build. *The Five* meant everything to her, and she needed to make the numbers fall back into place.

And Rufe was just…out of place. He was routinely ahead of the curve. He had an uncanny way of knowing what came next before anybody else. This time it was different. He tried, so very hard, to use his mind to think clearly and see the future. But the noise level was too distracting. He was unable to block out the diversions, and this was unacceptable. He was running on instinct instead of a planned path and didn't like it.

The fire was burning bright, but the wind was pushing it toward the rocks, causing it to slowly die out. As they stood just outside the fire and the tall pillar, the light flickered, showing words etched into the wall of rock.

"Can you make it out?" Danielle was asking anybody with a better view.

Jay's height gave him the best advantage.

"It says, V – Thou shalt not kill."

They all looked at each other in frustration. There they stood, in Mount Horeb, Wisconsin, looking at a wall of rock with the Roman Catholic fifth commandment etched into it.

Jay took a closer look at the fire. "It was definitely a man made fire." Stacks of tree branches were placed in a mound and a circle was dug around it in order to contain any further burn.

As the fire lost its brilliance, the crackle of the blaze was replaced by the sound of nature. The wooded area was thick with owls, frogs, rustling squirrels, and, in the distance, coyotes. They all seemed to do their thing at once, and Jay wished he had a switch that would shut them to hell up.

Twenty feet to the left, the group heard Danielle calling.

"Here, come here…foot prints."

When they found her, she was kneeling and pointing the light of her open cell phone to the ground. Phil made a sound from his big face that was either a grunt of dismay for humankind, or he was exerting himself too much by reaching in his pocket for his keychain. The keychain had a small flashlight attached that illuminated the area surprisingly well.

"There…that way!"

The wet ground and leaves left over from last fall had made the imprints of each step easy to spot. They followed the prints to a well-used path. The path took them directly to the back of an old farmhouse.

Jay knocked on the back door with his left hand and covered the right over his revolver. The old house was dark and quiet. The big man wasted no time forced the door open with his shoulder.

Rufe ducked under Jay and darted toward the dim light coming from a large room. Dozens of candles, lit some time ago, flickered. Most would last only a short time before the last of their wax was to render them useless. Others had already expired.

Jay was not the only one who recognized much of what the room was decorated with. "So this is where he moved everything."

Rufe turned and looked up at Jay. "Ted's basement was the original meeting room. After Amalthea was built, we moved our meetings there. Ted left his basement the way you saw it until after we went through it. He never told us where he moved all of…this."

His work at the farmhouse was not near completion. The walls of the bedrooms, kitchen and a bathroom were smashed to the ground. The room was big, but littered with studs that held protruding nails. Drywall lay broken and covered with its own powdery insides.

"He's replicating a pentagonal room." Phil Garnett said. "He's nothing if not determined."

Danielle walked through unopened boxes scattered on the floor and hit her head on a couple of metal wind spinners. Dozens of the spinners were stringed from the ceiling, making the light of the candles flicker even more. "Here, inside the glass case. Phil, bring your light."

Phil shined his key-light into the thick glass case that had held a key when it was in Ted's basement. A singular note with a barely legible poem was hand written.

To make things right we need to be five
and let destiny tell us who will survive.
Over the sweet river to the south we'll wait,
but not for long – don't hesitate.
You have until 5 AM to change her path.
That's not long, just do the math!
Phil read the riddle aloud.

Laura Juul was a born leader. Taking over, in most circumstances, was something she felt at ease with...until today. Since Ted almost singlehandedly had taken it upon himself to disrupt the world she lived in, she no longer held the confidence to lead. She was a part of something that had led to personal injury and even death. Now, and for every future moment in her life, she would carry that guilt, along with an immeasurable loss of conviction. Laura had been bearing a heavy load ever since Ted attacked Bernie Tennison and destroyed his eyesight. She was caught up in protocol, rules, and the laws of *The Five*. She believed that what Ted was telling her was the only way to correct a wrong. The truth was a way of life for *The Five*, but what had made Ted snap?

"He wants us all together. He will free Phoebe if we come to him." The weight felt unbearable and Laura's breathing became heavy.

For Danielle there didn't seem to be any other way. She concentrated on the words. "He's probably talking about the Sugar River. The Sugar River runs south through Green County. But where along the river is he?"

Jay grabbed a two-by-four and slammed it into the glass case. He retrieved the note and read it to himself. "It says "over" the river, not along it. It has to be a bridge. There are at least four bridges that go over that river."

Rufe didn't know the area as well as Jay did. "Is there a bridge that wouldn't have much traffic?"

"There's one called The Stone Bridge—an old railroad bridge. I don't think it's been used for quite some time. We have to chase kids off of it occasionally." Jay started toward the door. "Now that I think of it, the bridge has five arches."

Danielle followed him. "That sounds like Ted." She looked back at the others. They weren't moving. "Let's go! He lost his mind—can his patience be far behind?"

Rufe saw the dark images of Phil and Laura in the room. Only a half-dozen candles remained lit. The fumes from the candle smoke temporarily replaced the dank stench of the old farmhouse. "We know, Danielle." He rubbed his eyes. "Please understand that for the last few days Ted has been pushing the readings of the book of *The Five* in our faces. He's been muttering rules and regulations. Most of it had to do with consequences. What happens to those who leave *The Five* of their own free will? What happens in the event that the *Elite Five* do not follow the rules?"

"And?"

Laura drifted over to Danielle. "He means to kill us, Danielle. We had hoped to remove Ted...in one way or another, but he turned the table on us. In some ways, I feel like maybe we deserve what lies ahead."

"You don't deserve this from Ted. He isn't right, in what he's doing or in his head. I can't ask you to put your lives in danger...but Phoebe...she didn't do anything."

Phil walked slowly to the door. "No, of course you're right, Danielle. We should go." He hid his face, but his voice revealed a fear that made his legs move as if walking knee deep in mud.

35

Back down the path they went. Passing the pillar, they ran toward the vehicles. The clock was ticking and there wasn't any time to waste.

Up and down the winding road they drove, and as they did their minds were the only place holding a conversation. The air was cold and damp. Jay's grip on the steering wheel was tight. He drove in a calculating manner, trying to push out any interference that might pop into his head and concentrate only on Phoebe. He hadn't even met her and she had already meant more than anything to him. He saw the time on the dashboard. They had fifteen minutes.

The last few years was the first time since he left his hometown in Campbell Hill, Illinois that Jay felt truly alone. His parents were deceased, and his brother had his own family. He'd met women since his breakup with Danielle, but none of them stuck. His Thursday poker night with the boys had gotten old a while back and deep conversations on the internet weren't even in his top three thousand things to do.

Danielle finally broke the silence.

"I'm sorry things got to this point." She turned her head away from Jay, trying to hide the fact she was crying. "Maybe if I had come to you earlier…if I had talked with Phoebe more…if…."

Jay butted in. "If you had been a better shot."

Now Danielle was crying and laughing at the same time.

"Laura's right, you know. Ted will want to punish us in some way, maybe kill us."

With the bridge just minutes away, Jay still hadn't formulated any kind of plan in his head. He knew that Ted had a road map of how he wanted this to end, but there were no solutions because the future was unknown. If he or Captain Laura Juul called in for more help, it would be the end for Phoebe. Danielle was right, and much to Jay's frustration, he didn't have an answer…much less a plan. He reached over and tenderly squeezed her shoulder.

To Danielle, Jay felt strong and secure. She understood that her ex-love would do anything he could to save her and Phoebe from harm, and at this point, she had to hope that would be enough.

Jay took a right onto Town Line Road. Sunrise was getting closer and the morning sky was beginning to lighten up in the east. Tracks in the dirt road led to the bridge. Both sides of the road were thick with trees. Jay opened his window. He could smell and hear the Sugar River, its water rushing to get somewhere fast. He parked to the right, just before the bridge.

"Take this." Jay handed the gold .38 special revolver to Danielle. He put his own pistol inside his belt and covered it with his jacket. Opening the back door, he reached for his rifle. "My shotgun is missing," he said.

Rufe, Laura, and Phil pulled in behind them. Rufe walked over to edge of the bridge. There was a light pole on each side of the old structure.

"The current looks strong," he shouted as he leaned on the railing. He could make out three of the five arches. Only three of the spans dipped into the river, the other two rested in the marshy overgrowth on either side.

Silently, the five of them stood on the east side of the bridge. On the other side, Ted drifted out from behind a thick collection of trees, his steps hesitant, almost painful. The scent of dead fish was faint, but there. Ted took a deep breath and found the odor fitting.

Jay could see he was carrying a familiar shotgun. The police-issue pump-action seemed a heavy burden for the little man. Jay could possibly pull out his revolver and kill Ted, if he hadn't been holding the Phoebe card. That riot shotgun held 10 shells. If Ted got close enough, he could annihilate everybody.

Ted lumbered to the middle of Stone Bridge and stopped.

"Where's Phoebe?" Danielle shouted.

Without a word, Ted pointed the rifle toward the edge of the bridge. They all raced to see what he was pointing at. Five feet below the steel railing was the top of the middle arch. A small ten-inch ledge protruded out around it. The sun began to show itself as they peered down to where Ted Paulson was pointing.

The only one with enough length in his body to see what Ted was pointing to was Jay.

Phoebe stood, almost inconceivably, on the rounded ledge. This was not what he'd pictured life would be like the first time he laid eyes on his daughter.

"She's standing on a ledge. Her hands are bound behind her, and…and there's a noose tied around her neck."

Ted Paulson felt like his labyrinth had become untwisted. Now the road was getting clearer and more precise. He looked down at his watch and stood as straight as his aching body would allow.

"You all made it here, and with six minutes to spare, at that. It is gratifying to note that your problem solving skills are unique and quite scholarly. I think you all know the consequences if you don't do as I say. Think of this as another test of your character. You may or may not live, but Phoebe will certainly die, unless you follow along. Seems simple enough, don't you think?"

He stepped to the railing and glanced at Phoebe.

"One of you, perhaps all of you, will need to pay the piper. And then, in a whisper, "Oh yes...fitting...pay the piper."

36

Ted Paulson had grown up a loner. His birth had come as a complete surprise to Harold and Molly Paulson. They'd been in their mid-forties and the thought of having a child of their own had long passed. His father had not been a bad person, just not a particularly good parent, and a very average man. In high school, he'd rarely strayed from his "C" grade. The only higher grade he'd consistently achieved was for gym, since most could score an "A" just for showing up. He'd made the basketball and baseball teams, but played sparingly. College had not been in the cards…it wasn't even a thought. Ted's father had started working at Schram Chemical two days after his high school graduation. He'd spent the next forty-seven years inserting, packing, and shipping barrels of some of the worst God-awful chemicals ever created. Ted could never understand how his father had lived as long as he did. He'd died three months after he retired.

Ted's old man had addressed him as Theodore, when he'd addressed him at all. Harold had hoped that his only son would improve upon his own mediocrity, especially in sports. As it turned out, Ted had been miserable at any sport he'd tried. Harold had told anybody who would listen that his boy got his lack of height from his mother. Further, he'd explained that his small stature was the cause of his boy's minimum athletic abilities.

Ted had come to realize that the truth was, short or tall, he was awful at anything that called for physical coordination.

Ted had eventually withdrawn from much of the human race and set out to find his true calling. He'd found his only high-level ability had been in numbers and equations. His memory for anything mathematical had become quite phenomenal. Had he an imagination and a touch of creativity, he could have been something incredible. Instead, he'd become a bean counter—a very accurate one, and reasonably successful as far as accountants go, but a bean counter just the same.

It was *The Five* that had brought Ted the dignity that he'd felt he deserved. It had made him a part of something that fit like a custom suit. The only problem he had with the source of his newly found decorous position in life was that he couldn't tell his father. Even when the elder Paulson came home at night looking like his yellow skin was going to fall from his body, Ted hadn't been able to keep his father abreast of his latest achievements. *The Five*, after all, was a secret society and, truth be told, his beaten down old man wouldn't have understood anyway. He'd wanted to tell him, "I found something I'm proud of. I'm not the loser you think I am."

His mother, who was still living in the same house he grew up in, received a weekly call from her son. She expected very little from her life now. She'd lived a long life, and, now at the age of eighty-six, she had no problem leaving this earth before the next Wheel of Fortune show. She supposed she'd prefer that her exit happen after the show was over.

37

A member of *The Five* had come to Ted, not the other way around. They'd sought him, tested him, and found him to be the type of recruit that would make their people better and stronger. *The Five*, in turn, promised to bring him along on a journey and eventually teach him both ancient and current secrets to living life with deep wisdom and knowledge. In *The Five* he'd found a mentor, someone like a real father. His confidence had grown stronger every day. With his newly found purpose, he'd been able to put himself into the world without feeling inadequate. He had found his mate, a woman named Mary, and together they would foster many children, including one that they loved so much that they wanted to keep him. With his wife Mary, and their only son Wayne, life had been good in the early years of the Paulson family.

Wayne had been Ted's chip-off-the-old-block. Like Ted, he'd been athletically deficient, but had a memory for numbers. If one looked hard enough, however, they could find small differences. Wayne could, at times, be creative. He was infinitely more efficient with a computer. Lastly, he had a conscience. Wayne's own needs were not nearly as important to him as the needs of others. His father, on the other hand, put himself before any people or concerns. It was that last difference that changed both of their lives.

Wayne's death happened on a cold April day. Wayne had been out all day and Ted had remained in his home office working through difficult tax returns.

It was still light out when Wayne came home. He gently knocked on his father's door and stepped in.

"Hi, dad. You're still working on those returns?"

"It's a mess. I don't know how people can live with such disorganization."

"Anything I can do?"

"No, I'm almost finished. How about we order out tonight?"

"That's fine. Listen…I've got something we should talk about."

"Something good happen on your job hunt?"

"Oh, a couple of things are starting to pop up, but nothing for sure. No…I wanted to discuss something else."

Ted turned his chair around. "No time like the present."

Wayne was physically bigger and stronger than his father was, but at twenty-five years of age, he still feared his father's temper. His father had never actually hit him, but something in his father's voice was usually a forceful signal, and Wayne understood he'd better let things be. Of late, however, Wayne felt the need to go beyond the usual process. If he was ever going to be his own man, now was the time.

"I've met someone."

"Who might that be?" He asked without looking up.

"A girl…her name is Caroline Weber. We've become pretty serious. Caroline is pretty and smart. I think she would like you, dad. The problem is…she'll be transferring to another school…a school in New Mexico."

Ted had his full attention now. His boy was growing up, and that was okay. "I'm sorry that she'll be leaving, son.

She sounds like a wonderful girl. Those long-distance relationships can be a nightmare."

"That's just it. There aren't a lot of jobs here. She's invited me to go with her. I've decided to take her up on it."

This had been too sudden for Ted. He was used to having more time to absorb life-changing decisions. His first reaction was to make corrections. Though he'd known he was being selfish and inwardly feared for his own loneliness, he'd decided it better to attach such news to the rules of loyalty and trust.

"How can this work? What about *The Five*? You've worked so hard to achieve your status. Did you check with the New Mexico branch? Do they have an opening for you?"

Wayne had known this time was coming. He had rehearsed in front of the mirror many times.

"I'm going to need to leave *The Five*. Caroline would not be a candidate. You know as well as I you need to have a certain quality to be a member. I've decided that I cannot live a whole different life and keep that life separate from her. It has come down to keeping her or keeping *The Five*, I've chosen Caroline."

At that moment Ted Paulson's noodle had taken a sharp left turn and crashed. His mind, like a well-aged bottle of wine, now had a permanent ullage. A part of his brain, perhaps the part that held reason, had become vacant. Part of the open space was replaced with his own version of right and wrong. Ted knew that if every word in the bible were taken literally, most people on earth would be dammed to hell. At that moment, he'd made a mental note to correct the wrongs of all those who violated *the book of Ted*.

Ted stood and looked strangely at his son, cocking his head. "You understand that there is no avenue to take in this matter, don't you? Once you've achieved the status of the pentacle, you've learned nearly all the secrets and methods that are available. You've signed on for life. Leaving is not an option."

"Dad, this isn't the mafia. I have a life outside *The Five*, and I plan on taking that path."

"Your right, this isn't the mafia. You are in it to make this world better…to make you a deeper thinker. How can that hurt you? Why leave something that can only help you?"

"I've made up my mind."

Ted quickly envisioned the equation before him. There seemed to be only one solution. "Very well, son, I'll call for some Chinese food. We can eat in about an hour. Perhaps you could tell me more about this Caroline of yours later."

Wayne felt that this had gone far too easily and probably wasn't over, but he was tired and happy that round one had ended with so few jabs.

A half hour later, Ted had entered his son's room. Wayne was sitting in his desk chair, busily instant messaging Caroline. He heard a slight creak in the floor, but before he could turn around, a rope tightened harshly around his neck.

Ted's face had shown little or no emotion as he strangled the life out of his son. The physical aspect had proven itself much easier than expected. "It's okay, son," he whispered as he held tight to the strong manila rope left over from a scratching post he'd built for an old pet that was long gone. Wayne's face soon turned a dark shade of purple, as the blood in his brain had nowhere to drain.

"It's okay, son," he continued to whisper, repeatedly, until he laid Wayne's body down on the carpet. Ted had noticed his son had soiled himself, but like everything else that had happened since Wayne came home with his news, he'd felt nothing. He'd known from the time he entered the room what had to be done. From the moment Wayne said he was leaving *The Five*, his decisions had become quite obvious. It was as if he merely had to follow the instructions on a teleprompter.

Ted dragged Wayne's body to the closet and set up the suicide scene. He felt he had most of the county sheriff's department in his pocket, if a favor was needed.

He put together a suicide note on Wayne's computer and made sure to print it out without saving it. Ted noticed a saved folder called *résumés* and found Wayne's list of failed employment attempts. He'd printed that out as well, and it was then that he knew who to blame for his son's death. After all, if only one of them had hired Wayne, none of this would have happened.

"My son had been very discouraged of late, you know, looking for jobs," he told anybody who wanted to know and some that did not. He was able to push the entire fault onto the employers, and that helped him to sound completely believable. Believable to everyone, except one...a young girl by the name of Caroline.

38

An hour earlier, Ted and his hostage had been rambling through the dark, winding roads. Phoebe felt certain Ted would end her life on her fifteenth birthday, though she wasn't sure why? He drove to his semi-remodeled farmhouse, helped her from his car, and escorted her inside. He had already secured her wrists by binding them behind her. Phoebe recognized many of the symbols lying boxed and unboxed throughout the makeshift room.

"So this is where you've been hiding out lately. We were wondering where you were running off to." Phoebe sounded remarkably calm, considering the circumstances.

Small talk was doing nothing for Ted at this point. The path that he'd chosen was going downhill without breaks, and all his attention needed to be on point.

"Sometimes a person's best laid plans need to be altered. We'll be leaving in just a few short minutes."

Phoebe continued in her attempt to derail Ted's current state of mind. "What are you planning on doing with this place?"

Her captor sat at the kitchen table and, at least at that moment, didn't allow for distraction.

"Ted…what are you…what are your plans?"

He finished writing and looked up. "Concerning what?"

"For this place."

"Nothing…anymore. I…it's time to go."

Ted put the words he had written in a big glass case. Phoebe recognized it as the case that, at one time, held the book of *The Five*.

Ted lit dozens of candles, guided Phoebe back into his SUV, and drove south.

Phoebe held her composure until they approached the Stone Bridge. As a young girl, she used to have recurring dreams about falling into the deep dark water from a bridge. The sun hadn't quite shown itself yet, but Phoebe felt that she could handle things, if only the darkness became light. The meaning behind dreams was something that Phoebe studied. Her logical mind didn't help when it came to the sight of the bridge before her. She made it difficult for Ted to pry her from the front seat. She kicked him as he opened the door to pull her out.

He hit her with the butt of his stolen rifle. Not a hard jolt, but just enough to get her mind off the bridge.

She relented, dazed, as blood dripped down near her temple.

Ted was oblivious to his hit to Phoebe's head. She was getting in the way of his plan and he wasn't about to have another distraction. "It's May 15th, Phoebe. You don't want to miss all the festivities I have planned for your birthday, do you?"

Ted parked off the road, in a space large enough to fit his SUV and yet hide it from anyone approaching from the other side. He pushed Phoebe toward the bridge and didn't stop until they reached the middle.

The bridge was not the type that she had dreamt about. In her dreams, the black bridge turned to accommodate other trains from multiple directions. The gears made awful, deafening grinding noises. It was in her dream, during one of those times when the bridge moved that Phoebe fell from it into the dark, choppy water below. She hadn't had the dream for years, but the memory of it was still there. She knew one thing for sure...if Ted wanted to scare the shit out of her, he had accomplished his goal.

The bridge was a light colored stone. It was strong and sturdy. Phoebe noticed a plaque at the front end that dated the bridge at 1887, but to her it looked like it had been reconstructed.

When Ted forced her to stand on the middle arch, she noticed the rope tied into a noose. She began to shake and found it difficult to breath.

39

The sun was just coming up. Ted stood in the middle of the bridge, the barrel of his rifle nudging Phoebe's back. It wouldn't take much of a push for Phoebe to fall from the ledge.

Ted shouted toward the end of the bridge where all those who'd followed his planned meeting were huddled. "Drop your revolver over the railing, Lieutenant. I may have my faults, but I am one to keep my word. Young Phoebe will live if you all follow along."

Jay thought again about taking a shot at Ted, but he was about 100 feet from Ted and chances were good that, even if he hit his target, Phoebe would be pushed to her death. He threw the gun into the river.

They watched as Ted backed up a couple of feet behind Phoebe.

"Come along, Danielle. You were the first to show opposition to the laws of *The Five*. It's only fitting that I start with you."

Ted motioned with his rifle.

As Danielle took a step toward Ted, she reached behind herself and flung the gold .38 special back to Jay. The perfect toss was hidden behind her body, and Ted didn't notice. She continued to walk slowly toward a man she no longer understood.

She stopped when the barrel of Ted's rifle was pressed to her chest. Looking to her left, she could see the back of her daughter's head. Phoebe was afraid to turn her body around to see her mother; even the slightest movement might cause her to slip.

"It'll be all right, Phoebe. Don't move…Ted gave us his word." Danielle said the last words for her own peace of mind as well as Phoebe's.

As the sun rose and lightened everything around her, Danielle could see Ted's eyes. They seemed dark and lifeless. The bandage on his head was three-quarters blood. She looked away.

Ted's gaze went past Danielle and focused on her daughter. "Stand tall and steady, my young one. There is much to be done before I can let you go."

Ted pushed Danielle toward the far end of the bridge. There, he put a second noose around her neck and instructed her to join her daughter on the precarious ledge above another of the five arches. Ted reached over the railing and placed a thick band around Danielle's wrists, like the one used on Phoebe. Ted smiled as he saw the humor in keeping his victims captive using yellow bands that he'd received free during a festival. They were designed to be symbols of freedom.

On the other side of the bridge, Jay put the revolver in his back pocket and moved toward Ted and Danielle. He could barely make out what Ted was doing to her. As he moved closer, he began to see the horrible truth. When he reached the center of the bridge, Ted simply pointed the rifle at Jay and pulled the trigger. There was no hesitation; he just aimed and shot. Phoebe screamed from the blast behind her and nearly tumbled off the ledge.

Jay was hit in the right leg. The pain was excruciating as he stumbled to the opposite side of the bridge from where Phoebe stood. Reaching for a railing, the strength in his leg evaporated and he slipped over, into the choppy river below.

Phoebe screamed again in anger and fear, but this time she had thought that the splash she'd heard was the body of her mother. She turned her head and was relieved to see Danielle still marginally safe on the ledge.

Danielle hadn't seen what had happened, but heard the gunshot. She struggled to keep herself from losing all concentration. The reality of what was happening and who might be getting hurt by Ted Paulson began to overtake her emotions.

"Ted...Ted...this has got to stop. Don't you see what you're doing?" She tried to look behind her. *Was it Jay...is he hurt?* She slipped and corrected her balance. It was then that she noticed, unlike Phoebe, she was not above the water, but stood precariously over weeds and bushes, just a short distance from the river's edge.

Ted turned. Danielle could see he was breathing hard, and sweat poured from his forehead.

"I know exactly what I'm doing. Except for a few small details, it is all working magnificently. Excuse me, Danielle. I'm on to the next step."

He ambled down to the next arch. "Jim Ruferd, come along. Join us, won't you?"

Rufe walked up to where Ted loomed. It was as if he was headed to a much deserved retirement party. There was no hedging...no remorse...only sadness. Rufe saw no way out and only one way to save Phoebe. He crossed over the railing and situated himself on the second arch.

Ted leaned over and adjusted the noose of his third victim. "You seem rather resigned to the state of affairs, Rufe. What makes you so calm?"

Rufe gazed out to the long river before him. He smiled to himself as if he'd found a certain path that everybody was looking for but only he knew where it was and where it led. "Did you ever see the movie *The African Queen*, Ted?"

"Yes Rufe, a long time ago, but I recall the film."

"Well, toward the end, things weren't looking too good. Rosie wondered if Charlie was afraid, and Charlie said, "I gave myself up for dead when we started this journey. So, you see, I figure I'm already gone. If I die, it's expected. If I live, it's a hell of a bonus.""

Ted turned away. "You have a full decade of incredible learning under your belt and you take your final lesson from a movie. Never did understand you, Rufe."

Ted moved on to the middle arch, where he stopped for a moment to glance at Phoebe. Then he dragged himself and his rifle on toward the fourth arch.

"Laura, if you please."

Ted pointed his rifle and kept his finger on the trigger. He'd known Laura the longest and respected her cunning. She wasn't just a figurehead as captain of the Sheriff's Department. Ted was well aware of her knowledge in weaponry and the criminal element.

"Ted, I'm not going to lie to you. There is no way out for you anymore. The only thing left to salvage is a few lives. Let's say we close this chapter and call it a day." She reached for his rifle, but Ted backed up.

"Sorry, Laura, but I'm going to have to see this one through to the end."

He handed her a freedom band.

"Put this around your ankles. You can't fault me if I'm a little more cautious with you, can you?"

She reached her hand down to her feet. "I understand Ted. You do what you...."

Laura pulled a knife from inside her sock and slashed at Ted.

Ted stepped back and fired, pushing both of them back and onto the train tracks.

Laura lay motionless. Blood poured out from her chest.

Ted sat up and noticed Phil Garnett, wide-eyed and looking like he would run off if his fat legs were capable of doing the work.

"Don't do it, Phil. You wouldn't get three feet. And then there's the matter of Phoebe. You don't want to jeopardize her life, do you?" Ted said it with a hint of sarcasm. He felt that Phil, given the chance, would save his own life before any thought of Phoebe's.

Phil, on the other hand, wasn't so sure. Phoebe was one of the few from the young generation that he had any respect for. It was Phoebe who allowed him to keep some faith in the future of this planet. Early in his career, he'd done much of his practice in Chicago. He'd seen a boat load of the bad, and very little of the good.

Ted, satisfied that Phil wasn't going to attempt an escape, got to his feet and called him over.

Laura lay just off from the fourth arch, her head on top of the train tracks. It was obvious to Ted that she'd died quickly. He was still standing over her when Phil came as ordered. He shook his head and moved her sleeveless vest with the barrel of the rifle. Her chest was a bloody mess with a large hole. She was so close to Ted when he'd shot her that it looked like she had fallen on a terrorist's mine. He knew that at times Laura's job required her to wear a bullet-proof vest. He wondered if it would have mattered.

"I'm going to need you to help me fix this, Phil. She needs to be on the fourth arch."

Phil looked at Ted in disbelief. "Can you hear yourself talk, Ted? You shot Laura in the chest, and now you want to hang her body from a bridge. You're completely insane."

Phil was finding all of this too hard to comprehend. The bridge, Phoebe and her mother balancing dangerously, Laura dead, the detective shot and in the water somewhere…it was easier to emotionally shut down than to struggle with it.

The big guy sat down, leaning his back to a railing next to the body of Captain Laura Juul. "You might as well shoot me too. I'm done. Do what you want."

Ted glanced at his lawyer and sighed. His wounded head felt like it would explode any second now. Now that he thought about it, he wasn't even sure who had shot him back at Amalthea. If he was a betting man, however, he would have put his money on Danielle.

"Listen, Phil, just do as I say a little while longer. It could be much, much worse." His voice started to change octaves, as if it was coming from someone else. "You don't want anything bad to happen to your lovely wife Sherry, do you? I have someone sitting just outside your home as we speak."

Phil bent his head and then covered his eyes with his hand. Sweat rolled down his forehead. He rolled over and used the railing to get back to his feet.

They pulled Laura's body to the fourth arch, sat her there and propped her head back to fasten the loose.

Phil stared at his bloody hands in disbelief. He didn't know if Ted was telling the truth about his wife, but he wasn't going to take any chances.

"You're up, Phil. You did well. Your family will not be harmed in any way. They'll miss you, of course. You were a good provider."

Phil took a deep breath and submitted to his fate.

Ted pushed the lumbering lawyer to his assigned arch.

The fifth and final position was filled. Phil stood on the opposite side of the bridge from Danielle and, like her, there were trees and bushes beneath him instead of water. His balance was a particular challenge because this arch was mossy and slippery.

40

Ted left his rifle where it lay and walked to the center arch as if carrying the weight of the world on his shoulders. He took slow, deliberate steps, each one building on the next. Each movement forward pushed his pride to higher levels. His plan was nearly achieved, and soon, all would be right again.

His life had been one of order and discipline. Every paper, every file, every decision was in its proper and correct position or had been until the moment he took the life of his son. At that moment his life, based on mathematical perfection, had been losing digits.

Ted stopped for a moment, looking over his five captives. The morning was now reasonably quiet. The river was not flowing as rapidly as before. Even the birds seemed to have stopped their morning concert. "I've calculated all of it, you know." He seemed to be talking more to himself than to anyone else. "The rope drop-length is perfect for weight…the more weight, the shorter the rope."

Just then, Phil vomited profusely and nearly slipped off his perch.

Ted looked over at Phil as if watching the wind blow and then glanced at his watch. "One or two annoying mishaps can throw one's timing off completely. Sunrise was to be at exactly 5:32 this morning, as well as the conclusion to my little plan. Here it is, already 5:40. Well, better late than never, my mother always said."

Ted walked to the center of the bridge and got down on his knees behind Phoebe. Reaching in his pants pocket he removed a knife. He leaned over toward her and cut the thick rubber band.

"Give me your hand, Phoebe. You did your part. You are free to go."

Phoebe turned and, with some hesitation, grabbed his hand. Ted pulled her up and removed the noose from around her neck.

He held his knife as if to warn Phoebe that she could still be in danger.

Phoebe moved back a few feet.

Then, to Phoebe's surprise, Ted raised his leg and eased himself over the railing. He put the noose around his own neck and threw his knife back unto the bridge. He turned back to glance at Phoebe, for just an instant, and then flung himself down and out toward the water.

Phoebe watched in horror.

Ted's calculations were based on math as well as miniature experimentation that he conducted at his cottage. His drop was long and his flight downward ended at exactly nine and a half feet. Under his jacket he wore a weighted vest, used for exercise. As he fell, he held onto the rope above the noose because calculations told him the rope length and the added weight would decapitate him. He needed the weight to help further his plans, and losing his head would have interfered with the outcome.

Ropes connected to each of the five, set at precisely fifty feet apart, pulled Rufe down on Ted's right and Laura's body on his left. Ted's added weight and the force assured it.

Their noose was cut to a six and a half foot length. Their weight, together with Ted's, then pulled Phil and Danielle over. Danielle's drop was set at seven feet, while Phil's was five feet. Ted's domino affect had worked.

"Nooooooo!" Phoebe yelled, as the shock of what was happening consumed her. Seconds' later instincts pushed paralysis aside, and Phoebe began to run toward her fallen mother. She stopped, ran back for the knife that Ted had thrown onto the bridge before he descended, and again started running toward the far end of the bridge.

The fifth angel sounded, then I saw a star from heaven fallen into the earth; and there was given to him the key of the pit of the abyss. To the locusts that came out thence it was said that they should not kill the men who had not the seal of God on their foreheads, but that they should be tormented five months (*Rev.* 9:1, 3-5, 10).

41

After being shot by Ted, Jay fell into the cold water stunning his bloody leg. His first reaction was good—the pain seemed to subside. His second wasn't—he'd been taken down river by the strong current and found it hard not to drown.

Jay struggled mightily, but made it to the far shoreline. He turned over on his back, breathing hard. From a distance he could see Ted and Phil placing a limp Laura onto one of the pillars. He'd heard a gunshot, but was too far away to tell if she was alive.

He strained to get to his feet, but the pain made a triumphant return. Jay tried to run but his leg had none of it. He fell to the ground and tried to take stock of the situation. The strength in his right leg was virtually non-existent. The blood however, was not. He didn't think a main artery was hit, but still, he knew it was a mess. He'd begun to unbutton his shirt when he realized that taking the time to undo it with hopes of using it again was purely ridiculous. He ripped his shirt off and tied it just above the wound.

When he looked toward the bridge again he could see Phil's large frame being positioned above the final pillar. He got to his feet again and knew there would be no more time for executing a plan. Adrenaline and luck would have to suffice.

He limped his way through bushes and trees, fighting his way toward the horrible sight before him. His daughter and her mother were among five victims who were perched above the Sugar River. He made his mind up: find a way to help them or die trying.

Jay's lungs felt as if they were filled with desperation as he came closer and closer to the bridge. When he ducked under a large birch tree he saw Ted pulling Phoebe up from the middle pillar. His breathing became a touch easier when Phoebe stepped away from the railing. As he hobbled closer, he could see Ted replacing his daughter on the pillar.

Jay heard his daughter scream and could see Ted dropping toward the river.

Ted's plan to hold the rope just above the noose worked, to a point. He was not decapitated. The long drop, despite his hold above the noose, still caused a severed vertebra. He died, however, as he had hoped—quickly.

Danielle had watched Ted replace her daughter on the middle arch. She'd struggled to get her hands loose, but could not. Each second seemed to take minutes, and the helplessness was overwhelming. She didn't notice the connecting rope tucked under the bridge railing until seconds before Ted plunged downward. As the force of the rope pulled her to the left and off the arch, she felt something block her fall.

Jay caught her legs with only inches of rope left, saving her from instant death. But while Jay held her with everything he had, she was still choking from the tightness of the noose.

"Mom!" Phoebe yelled as she grabbed the rope that held her mother and sliced into it.

Danielle fell into Jay's arms and they both tumbled to the ground.

Phoebe ran off the bridge and into the thicket to find Danielle.

"Mom, are you all right?"

Danielle's neck was scraped and bloody. She was hugging Jay so tightly that he could feel every heartbeat. Phoebe got down on her knees and they pulled her in, close and tight.

Danielle cried uncontrollably. Relief, anger, happiness, confusion—it was too many emotions to deal with at one time, and so she cried. She would only give herself a minute. Sixty seconds of release was all she needed. Ted Paulson has finally expired. She and her daughter had made it out alive, but at what cost? Her legs were as wobbly as, perhaps, her mind. She'd lost so many people she'd known, and much of herself in the process.

After helping Jay get to his feet, Phoebe wondered about the tall man standing beside her. "Do I know you?"

Jay looked at Danielle and then back at Phoebe. He wanted to grab her and hug her. He wanted to look at her closely and see what he had been missing for so many years, but understood that this wasn't the time or place. "We'll talk later. Would you fetch that old branch for me? I may need something to lean on.

She quickly did as he asked.

"Thank you, Phoebe. Help your mother get to the car. I'll be up in a minute."

Jay limped to the river bank. There, he glanced up to see a sight he would never forget. Three bodies swung from the bridge. Jim Ruferd and Ted Paulson had a horrifying purplish tint to their faces, while Laura Juul was pale and bloody. Phil Garnett's body was not one of those that hung from the Stone Bridge. Jay wondered what had happened to him, but was too tired to think about it. He leaned against an oak tree. Closest to him was Rufe, his partner. "You lied to me and tried to steer me in a different direction," he whispered. "But, in the end you did what was right. I'm going to miss you, Rufe."

Jay's expression as he saw Ted Paulson hanging, with his neck abnormally stretched, said it all. He thought, *"You took so many lives and hurt many people. For what? To make things right…to follow the rules. No Ted, there has to be more to it than that. Nobody goes to these lengths just for some payback. What else was going on in your sick little mind?"*

Danielle and Phoebe waited for him at the foot of the bridge.

Phoebe replaced Jay's walking stick with herself and smiled, just a smidge. "Take me to a ball game?"

"What?"

"Isn't that what father's do…take their kids to a ball game?"

Jay gave Danielle a quick glance. "You didn't mention anything to me about being a father for fifteen years, and now you couldn't wait five minutes?"

"Being one step ahead of you is what I do. It's a habit that can't be broken." She looked around and saw Captain Laura's blood on the bridge. "Besides, I'm a little sick of secrets."

Danielle saw it first. Jay's face was getting pasty white and the blood dripping from his leg was not letting up.

"Jay, are you okay? Your leg, it's…we need to get you to a hospital…fast."

Jay's body went limp as he passed out. Danielle and Phoebe was no match for the heft of the big man and they all tumbled to the ground.

Danielle scrambled to the car and called in for help while Phoebe tried to comfort her newly found father. In short order the place was surrounded by police and medical vehicles. They found Phil's body in the marsh below, his neck severed from the force of the drop against the weight of his body. Phoebe rode with Jay and her mother to the hospital. Danielle and Phoebe held Jay's hands until the emergency room attendants pried them apart.

"To be able to practice five things everywhere under heaven constitutes perfect virtue" – **Confucius**

42

Life in Granite slowly became easier for Danielle. She no longer had the feeling of doom or the need to always look behind her. The pressure was diminished but for one thing...the media. The rest of the town, most of who were not used to getting any kind of attention outside of their little world, were still feeling out of sorts. Danielle understood that the circus would leave town on its own sweet schedule, and so far, the end date was undefined.

Though all charges were pinned on the late accountant, Theodore Paulson, his involvement in a secret society was the real news.

Jay had actually gotten off easy, his physical state notwithstanding. He was stuck at a hospital in Milwaukee under orders to have no stress, which included media. His leg was a mess, but except for a noticeable limp, he would be okay. Besides, Danielle and Phoebe had promised to take care of him when he was released, and he was happy with that proposition.

After three weeks, Danielle was getting sick of the media's constant intrusions into her life. When Jay grumbled enough, the hospital sent him packing and Danielle brought him to her house. Jay considered this the best intrusion into his life that he could have wished for. He'd never been fussed over much and he loved it. It didn't last long, but those few short weeks were something he could have gotten used to. Danielle was happy to do the cleaning, make meals, and care for Jay's fox red Labrador retriever. When the dog's owner had moved away Jay decided to take him in. He'd been Jay's companion ever since. Though, at the time he was only two years old, the canine had the face of a distinguished old man and tended to act like one as well. Jay called him, Geezer.

Danielle agreed that the dog acted twenty years older than he was, in that he could use a box of Depends. He leaked on most anything within eyesight when nervous. Between the constant media intrusions into her life and the bad habits of Geezer, her patience was running thin. The media, however, won top prize for in Danielle's list of most irritating.

"I go to work, they're there. I come home, they're in the driveway."

"Tell them what they want to hear and they'll never go away. But, preach to them about virtue and morality…and they'll run away." Jay was in the living room lounging on the couch. Danielle could barely hear him from the kitchen.

"What?"

"Tell them about *The Five*. The jig is up. People know they exist. Just give them enough to satisfy. Make it boring and deeply philosophical. They'll move on to something else if the people lose interest."

Phoebe paused as she was going to the kitchen for a bite to eat. "Boring…hey Mom…you can do boring."

"Hey." Danielle felt mildly hurt, but thought about it. "You're right. You're both right. I'm good at boring. I could put them asleep in ten minutes if I try."

"That's right Mom, let 'em have it. They'll never come back again."

Danielle opened the front door.

Jay could see the crowd gather from his vantage point through the sheer living room drapes. "They'll never know what hit them," he whispered to Phoebe. Jay has gotten to know and love his daughter. It wasn't a father/daughter relationship yet, but they both felt comfortable around one another and Jay thought that was a solid start. They sat together to watch Danielle do her thing.

"Gather around, boys and girls." Danielle suddenly found herself feeling relaxed in the presence of the eight or ten reporters that had made her driveway their home. She felt more in control. Despite the warm temperatures, she wore a scarf around her neck to hide the remaining redness from the noose that had nearly killed her a few short weeks earlier.

An elderly man with a flat hat started the questioning. "How are you doing, Danielle?"

"I'm doing well, thank you."

"It was quite an ordeal you went through. Can you tell us about Theodore Paulson? What made him do those horrific things?"

"I knew Ted through a club that we belonged to. We were good friends until he snapped."

A lady with startlingly red lipstick from the Chicago Tribune spoke up. "I heard it was more than a club. Can you elaborate on…what were they called…*The Five*?"

This is the opening she had been waiting for. "Oh, yes *The Five*, yes…what a wonderful group of people. I've learned so much from them. They teach Pythagoras, Confucius, readings from the bible and many other great writings. Of course, they thought it best to move on, get out of Dodge, as they say. Did you know the Washington Monument is 555 feet tall?"

She spoke endlessly on mathematics, moral concepts, and how life itself could be changed and enlightened. All in all, she did her job.

About half way through her oral dissertation she momentarily stopped when her eye caught a reporter who remained curiously silent in the background. He took notes, but did not have a recorder or a camera. This man in a well pressed suit was more serious than the others. It was a brief encounter, but it bothered her.

After forty minutes, they began to amble back to their cars. By the time she was finished, the only media remaining was the humorless man she had noticed earlier.

As she turned to go back into the house, the strange man finally spoke. "How did you feel as your friends hung from the bridge and you...you were not among them?"

It was a startling question. She didn't know if she should answer it. For that matter, she didn't know that she had an answer.

She looked back at the man. "I hadn't had much time to process what happened. True, I was lucky to get out alive. My friends didn't deserve what happened to them."

Danielle felt a need to finish. "Except Ted...Ted deserved how he died, and more."

Ever since she was little, Danielle had a sense inside her that squeezed at her gut when she felt uncomfortable. This guy made her want to vomit.

Before he said anything else, she said goodbye and left him standing there. All she wanted was to return to her main squeeze on the couch. She found both Jay and Phoebe asleep. She could only conclude that her speech had been successful. She talked about *The Five* without actually giving them any inside information on the sect itself. The plan had worked.

43

Exactly one month after the grisly May 15th attack by Ted Paulson, things were finally beginning to quiet down in Green County. There were still whispers and small discussions among the townspeople, but the sense of returning normality was measurable. Three of their citizens were maimed forever. Marcus Wingate, who had lost his hands on the saw table, was dead, as well was Green County Sheriff Department Captain Laura Juul, Sergeant Jim Ruferd, and Chicago lawyer Phil Garnet.

The other possible victims of Ted Paulson had been listed as accidental deaths by the coroner. Perhaps, in the future, friends and relatives might decide to dig further into their deaths, but for now, the cases were closed.

In Danielle's mind, Martha Wycoff, her schoolteacher, Herbert Yates, her grandfather, and Johnny Silton, her little cousin, were all victims of Ted Paulson. She told Jay that it would only bring more anger and hatred to investigate, and the town needed to heal, not open more wounds. Danielle did not pursue or ask for an inquiry into those deaths.

Since they were still getting the occasional call from the media people, Danielle and Phoebe agreed to move into Jay's home in Granite. Perhaps the location would throw the reporters off for a while.

Jay put his copy of Sports Illustrated aside, pushed his covers away and sat on the side of the bed. It was a beautiful Saturday morning. "I'm going back to work Monday." Without saying another word he headed for the bathroom.

Danielle watched from her side of the bed. His right leg still looked as if he'd been attacked by a great white shark. His limp was pronounced, with little improvement since the day he'd been injured. Though he tried to stretch and exercise, he still hadn't been able to straighten it out all the way.

"Are you sure that's smart? You still have some rehab to do on that leg."

Jay finished doing his business, washed his hands and face and jumped on top of Danielle. In his mind the attack had all the grace of a gazelle.

Danielle thought he was more like a wounded moose.

He kissed her.

"I get half my rehab done right here, and I think I can get the rest of it done by going to work and chasing bad guys," he said as he held his body above Danielle in order to prevent his weight from squishing her.

"Are there any bad guys to be chased?"

"Nope, bad guy is dead. No more bad guys left. Looks like I'll have to complete all my rehab here."

He lay on top of her, still using his arms to defuse the weight. He kissed her neck, then lips, and finally her breast.

"I'm not sure that your therapist had any of this listed on her notes."

"If she asks, should I show her what type of exercises I've been doing?"

"If you do, I'll sign the divorce papers in record time."

Jay arched his back and gave her a look as if he missed something. "Don't we have to be married before we divorce?"

"Oh…yeah, that's right. We'll need to do something about that, don't you think?"

"Well yes, strictly speaking…it would be the thing to do, you know, make a proper woman of you."

Danielle wiggled herself out from under the big guy. She got up and looked out the window to Jay's backyard. The flower garden looked healthy and colorful, a completely opposite outcome from his usual patch of whatever cared to grow there. Though it had only been a short time, the difference maker was his daughter Phoebe, who had an uncanny association with nature. She was there now working away with a wheelbarrow half full of weeds. She'd been spending a lot of hours out there since their move to Jay's home.

"Sometimes I worry about her, Jay. She'd been through so much."

Jay sat up and folded his hands behind his head. "She's doing fine, Danielle. She's an intelligent, healthy young lady. Sometimes I think she's handling what happened better than we are."

"That's just it. I feel like she's hiding something. She never talks about it. I don't know if she's keeping it locked up somewhere inside of her, or if she just doesn't feel things the way…others might feel. She's only fifteen and she's seen enough horror to last a couple of lifetimes. I know it's difficult to believe, but I think she misses her life with *The Five*. She soaked up years of deep learning and understanding. There isn't a place for her to go and carry on discussions like she used to, and I'm afraid that leaving her old life behind will be an impossible task."

Jay walked over to Danielle and held her as they watched Phoebe work below. "Come on to bed, I need some rehab."

Danielle was being serious, but she knew Jay only wanted to take her mind off of the bad things. She didn't know if she should be mad at him for not putting a higher priority on her concerns or if she should temporarily put it on the back-burner.

She chose the diversion route and jumped into Jay's arms. "I think I can help you with your rehab," she whispered, as he carried her to his favorite gym. He may have had a bum leg, but everything else worked perfectly.

That night Jay set out to celebrate Phoebe's fifteenth birthday the way it should have been the first time around.

"Phoebe ought to have a birthday like any other girl her age. I've only known her for a few weeks, but I think she should know I'd do anything for her."

"So you're showing her that you're her security blanket by taking us to Moose Droppings Bar and Grill?"

"It's not the place but the people you're with that count. Besides, MD's has great food."

Phoebe was in her bedroom working on ideas for her future. She felt lost without some sort of path and needed to begin the process. She overheard Jay talking and started for the stairs, and suddenly stopped halfway down.

"Are you still talking about going out tonight? Its okay, you don't have to go to any trouble. Things…happen you know! My birthday is over. The further we get away from that day, the better."

Jay limped up the stairs and sat next to her.

"Don't you think it's time to get out of this house and loosen up a little?"

"I wouldn't know anybody, except for you two."

Danielle peered in through the railing.

"You might remember somebody from first grade before you were home schooled."

Phoebe knew this was not a winnable battle and decided that the sacrifice was not as difficult as the fight.

"Fine, but I'm going to need time to get ready. If I'm to be put on display like a piece of meat for all the eligible bachelors that frequent the local pub, I'm going to have to look my best."

For the first time in Jay's life, he felt what every father feels about their daughter's boy prospects.

"If one boy touches you, his offending digits will be forcibly removed."

"Easy...I was just kidding."

"Yah...well...just the same."

Danielle smirked, "Were you ever that protective of me?"

"From what I've seen, it's the guys who need protection from you."

44

The mild mid-June weather was not something to waste. Jay knew Phoebe enjoyed the outdoors and couldn't wait to bring her to places that she had never seen. Tonight, however, he needed to relax and have a few beers.

Jay, Danielle and Phoebe found an open parking space and strolled into Granite's Moose Droppings Bar and Grill.

Phoebe was a little startled by the animal heads that hung on the wall. In her study of Pythagoras, she was taught a certain kinship to animals. They were to be treated with respect. The walled trophies seemed to her more of a display of winner versus loser.

Danielle hadn't joined *The Five* until she was twenty-four years old. She'd lived a very normal life up to that point. She grew up in the typical Midwestern family way. She lived four years at a major college and learned how a diverse set of people conduct themselves. In other words, she lived her early years learning about life in person and not necessarily through books.

Phoebe's life, in contrast to her mother's, had been a study in isolation. When most people need to seek the meaning of their existence, Phoebe had resided in the life of learning.

She stayed there for all of her fifteen years. Despite the recent bad memories, she was as mentally and emotionally advanced as most people twenty years older.

It didn't take Phoebe long to strike up a conversation with a couple of boys her age. Though she had never played pool before, she quickly picked up on the correct angles and the likely speed of the ball.

Danielle and Jay were surprised by her outgoing manner and pleased that she seemed to be fitting in; but, as they sipped on their brews, that laid-back feeling began to unravel.

"Did you hear that?"

"Yes, what was that?"

Danielle and Jay put down their beers and surveyed the bar. They said it at the same time.

"Phoebe!"

They ran outside. Off to the left, one of Phoebe's new friends was on the ground holding his balls in a fetal position. She held the other on the hood a car with his arm bent behind his back.

Jay ran to Phoebe. "It's okay, you can let him go now."

The parents of the boys stumbled out the door. One of the mothers tried to help the one on the ground.

Phoebe was breathing hard. She slowly let the boy's arm loose and composed herself.

"I think I'd like to go home now," she said.

As they walked with Phoebe to the car, Jay could hear one of the fathers of the boys say, "You let a girl whip you?"

Jay went back into the bar, paid his bill and hobbled into the driver's side of his car. He glanced at Phoebe in the back seat. "You gonna tell me what happened?"

She looked at her mother, who gave her the international nod for "well, go ahead."

"The one called 'Marty' just turned sixteen and wanted to show me a car that he and his dad fixed up. You both looked like you were having so much fun…I didn't see any point in telling you where I was going. Marty got behind the wheel and started pointing out all the things they added to the dashboard. As I bent down to see, the other guy, Paul, got behind me and was…well, he was…I could see him in the rear-view mirror. He was acting like a…teenager. I don't like being made fun of, so I kicked back and hit him in his testicles. Marty knew what Paul was doing, he even laughed a little. They're such creeps."

"Then what happened?"

"I felt bad at first. I wasn't sure if, maybe, it was normal behavior. I wondered if they all acted like that and I took it too seriously. Anyway, when Marty got out of his car, he shoved me. I nearly fell. He started to laugh and called me something. I didn't want to hurt him so I started walking away…toward the bar door. He ran to the door and wouldn't let me get through. I asked him politely to get out of the way, but he refused. I told him I didn't want to hurt him, but he just laughed again."

Jay thought it odd that she stopped at that juncture.

"Well?"

"I hit him in the laryngeal prominence."

"The where?"

Danielle volunteered, "The Adam's Apple."

"Then I grabbed his arm and pushed him on the car. It's okay, he should be able to speak normally again by tomorrow."

Jay put the car in drive and could only think of one word.

"Wow!"

Danielle looked at him in astonishment. "That's it. That's all you have to say?"

Jay thought he'd better become more fatherly, and fast.

"You can't go around beating people up, Phoebe," he said with a smile on his face that wouldn't vacate no matter how hard he tried.

Danielle volunteered, "You could have walked away before you hit the boy in the balls."

"Yes, of course, you're right mother. I could have, but I don't see how those boys would have learned what they did was wrong."

Jay looked over at Danielle.

"Are you sure she's only fifteen?"

Danielle was frustrated. "That's the hell of it. I'm not sure she didn't do exactly what the situation called for. The problem is that I can't go anywhere without people looking at me as if I just boiled their children in a cauldron of soup. Now...this!"

The rest of the drive home was silent. Everybody in that car had once had lives, predictable lives with set habits and rituals. That had all changed.

Just days earlier, Jay had gone to the department to see some of his old buddies and talk about returning. He thought he would be welcomed as a guy that did all he could to save lives. Instead, he'd felt like an outsider, like perhaps he should have died with the others.

Danielle had recently taken an extended leave of absence from her company. She was contemplating leaving for good.

Phoebe wasn't sure what direction her future was headed in.

Things were in disarray.

As they entered the driveway, something wasn't right. It wasn't anything obvious, but all three saw it at the same time. On the front porch, a lamp on top of a small patio table was lit. This was unusual enough, but as they approached the door they noticed a tiny rope tied into a noose next to the lamp.

"I'm not liking this," Jay whispered.

The front door was still locked. Most people in Granite did not lock their doors. After his years in Chicago, Jay made it a habit and did not follow his townspeople's lead in that respect. Much to Danielle and Phoebe's dismay, he kept his house locked up like it contained the Ark of the Covenant.

Jay unlocked the door.

"Stay here."

"Are we really safer out here on your porch?" Danielle said with noted sarcasm.

"Good point. Come on. But stay behind me."

The living room looked untouched, as did the kitchen just beyond. As Jay entered his office, Phoebe broke rank behind Danielle and ran upstairs.

"I'll get her!" Danielle said, with urgency in her voice.

Jay took a quick look through the office. At first glance, nothing seemed different except for a type of playing card on his desk. He put the card in his pocket and turned to follow Danielle.

Jay heard a muffled scream outside his house and at the same time, he locked eyes with a frightened Phoebe at the top of the stairs. They both ran toward the scream.

Just outside, two men dressed completely in black were dragging a dazed Danielle into the woods across the street. The plot of land, a half-block down the road, was thick with trees.

Jay tried to sprint toward them, but his gimpy leg made him look more like a wounded Frankenstein's Monster.

Phoebe yelled, "Mom!" She soon reached two men as they dragged her mother into a dark car parked in a clearing. She could see the car was heavy, yet smooth in its curves. The men were attempting to put Danielle inside the back seat, but she seemed to be coming out of her dazed state and began to struggle. Phoebe ran to her and helped her mother battle the would-be kidnappers. The women held their own. Each attempted blow was blocked and returned. It was as if they had been given the same game plan as their assailants, and neither side could penetrate the other's defenses.

When Jay finally approached them, the two in black pushed their way back inside the car and wildly drove off.

Danielle sat down on a large boulder. She felt like she had just finished a triathlon.

Jay hugged Phoebe and then went over to Danielle. He raised her head from under the chin and looked her over. The moon's light was just bright enough to see Danielle's face. She had a couple of scratches and a little bruising. He felt the top of her head and located a bump the size of a golf ball. Blood dripped down her forehead.

She smiled and said, "I know...I know...no real damage, we'll just buff it out."

Jay pulled her up, gathered Phoebe in his other arm, and walked them back to his house.

"I don't think we'll be able to polish this away. It was them, wasn't it?" Jay's voice was hesitant and halting, like each word was not only thought out, but as though the more he talked the deeper and more puzzling things became.

Phoebe spoke over her mother. "If you mean somebody from *The Five,* yes, I think it was. I didn't recognize them, but one had a symbol tattooed on his hand."

"Did it look like this?" Jay took out the odd card he'd found in the house.

Phoebe took the card. It was the size of a regular playing card. One side was blank, but the other side had two roman numeral fives divided by a row of five stars.

"That's it. That's what I saw on the man's hand."

Jay put it back in his pocket. "I think it was left as a calling card. They wanted us to know who was responsible. The question is...why?"

Phoebe was tired and like Danielle, bruised. She'd taken a shot in the ribs and was finding it difficult to take a full breath. Despite the pain, she helped Jay put her mother on the living room couch. "I'm sorry."

Jay went to the bathroom to rinse out a warm washcloth and moved on to the kitchen for an ice pack.

Danielle's head was throbbing. "Sorry? Sorry for what?"

"I think it's my fault that they came here."

Jay placed the washcloth on Danielle's face and the ice pack on the mountainous bump on her noggin.

Phoebe was in the corner of the room. The light was dim, but it didn't take a psychoanalyst to figure put Phoebe had some explaining to do and it had taken tonight's attack to bring it out.

"Danielle…ah, mom…I think you know how much I miss my old life. *The Five* was my family as long as I can remember. After everything that happened, I was curious about everybody in our chapter. What happened to them? Were they transferred to a different part of the state?"

Danielle pulled the wet cloth off of her sore face. "I think we were all wondering about that. Did you hear anything?"

"After things settled down a little, I talked to some of my friends. They were beginners, you know…auditors. But, they wouldn't say anything. It was as if they were told to be quiet. I decided to let it go for a while…until I got a phone call last week. The voice said it was one of the *Pentium Five*."

Jay looked up. "Ah…one of the big wheels, what did the boss man say?"

"He said they were aware of my abilities at such a young age and wanted to talk to me about my future with *The Five*. He knew what I went through and thought I handled everything with strength and wisdom."

Danielle was proud of her daughter as well, but didn't like where this was going.

"He said he would be in touch, but would need to know where we were staying so that, when the time was right, they could meet me. We agreed that it was best to keep this secret until arrangements were made. I was thrilled that they would want me. I'm sorry, but I told him everything he wanted to know. I feel so stupid."

Danielle got up, still holding the ice pack to her head, and walked to her daughter.

"First of all, God knows where I would be tonight if it wasn't for you. And second, no more secrets, okay?"

"You got it."

"Jay, where do we go from here?"

"When I was a boy, halftime of the Green Bay game was my favorite time. My dad's way of relieving the tension of the first half was to toss the football to me in the backyard. He would have me do a down-and-out and threw the ball to me as he counted down the last seconds of our imaginary game. Then I would catch it, followed by a victory dance."

Phoebe smiled. "I don't think we need to see that."

Jay glanced at his gimpy leg. "I don't think I can do it anyway."

He continued, "My dad would wave his hand at me and say, "Act like you've been there before, boy." Jay gathered his girls back to the couch. "I think we need to do that. I think we need to find the end zone before they do and tomorrow morning it's first and ten."

Danielle rolled her eyes. "Football analogies aside, you're probably right. If we sit here and wait for something to happen, it probably will end in a bad way. We need to find out just what we're dealing with and put an end to it."

With locked doors and firepower always close by, they made it through the night without any further incident. All three knew it would be a while before they actually had a night's sleep with both eyes closed.

45

Jay didn't sleep much. By the time the sun began illuminating the sky, he was in the kitchen having coffee. His life had become complicated again. A few short months ago, he'd wondered if the rest of his time on this planet would be an unwavering rehash of the previous day. His existence had consisted of going to work, shooting the shit at the local pub, crashing in front of the tube, and doing it all over the next day. As bad and monotonous as it was, he kind of missed the old Jay. The new Jay Barthus has a daughter, with luck a future bride, and a promise to keep them safe. The old Jay Barthus had next to nothing in the area of responsibilities outside of his job. If it wasn't for his brother, who was living in Maryland with his wife and their twin boys, he could have been a complete loner. The twins had gotten used to their uncle visiting on Christmas loaded with gifts.

His mind snapped back to the present. *What about Ted's place,* he thought. *The cottage in the woods…it should start there.* He put on his shoes and started for the door, then stopped. *You can't leave them alone anymore. They may not want to go back there, but you have to bring them along.*

He walked out of the kitchen just as Danielle and Phoebe reached the bottom of the stairs.

Jay said, "We need to go."

"You mean Ted's cottage out in the woods? Are you about ready?"

Danielle and Phoebe had already slipped on clothes that were usually saved for painting or gardening and were headed toward the door.

Jay was beginning to wonder if they needed his help at all. "It may be a long day. Don't you want a little breakfast or something?"

Phoebe gave her dad a little pat on the back. "Oh, we ate before you got up. You looked so tired on the couch we didn't want to wake you."

When he opened his SUV, Geezer pounced, taking over the back seat. Jay was in no mood to persuade his lab to give up his place, so he relented. The sun was fully out and the 50-degree night was slowly giving way to what looked to be a pleasant day. Jay, rarely the most optimistic fellow around, wondered if the weather was going to be the only bright spot in what could turn out to be a hellish day.

Traffic was minimal as they squirreled around the multitude of woodsy curves and dips. The daylight made the drive much different than it had been that early morning about a month ago.

Danielle noticed Phoebe was uncharacteristically acting like a teenager and listening to her iPod. She seemed oblivious to anything going on in the world save Geezer, who sat beside her and was smearing up the window with his big nose.

Danielle could sense that Jay was in one of his quiet moods. Back when they'd first dated, he'd worn that game face whenever his job pushed stress his way. She also remembered seeing it toward the end of close football games, especially when she would annoy him with questions at the precise moment his team needed a first down.

Danielle broke the silence. "Remind me never to go on this drive with a hangover."

"Sorry, I drive fast when I'm keyed up."

"We'll get there soon enough. I hope the department didn't take everything for evidence. This could be a wasted trip." Danielle was wearing old blue jeans with a brown shirt and a leather vest. The vest had a pocket on the inside, where she had Ted Paulson's prized gold colt revolver. She tapped it lightly and thought, *Ted's not going to be using it anymore.*

Jay remembered the dozen or so boxes of evidence that were taken from the old farmhouse. "I went through everything that was taken from Ted's cottage a couple of weeks ago. There has to be something we're missing. He was in contact with *The Five's* top dogs, and we need to find out more about them."

As they rounded another curve the tall pillar of Donald Rock stood before them. This time, with the sun shining through the trees, they could see a dirt driveway that led to the front of Ted's cottage.

They walked to the back. The door that Jay kicked in on that horrible May night was still broken. Across the entrance was yellow *"Do Not Enter"* tape.

Phoebe noticed that Geezer stayed in the car. "Come on out, Geezer. You need country air as much as we do."

Phoebe knelt down and gave a tail-wagging Geezer a hug. Geezer, however, quickly pulled away and darted for the woods.

"He just wants to do a little exploring." Jay said as he pushed the yellow tape out of the way.

"When he comes back all dirty, you're the one cleaning him up. He's not going to make a mess in…God, I sound like my mother." Danielle was disgusted with herself as she ducked under Jay's arms and entered the cottage.

Jay followed her in and jokingly said, "We're not married yet, ya nag."

"Oh, shut up!"

Phoebe entered as well. She certainly hadn't liked this place when Ted brought her here on her birthday, but today seemed almost worse. The candles that had burned brightly that night had been left behind by the sheriff's crew. Despite the fact that the temperature was now in the mid-seventies outside, she felt a chill in the air. She'd walked back into this bad memory knowing it wasn't something she'd really wanted to do. She'd repeated over and over in her mind that she was strong and would not let Ted Paulson call the shots from the grave. It settled her down and lowered her fears, but just the same, under no circumstances would she ever return to the Stone Bridge. There were some things she knew would be too hard.

"The electricity is turned off." Jay pushed aside the drapes of each window to let more light in.

Any paperwork and boxes of material that had anything to do with *The Five* were already gone. The department had left behind furniture, kitchen utensils, along with smashed drywall from Ted's attempt at reconstruction.

Jay pounded on walls and floor boards, while Danielle and Phoebe checked cupboards and any other nooks and crannies. Jay began to give up the hunt.

"If we don't find anything here, we'll check out the mansion, Amalthea."

"That makes a lot of sense. We aren't finding anything either." Danielle was running out of places to look as well. Hey, where's your mutt?"

"I'll get him. Keep looking, I'll be right back. Geezer, come here, boy." Jay stood for a while, groaned, and entered the same patch of thick pines and birches his pooch ran into when they arrived.

Jay heard his dog making the same noise he'd made when Jay forgot to feed him. There wasn't a path to follow and much of the ground looked as if it was trying to grow rocks. Some protruded just barely out of the ground; others were quite enormous. Moss grew on many of the less-noticeable outcroppings, making it slippery. Jay found it easy to follow Geezer's footprints in the moist ground.

"Geezer, what are you…" He stopped in mid-sentence and knelt down. Geezer had been a busy canine. He'd been digging in an area that lacked rock. Danielle was right; the dog looked as if he were rolling in the dirt. But what caught Jay's eye was what lay just beyond the nose of his red lab.

Almost a foot into the ground, Jay could see a shoe. Next to the shoe a bony hand rested in the soil, coming from the opposite direction. Jay didn't smell it until he looked closer, but a familiar rotten-egg odor was bringing back some old and disturbing memories.

Jay, Danielle, and Phoebe felt extremely uncomfortable as they stood outside the cottage waiting for the officials to finish digging up the body.

Jay was asked to wait outside of the perimeter of the dig. He was leaning against a tree when an old colleague stopped to talk to him.

Danielle felt Phoebe's anxiety.

"What's wrong, Phoebe?"

"I don't feel safe here. It's too…open."

Danielle put her arm around Phoebe. "Maybe we should go to Amalthea. I'm sure they can call us when they figure out who's buried there."

Jay didn't know where he stood with the department, but he was friends with enough of them to find out what he needed to. Carl T. was the old man he was talking to. Carl had been on the force for over forty years. He only worked part-time now. Jay called him Carl T., because his last name was too hard for anyone to pronounce.

"Carl T. filled me in," Jay told Danielle. Even though the Green County Sheriff's Department is in charge of the excavation, officials from the University of Wisconsin Geology Department are supervising the dig. Carl told me the body was a female and was lying in a fetal position. It appears there's nothing left but clothes and bones. The maggots and beetles did their job. Oh, and they found a clutch purse with a metal detector about fifteen feet away."

Danielle could not think of one reason why a dead woman would have been found behind Ted's cottage. He hadn't seemed to have had his breakdown until recently.

"Do they have any idea who it was?"

"They think she may be Caroline Weber, a missing person from nearby Lafayette County. She was twenty-eight years old when she was discovered missing. The purse didn't have anything inside, but they found one of those return address labels taped to the inside. The Geology Department thinks the body had been there between one to three years. The timing fits, since she went missing about two years ago."

Jay reached inside his pocket for his car keys.

"Carl said he'd keep me posted. I think we should go now."

Phoebe, who just got her temps, snatched up the keys from her dad.

"I'm driving! I take it we're going to Amalthea?"

Jay hit the back of her hand. The keys popped up in the air and he completed the pass to himself.

"One, you can only drive with one passenger. And two, I would prefer to get there alive."

46

To Danielle and Phoebe, Amalthea looked like home. To Jay, it turned his stomach.

Phoebe and Geezer raced around the compound. Phoebe hadn't been back since her birthday, but despite that awful day, she still felt attached to Amalthea. Her mind understood and longed for the good years, and those times had taken place at Amalthea. Her best memories were of the outside. The outdoors were for life; the inside, study, discussions, and research. The trees were now full and most of the flowers were in full bloom, except for the tulips, which were struggling to hang on. Nothing was trimmed. The grass was long and poked out in the cracks of the sidewalks. The clear stream that snaked all around the compound seemed dirty and still. Phoebe was sad to see the landscaping and gardening that they had taken such pride in replaced by neglect.

Jay double-checked the revolver holstered under his shirt. He looked up and stared for a while at the clock tower high above. "It looks like time has stood still."

Danielle scanned the length of the property. "That's what happens when nobody is here to take care of the place."

"No, I mean the clock. It looks like it's stuck."

Danielle put her hand over her eyes to see the familiar tower clock. "Well, at least it stopped at the appropriate time."

The clock held its hands at exactly five o'clock.

Danielle had a golden skeleton key that each of the *Elite Five* were given. To her surprise, it still worked. They entered the mansion and noticed that all of the furniture was gone.

"This will be a quick search, what with everything gone," Jay said. As he started to check the many rooms, he got a phone call from Carl at the department.

"Jay, it was the missing girl, Christine Weber. We're trying to find a connection to Ted Paulsen, but haven't found anything yet. Many of those that belonged to that sect your friend Danielle belonged to have moved out of town. We're finding it a little difficult to get answers, but we'll keep trying. I'll send you a picture of her."

"Thanks, Carl! Carl, one more thing…someone's been keeping an eye on us lately. In fact, they tried to snatch Danielle. If you hear anything, anything at all, let me know."

"I will, Jay. Watch yourself."

Jay started up the steps to the second floor with Danielle and Phoebe, and then suddenly, stopped.

"Did either of you ever hear of the name Christine Weber in connection to Ted Paulson?"

They both shook their heads. But as Jay started back up the steps, Phoebe remembered something.

"I do remember a Chrissie, but it wasn't from Ted. It was from Wayne."

"Ted's son?"

"Yes, he mentioned a girl that he'd been dating. I remember thinking that it was unusual, because I'd never seen him with a girl before."

Danielle began to recall the girl as well.

"Now that you mention it, I think he showed me a picture of the girl during one of our meetings. Wayne was really shy and I didn't know whether to believe him or not. I thought he might have made it up."

"Do you think you could remember the girl if I showed you a picture?"

"It was over two years ago, but maybe."

Jay's phone beeped and Jay retrieved the picture Carl sent him. "Does this ring a bell?"

Danielle took a long look at the smiling young girl on Jay's cell phone. The girl was throwing a graduation hat in the air. Her smile was ear-to-ear. Her face portrayed confidence and like those around her, enthusiasm toward what was coming. Though Danielle had never really met her, she had something in common with her—what it felt like to know that Ted Paulson may be the last person she would ever see alive.

"I can't be positive. It's not the same picture I saw, but it does look like the girl he showed me...maybe a little younger."

Phoebe listened intently until something triggered another memory. After all, she'd known Wayne Paulson all of her life. When she was twelve years old, she'd had a short crush on him. He was easily the youngest of *The Elite Five* and he'd made an impression on her.

"He told me, before the suicide, he was wondering what would happen if he left *The Five*. He was always one to study every side of every situation. I thought he probably was doing a study on percentages. Maybe he was leaving. He could have decided to leave because of the girl."

Jay stepped down all the way to the first floor and paced back and forth. "Maybe it wasn't a suicide? Suppose Ted flipped out because his son was leaving *The Five*." He stopped to think about the possibilities. "He killed his own son."

Danielle followed, "And then he killed Wayne's girlfriend, because she knew the truth. She knew they were planning on being together, but nobody else did. Wayne would have told her to keep it quiet until he could figure it out or until they left."

"Father, can we find out if Wayne had plane tickets to leave, or if he died from something other than suicide?"

"I think we can now. Back then, Ted had a lot of people in his back pocket. By the way, what's with the father thing? I thought we advanced to dad."

"You're dad at home...you're father on the outside."

"All right, you two, can we get back to the business at hand?" Danielle turned to continue their search. "Knowing what happened doesn't change the fact that somebody wants me dead, does it?"

Jay started back upstairs. "You're right. Let's keep looking."

Phoebe went outside to check the shed in the back.

Danielle was getting frustrated with their lack of anything substantial.

"Anything, Jay?"

"No, nothing."

Then Phoebe ran inside.

"The tower clock! We need to go upstairs!"

They ran upstairs to the fourth floor.

As Phoebe reached the door she said, "Like you said, the clock is stopped at five o'clock." She tried the door. "It's locked."

Danielle again retrieved her gold skeleton key.

Phoebe opened the door and flipped a light switch. The pentagonal room housed only a white marble floor with a railing along the outside perimeter. The pendulum stood still exactly in the middle of the sunken floor.

Phoebe knew the workings of the clock about as well as anyone could. "It's a two-second pendulum...one second each way. The best pendulum clocks that were ever made had an accuracy of about a second per year. This pendulum is thirteen feet in length. These invar rods are specified to an exact length. The best that Ted could do for this one was around ten seconds a month. He showed me how to add adjuster weights to the top of it." She pointed upward.

Jay and Danielle both stared at their daughter.

"What...I liked listening to the tick-tock."

Jay looked up at the top of the pendulum and then back down to the floor, some five feet below them. He hadn't seen see it before, but under the pendulum bob was a large book.

"Look, under the pendulum." Jay made his way over the railing and knelt down next to the large pendulum bob.

"It's the book that I saw in the glass case at Ted's house. It's jammed!"

Jay started to pull at the large book.

Phoebe was worried. "Be careful, the bob has very sharp edges. If there's enough tension, the pendulum could start swinging again."

Jay pulled hard and the book slid out from under the bob. He dove toward the railing to avoid the pendulum's swing and hit his head on the upper rail. The pendulum never moved.

Phoebe laughed—just a little. She then added, "If the tension is slight, you need to push it to get it going again."

Rubbing his head, he thanked Phoebe for the warning.

They took the book downstairs.

Danielle ran her fingers over the leather bound cover with *The Five's* symbol. The symbol of the roman "V" with the mirror image of the "V" separated by five small stars was crested in blue. There was considerable damage to the book due to the pendulum. "It was exactly five o'clock that night when Ted hid the book up here. There must have been a reason for him to do that."

Phoebe seemed to know the answer. "I think he knew I'd find it. There must be something in it that he wanted me to find." In her usual logical manner she continued. "I would say he wanted *us* to find it, but I think he planned for you both to be…that is…for me to be alone."

Phoebe opened the book. It was about three inches thick. Much of what she'd learned was in that book. She sifted through the pages.

Danielle had seen Ted using the book to find certain answers to very deep philosophical issues. She and the other three of *The Elite Five* were occasionally allowed to read certain parts of the book, but only with Ted's supervision.

Phoebe turned to the page where the ribbon bookmark had been left. She glanced through the entire chapter.

"It lays out, in detail, what the *Pentium Five* looks for in each of the fifty factions. It describes how the *Pentium Five* are to help and instruct all of those factions."

Phoebe scanned the pages with greater concentration.

"I don't see anything noted as to where to find them. It repeatedly mentions another book located at the Quincunx. Only the *Pentium Five* have access to this book. It doesn't specify what the Quincunx is or where. Apparently, they live by a set of rules that only pertain to them." She pointed toward the bottom of the page. Here's something, the *Pentium Five* are the nucleus of the whole. They are a bound structure that contains the cell's hereditary information and controls the cell's growth and reproduction."

Danielle moved the book closer. She had been observing the words and was beginning to see some sort of pattern. She was extremely bright when it came to numbers and was well aware of how members of *The Five* used them to hide actual meaning. With pen and paper, she began to write down letters that seemed scrambled and nonsensical. She crossed it out and started again.

"It's the fifth paragraph. The meaning seems ambiguous.

Our effort in crafting tried heirs stays true. Taught to come into fifty ideal veins, every life tested, thrust. Each prehensible five digit effect tie a symbol.

Jay scratched his head.

"What?"

"There's probably another book worth of hidden gems in this thing. But for whatever reason, Ted wanted Phoebe to learn about the *Pentium Five*. He made sure she went to the correct page. This paragraph is the only one on these two pages that seems to have hidden meaning. Every fifth letter in the fifth paragraph forms a word."

She finished making out the answer.

"fifth – state – five – letters - fifty"

Phoebe reached into her pocket and began to tap away at her iPhone.

"Connecticut! It says Connecticut was the fifth state to join the union."

Jay preferred to do things the old-fashioned way. His fingers were too big to press such little buttons. Phoebe seemed to orchestrate it like Itzhak Perlman on his violin.

Danielle was getting excited. Though she had grown tired of Ted's games long before, this was different. It involved *The Pentium Five*. To her these people were an all knowing power source that helped others find wisdom, truth and love. If nothing else, she wanted to prove to Jay that *The Five* was a bucket of fresh, ripe blueberries with just a couple of duds. She admired their work and only had one misgiving—that they were unseen and untouchable. They were a mystery that could only be solved one way: to become one of them. Now she wanted to find another way, another path to the mystery that had long been awaiting an answer.

"Phoebe, let's look up some cities and towns."

Phoebe's fingers moved before Danielle finished the sentence.

"No problem!"

Danielle waited with pencil in hand.

"Give me all of the five letter cities and towns in Connecticut."

"Ahhh…well, there's one city and three towns; Derby, Essex, Salem, and Union."

Phoebe knew her mother was brilliant with numbers; she was, however, surprised at the speed in which the calculations came.

Danielle mentally computed the number attached to each alphabet and wrote the totals down for each of the four places. Her notepad read, Derby – 54, Essex – 72, Union – 73, and Salem – 50.

All three whispered the same town—*Salem*.

Jay smiled suspiciously. "Is that the witch town?"

Phoebe had this one. "No, *that* Salem is in Massachusetts. However…." She continued tapping away on her iPhone. "It was named after Colonel Samuel Browne, who was from Salem, Massachusetts. Oh, it also says that Captain Kidd was believed to have buried treasure in the woods of Salem, Connecticut."

Danielle stood, and opened the double doors leading to the outside of Amalthea. Geezer had been waiting for them at the porch and wagged his tail wildly at the sight of her.

She reached down to pet Geezer and took a deep breath. "I heard Connecticut is wonderful this time of year."

47

All three agreed on their need to pursue the path that was now taking them to Connecticut. Sitting back and waiting for something bad to happen was not an option. Someone meant to hurt Danielle, and they would find out who and why, or they would die trying.

The two-hour flight out of Milwaukee was uneventful. There wasn't any time to find someone to take care of Geezer, so they'd thought it best to take him along.

During the flight Phoebe rested her netbook on her lap and tried to scan the Salem area through satellite images.

"So what are we looking for?"

Jay glanced at her netbook. "You can look for an odd shaped building, but I think our best chances may be to ask a few questions around town."

Phoebe didn't see anything out of place or strange from the views she scanned of the Salem area.

From Connecticut's Bradley International, they planned to drive south to Salem and arrive in less than an hour. They rented a GMC Terrain with GPS and soon were on their way.

Heading south on Hartford Road they stopped at a shopping center and sat down at Uncle Chong's Chinese

Restaurant. They had made it to Salem's Four Corners and didn't have a clue what their next move was going to be.

As they filled their bellies, Jay finished ahead and took his coffee to a booth.

"Mind if I sit with you guys for a minute?"

The two old men looked a bit startled, but nodded just the same.

Jay wondered if they were being friendly or if his size had intimidated them into agreeing to the new sitting arrangement.

"Have you fellows been living around here for a while?"

The undersized one with the glasses spoke up. "Grew up in Montville just down the road, but mostly Salem. Earl here moved to New Jersey for a time, but he found his way back."

Jay introduced himself and shook their hands.

"What brings a big guy like you to a small town like this?"

"Did you ever lose something and all your instincts tell you where it's likely to show up, but you still can't find it?"

Earl spoke up this time. He was wearing a jean shirt and pants. The knitted words just above his pocket read, *Zemco Fields and Trails*. "I do that with my car keys all the time."

"Well, I'm helping my girlfriend look for her lost father and we're thinking he might be around these parts. He used to talk about this area once in a while. He said he spent some time here as a child and always meant to come back for a visit. Unfortunately, he's been missing for a couple of months."

The impish fellow, Benny, looked over at the table where Danielle and Phoebe sat.

"You sure have a couple of good looking girls over there."

Earl cleared his throat. "Easy Benny, remember your age."

"I may be old, but I can still see!"

"Our new friend Jay is looking for somebody who may be in trouble and you go on about pretty girls. You ought to be ashamed."

"I am ashamed, Earl—ashamed that I sit here every morning and have to look across the table at an old, wrinkled-up prune like you!"

"I'd say those are fighting words if my opponent wasn't a short stump who can barely lift his chin, much less his fists."

Jay was enjoying the good-natured attacks, but needed to reel these old guys back in.

"He may have joined some sort of strange group or following. He gets involved with people that are a little outside the box, if you know what I mean. Anything like that here?"

Benny, barely audible, mumbled. "Well, there's this group out in the woods."

Earl looked at his friend with astonishment. "They like to be left alone. You know better than that, Benny."

Jay knew he was on to something. "Benny, I wouldn't ask if it wasn't important."

Benny looked down at the floor. "If anybody asks, you didn't hear nothin from me. I'll deny I ever met you."

Jay could smell his fear. "I'm only looking for an old man. I don't care about anything else, but if you know something, I'd sure like to check it out." Jay thought a little icing wouldn't hurt. "The old guy is a diabetic. He may need his meds. Danielle, his daughter, is getting very worried."

Benny was about to spill when Earl butted in. "What was this guy's name?" Maybe I knew him or his family."

Jay was hoping that question wouldn't be brought up. "The family name was Pontes." It was close to Danielle's last name of Ponto, but with a small alteration.

Earl grunted and sat back for a moment.

"I think there was a family by that name around Norwich, but…not sure."

Jay felt lucky, since he'd just pulled the name out of his ass.

Benny started up again. "They lived in the "Big House" for a while, at the end of Horse Pond Road."

"Who?"

Earl was beginning to warm up to Jay. "Oh, we don't know much about them. They keep to themselves mostly. They talk friendly enough, but you really don't know who belongs to the thing and who doesn't. They have money to spend, so we just let them be. I couldn't tell you what they do. Neither could Benny."

Benny didn't let that stand. "I know more than you, ya old fossil. Years ago we thought they were some sort of witch cult…you know, because of the Salem thing. But, we never saw any signs of such things. They seem real smart, those people. I think it's some sort of government think tank."

Earl laughed.

"I read about those think tanks, ya decrepit bag of bones." Benny said, sounding defensive.

Keeping these two on track was beginning to get on Jay's nerves. "Where are they now?"

Benny pointed at Earl's shirt.

"Zemco Fields and Trails?"

"It's a bit south of the trails, but that's where they are. I'm not saying these are the people you're looking for. All I know is, you asked for people who are outside the box and these people aren't anywhere near the box."

Jay thought about Salem and this area in the country. From the few folks they'd met, they'd seemed to be good people and everything appeared landscaped and well kept. There was no sense in making ourselves visible to the townspeople if they didn't have to. These two old gentlemen knew a few things, and if he and the girls could keep their business quiet, even better.

"Benny, can you tell me more about this place?"

"Like I said, they moved from the Big House, oh…maybe twenty years ago." Benny paused for effect. He enjoyed a captive audience. "Well, you can't see the new place from above this time of year. The tree leaves are too thick. But Earl and I seen it. We went up in a hot-air balloon."

Earl made some sort of grunt. "It was on our bucket list."

Danielle and Phoebe finished their meal and curiosity got the best of them. They went over to meet the two old townies.

Jay introduced them, but made sure not to let the conversation stray.

"Benny and Earl here were just telling me about going up in a hot-air balloon."

Benny continued, "Like I said, this time a year the tall timbers hide the place pretty good. We went up in April. We didn't do it to spy on those people, but we couldn't help but notice their…aah…compound."

Danielle spoke up. "What did it look like?"

Benny didn't mind switching the conversation from Jay to Danielle. He could barely take his eyes off of her anyway.

"It's laid out kind of funny."

"How so?"

Earl interrupted, "Like on dice. Like the number five."

Phoebe whispered, "A Quincunx."

Danielle drew on a napkin. She showed Earl her outline of four circles in the outside corners of a square and added the circle in the center. "Like that?"

"Yes, but they looked like they were all connected."

Jay intervened, "To each other or to the center?"

Benny reached for Danielle's pen and finished the drawing. "Both! It looked like rounded cement walkways that ran to each corner and to the center."

Jay sat back and scratched the back of his head. "Did you see any people?"

"Nope, but there was some sort of parking lot that circled the whole place. Black or dark-blue SUVs were the only thing parked there."

Earl interjected, "A big mess of them."

Jay pressed on, "I suppose Danielle's father could have known somebody and was allowed in. Do you think they would let us in if we went there?"

Danielle and Phoebe weren't in on Jay's story about her father.

Danielle interrupted Benny's response. "My father…what?"

Jay kept the story going. "I had to tell them about your father settling up here and maybe getting himself involved with that cult or whatever it is."

"Oh, yeah, the cult," she answered with a slight roll of the eyes.

Benny laughed. "You wouldn't get anywhere near it. They have fences and the main entrance has at least one checkpoint. We rode our bikes up there once. They were friendly enough, but they made sure we turned around and scooted out of their view. I think its invitation only."

Jay got up from the booth. "Thanks, it's been a pleasure to meet both of you." He held out his hand.

Benny took Jay's hand and shook it with a surprisingly strong grip for such a small man.

"Like I said, no need to involve us two old boys in this search of yours. If somebody should ask, tell them you were talking to some retired folks over at the library."

Earl made that grunting noise again. "Yeah, you'd be pretty hard pressed to find this illiterate at the library."

"Shut up, you toothless, big-eared bat. What do you know about books other than porn?"

Danielle started to laugh as she and Phoebe followed Jay out of the restaurant. "We got lucky with those two, but getting into that compound sounds extremely tricky."

Jay nodded, "I just thought we would go in, guns blazing."

Phoebe looked up at her dad just to make sure he was kidding. "Good idea, father, you go first. Let us know when it's safe for us to move in."

Danielle leaned against the outside of their van. Geezer pressed his nose up on the window and let loose with one of his loud and startling barks. Danielle jumped. "I swear, if I wet my pants…."

Jay took out his cell phone, "Phoebe, could you take Geezer for a walk?"

As she strolled toward a small field, Jay made a call to his old friend Carl T.

Carl sounded relieved to hear Jay's voice.

"Where ya been, Jay? The interim captain had been asking about you. They're wondering where you are?"

"They didn't seem all that interested in me earlier. Why now?"

"I'm not sure. Anyhow, where are you?"

"I'm in Connecticut, but I'd like to keep that just between us. Anything new?"

"Funny you should mention Connecticut. When they went through Ted Paulson's house, they found a sort of memory box. It seems Ted had a half-brother on his father's side. I checked on Ted's mysterious half-brother. He's an interesting character."

"Tell me about him."

"His name is Leland Paulson. He was born in 1940. They both have the same birthplace, Sapulpa, Oklahoma. Leland was or is, six years older than Ted. He never married, as far as I could tell. He lived with his mother for all of his young life and shared the same father. Leland graduated college in the Midwest and got his doctorate at MIT. He also taught or did research there for a while."

"What did he teach?"

"His research was exclusive to number theory. He was unceremoniously dismissed from MIT in 1972."

"Why?"

"They wouldn't reveal that."

"You mentioned it was funny that I was in Connecticut."

"Oh yeah, this Leland's last known address is listed as Connecticut. It didn't list what particular part of the state he was located, however."

"Thanks, Carl. Tell the interim captain I have a few personal things to attend to. I won't be back until everything is taken care of."

"You got it, Jay. Let me know if you need anything."

"You've done enough, but there is one thing."

"What's that?"

"Call Danielle's folks and tell them their daughter and granddaughter are doing fine and will be home soon."

"Will do!"

Quincunxes in heaven above; quincunxes in the earth below; quincunxes in deity; quincunxes in the mind of man; quincunxes in bones, in optic nerves, in roots of trees, in leaves, in petals, in everything. Samual Taylor Coleridge on Sir Thomas Browne's "The Garden of Cyrus.

48

The next morning they drove back through the town of Salem and took a turn to the east on Round Hill Road. Ten minutes later they stopped in front of the checkpoint that Benny had mentioned.

Jay lowered his window and took a flyer. "We were sent a...message from Leland Paulson. He wants to see us."

The guard house wasn't your typical wooden shed. Though the building was not much bigger than a normal state park checkpoint, the height was striking. Spiral stairs in the center of the structure led to an extremely high lookout point.

Danielle whispered, "What is this, a penitentiary?"

Jay could see the guard call ahead. The wait seemed long and the tension was building. Geezer broke up the tension.

Phoebe reacted first, gagging from the aroma. "Oh...that's not right."

Danielle blamed it on Jay. "Why you didn't keep that dog home, I'll never know."

Jay stood up for his canine. "He hasn't had a proper meal in days."

Just then the guard spoke up. "Keep this in your front window and it will allow you to enter and visit for the day." He paused and replaced his friendly voice with one of authority and lack of emotion. "Don't stray from the road. That would not turn out well for you."

The winding road continued deep into the woods until they reached yet another guard station. This one was a half-circle building and did not include a tall lookout tower. The watchman simply waved them ahead.

Something was bothering Danielle. "I know your friend at the Sheriff's department told you about Ted's brother. What made you use his name to get us in?"

"The connection is too much of a coincidence. I took a shot that Leland Paulson is somehow linked to the *Pentium Five*.

Immediately after the second security check, they approached the circular road that Benny and Earl had mentioned earlier. The road was wide enough to allow for single-space parking, and sidewalks were placed just inside the road. There were blue SUVs parked around the compound.

Phoebe was excited. Inside this building were the *Pentium Five*—the best and the brightest. Through hundreds of obstacles, they'd achieved the highest levels of wisdom and truth. She couldn't begin to imagine what she could learn from them.

Halfway around the quincunx design, Jay slowed and parked. "This looks to be the entrance."

The three stepped down the walk, leaving Geezer in the SUV. The large wooden doors reminded Jay of those at the entrance of Amalthea. The only difference was the carving. There were five oval shapes. Each shape bore two Roman numeral fives. One mirrored the other and was divided by a line of five small circles. Five-point stars were etched inside the circles. Two ovals were on each of the two doors and the center oval came together when the two massive doors were closed. Overall, the door was very similar to the playing card that had been left inside Jay's home the night Danielle had been nearly taken.

Jay yanked on the large Victorian era door pull, and to his surprise, the doors were not locked. On a huge wall directly inside the doors was a three dimensional map.

Phoebe's eyes grew big. "The Great Principles," she said almost whispering. The quincunx in front of them was of the same pattern the two old men at the diner had described.

Danielle scanned the map and words before her. Though she wished she could study the map further, she realized, as did Jay, that their main concern should be their security. Despite the fact that no other people or cameras were visible, she felt they were being watched.

"It's like everything I imagined, Danielle…er…Mother," Phoebe said. She pointed at the map. "To the right is the west wing, the one that houses *Love*."

The wing seemed to glow. It radiated a bright beam that seemed to shoot out from the walls.

"To the left is the North wing. It represents the principle of *Justice*." The wing was dark and gloomy. Phoebe didn't find it inviting.

The quincunx pattern on the wall depicted all five wings, each with their own principle and each a certain color theme. The south wing represented *Truth* and had a red theme, while the east wing represented *Wisdom* and the color green.

Phoebe felt her mind was exploding with the possibilities she could sense within these walls. "The yellow center is *Virtue*, moral excellence. It is the umbrella of the other four principles." She looked at Jay and Danielle, not as her biological parents, but almost as her students. "Don't you see? Each wing is led by a member of the *Pentium Five*. *Virtue* is the wing that can make everything right."

Danielle knew her daughter well enough to understand when her mind's eye was using tunnel vision and not seeing the broader picture. "Phoebe, are you focusing on our lives, or on picking the brain of this *Pentium Five* member?"

The question took quite some time to filter through the hundreds of other thoughts shuffling in and out of Phoebe's brain. Phoebe evaluated all sides of it and finally found the answer to be both satisfying and troubling.

"It's both, mother. It has to be both."

"What do you mean?"

"I agree that we needed to come here to make some sort of agreement with the people who tried to abduct you, but it would be such a waste not to take advantage of the wealth of knowledge within the *Pentium Five*."

The corner of Jay's top lip rose slightly and Phoebe could see his anger. "My discussions with these people will be short and to the point, I promise you," Jay grumbled.

Phoebe had intended to point out the importance of the *Pentium Five* and the value of discussing orally rather than with violence, but the look on Jay's face scared her to silence.

The map showed that the path to the center of the quincunx buildings could not be reached without first going through either the wing of love or the wing of justice.

Jay considered both options. "Which will it be?"

Before saying another word all three of them crumbled to the floor.

49

Jay woke to a feeling of déjà vu. For an instant he thought he'd just awakened from his leg surgery the day after being shot by Ted. The same grogginess was there, but after the initial jolt of consciousness, he realized everything else was different.

This place didn't smell of rubbing alcohol, nurses and cleaned metal instruments. The aroma was, instead, of old books. The lighting was dim. The only sound he could hear was that of his own breath. He tried to adjust his eyes. He began to focus on a word carved deeply into the wall across from him.

He tried to say the word *justicia*, but it came out "*jestucha*"—his thick, dry, tongue was not working well.

On Jay's left an elderly man shuffled over. He wore a black shirt embroidered with the same *V* symbol that Jay had seen on the entrance doors.

The man reached into his pocket and retrieved a small device. "I wasn't going to hurt her," he said as he tapped the remote.

The room's lighting slowly brightened.

Jay's ability to focus became less fuzzy and the light gave his situation much more clarity. He immediately noticed the absence of Danielle and Phoebe. The large room was still dark in many ways. From the magnificent woodwork to the comfortably aged furniture and the wall-to-wall higher educational books, it appeared to be a room fit for an old defense lawyer or a retired judge.

Jay also realized he was tethered to a chair that did not fit the decorum.

"You were saying?"

"Yes, Lieutenant, I was saying I would have done my best not to hurt your friend Miss Ponto. I merely wanted to discuss her future. Things have changed, however."

Jay squinted and finally was able to make out the old man's face. He looked like a taller, more professional version of Ted Paulsen.

"As you may have surmised, I'm Leland Paulson. I am the High Cardinal for our Justice department. We merely wanted to make some adjustments concerning Miss Ponto. She broke a most quintessential part of our irreversible policies, did she not?"

Jay scanned the room to get a better sense of his surrounding, while listening to Leland.

Leland, mistakenly, took Jay's glances as interest in the fine architecture within the room.

"Much of the wood trim is black walnut. I often look at it with humility because I understand that its beauty will be here for all to see well beyond either of our lives. Beyond the inevitable decay of our bodies and our short existence, this beautiful art form will endure."

Even in his dizzy state, Jay could pick up the fact that the man in front of him could not be conceived as normal. He glanced down and took in a most unusual floor. It had the appearance of foggy glass and imprinted in the center was *The Five's* logo. Jay shook his head, trying to clear his mind.

"Where are Danielle and Phoebe?"

"I have them. They are comfortable." Paulson walked back and forth in front of Jay.

"My brother Ted got himself into a bit of a pickle. He respected our mandates and followed them as literally as he knew how. On the other hand, he dealt a sentence to his own son before any breach had been committed. That one mistake forced my hand."

Jay was surprised to hear this man divulging his own role in his brother's deeds. "Ted didn't do it alone?"

"Ted did very few things alone. I didn't even know I had a brother until my late twenties. By that time, I had access to people and records. I had always suspected that my father had a life other than what he divulged to my mother and me. It turned out that he had two families. We were only twenty miles apart. Neither knew of the other's existence. In 1969, I found Ted and confronted him with the news. He was a young accountant…just twenty-three years old."

Jay realized Leland was not really talking to his captor. Rather, it was as if he was instructing a class of students.

"After finding and being a part of the growth history of *The Five*, I saw an opportunity to help mold my half-brother from a meek accountant to a self-assured man with nearly the same interests as myself. I showed him only the basics. From there, Theodore soon learned how numbers could be used to develop a way of life."

He turned away from Jay and seemed to transform into a different person.

"My father didn't like me much. He thought of me as a mistake…an obstacle."

Leland Paulson's voice changed. He sounded and looked to be a meek, beaten soul, missing the ability to overcome the slightest of life's miscues or hurdles.

"My young life was that of a mouse in a maze. Father would watch me struggle. He made me do things…tasks I had no comprehension of how to complete. Don't get me wrong, he didn't hurt me in…that way. It was more like he kept asking me to cut the grass without a mower. I could go to the bathroom at the completion of my task. Many times I urinated in my pants. Since I had not completed my task in the allotted time, I was ridiculed and forced to remain in my wet clothing. My mother was a non-factor. She had nothing to offer, and father made sure she stayed that way."

Leland walked around Jay's chair as if sizing up his prey.

"I later learned that my brother Ted did not have such an upbringing. I don't know why."

He stood silently for just a moment, then spoke with a level barely over a whisper. "Ted did, however, inherit a genetic pattern quite similar to mine."

"Where are Danielle and Phoebe?"

Leland Paulson ignored the question.

"Do you suppose a person could survive without all five senses, Lieutenant?"

"Where are Danielle and Phoebe?"

Leland grabbed a handful of Jay's hair and pulled his head backward.

"How gratifying it is to find someone who cares more for others' well-being rather than his own. Sometimes it is noble to put yourself before others. But it depends upon the circumstances."

Jay's anger was mounting. "You have the same look in your eyes as your brother did…the one that says; don't look inside of me, it's dark in here."

It was as if Jay's words were sucked into a vacuum.

"Lieutenant, you've done nothing wrong. Unlike others, you didn't break the trust of your chosen society, disrupt an entire division, and then dismiss our fifth golden rule. No, your fate does not exactly fit the crime—not like your friend Danielle Ponto. I must make an example of her. As far as your newfound daughter, she has now become the life or death decision-maker."

Jay's eyes bulged. Every muscle in his body tensed. He knew if he could get loose of the chair, he could kill the old man in less than a minute.

Leland Paulson glanced at the large clock on the far end of the room and nodded his head.

"It's about that time. Let the show begin."

Leland reached for a touchpad on the wall. The floor's logo disappeared—replaced with the visibility of the room below. The clarity to the room below became vivid to Jay but, apparently, the conversion went unnoticed to the people below.

It took a few seconds for Jay to understand what he was seeing. Danielle and Phoebe were in a bright space that, like all the rooms in the quincunx complex, was pentagonal in design. Jay could see everything from above. To Jay, his confinement over the scene below made him feel as helpless as he had ever felt.

Danielle sat in the corner. She was strapped to a chair in much the same fashion as Jay. Her jeans and shirt had been replaced with a hospital gown. As with most such gowns, it wasn't form-fitting.

Phoebe stood nearby. She appeared to be holding a syringe.

Two older fellows walked out of the room and closed the door behind them. Jay thought they looked a lot like Benny and Earl from the diner. Then it dawned on him: they had been set up.

Leland sat opposite Jay on a small stool in front of one of his bookshelves.

"You see, for years now I have realized that my father left behind more than the memory of his less-than-perfect ability to nurture his sons. Though we didn't know the cause of his behavior growing up, his later years gave us the answer. He tended toward a lack of emotion, scattered thoughts, and delusions. Near the end of his life, the authority's found him naked in Ted's backyard, scrubbing his skin with a wire brush. Ted eventually had him committed."

Jay heard Leland, but the bulk of his attention was focused on the room beneath the floor.

Leland continued, hands clenching and unclenching as he spoke.

"What I have is highly hereditary, Lieutenant. That means it must have a strong genetic component. Scientists believed that the responsible genetic variants for schizophrenia disorder could be found and corrected. That may have been true if the variants were few in number, but it turns out that the cause may be at least 10,000 different disruptions. I'm quite certain my brother and I have received that gift from our father. Symptoms grow ever stronger as the years go by."

Leland put his hand around his forehead and massaged his temples.

"I have been doing my part in helping some old friends...scientists...to crunch variables. They've finally put together a drug that may correct all, or most, of the genetic disruptions. Tests on mice are not yet conclusive, but there have been signs of improvement. I'm afraid I don't have five or ten years to wait. Many humans would like to believe that one's life is just as important as another's, but that is simply untrue. Sometimes it makes complete sense to sacrifice a few lives for the greater good."

"What does this have to do with us?"

"I was able to acquire the test drug, Lieutenant. Your daughter is holding the drug in that syringe in her hand at this moment." Leland looked at the clock again. "She has been given a choice. She has two minutes to inject her mother with the drug. Then we'll wait for the outcome. The results won't help us in testing whether the drug will cure what I have, however, it will tell us if she lives or dies."

"And if she decides not to inject Danielle?"

Leland's appearance showed just the slightest of emotion. "Your daughter has been informed of the consequences." He put his hand to his chin and watched the scene below. "This will be interesting, don't you think?"

Jay grunted. "I doubt that you gave her much of a choice."

Leland pointed to the floor and said, "Look!"

Phoebe walked over to Danielle. She focused on the syringe in her hand. Jay could see her agonizing over what surely was an impossible choice to ask of a fifteen year old girl. As she approached her mother, she wiped her eyes with the back of her hand, fighting to keep her emotions intact.

Jay watched in horror as Phoebe inserted the needle deep into Danielle's arm. He jerked in his chair, attempting to break free. He watched in desperation as Danielle convulsed and slumped over. Then she was still—so still, that the life appeared to be sucked out of her.

The two old men had been keeping an eye on the captives from a small window in the door. They moved more quickly than old men should logically have been able to move and released Danielle from the chair, laying her on the floor.

Jay could see the disappointment on Leland's face as he ran from the room. A moment later, Leland entered the room below and stood over Danielle.

For a dead person, she moved quickly. She'd landed her foot squarely on Leland's testicles. As he collapsed, she spun him around and reached under her leg for the spent syringe that Phoebe had dropped underneath the chair. She pulled the plunger back to let air into the syringe, and then held it to Leland's neck.

Danielle now realized they were set-up by those two fellows' at the diner. "Benny...Earl, if those are your real names...you'll want to back away—now!"

The two makeup artists hadn't had time to remove the entirety of their disguises. Benny's neck no longer had the wrinkles it'd had earlier. The one that played the part of Earl removed his well-applied concealment.

Danielle looked more closely at Earl and remembered the young reporter that had stood out among the other journalists at her house when she'd bored them with her dissertation on the teachings of *The Five*. She wondered if he had been tracking her ever since the morning of the bridge murders.

Seconds later, the door swung open and several guards moved in, all dressed in yellow hospital scrubs with the mirrored V insignia. An older gentleman followed them into the room. The man had wavy white hair and was wearing the same type of shirt as Leland, except his was of a yellow shade.

"You have every right to hurt Leland, Danielle. He wasn't very hospitable to you. I can understand your anger. I wonder if you would consider putting that syringe down? The air bubble would likely be big enough to cause Leland to have a heart attack. I hope you can trust me to believe that we can take things over from here."

"Where's Jay? I'm not letting this bastard go until I see Jay."

The white-haired gentleman's voice had a soothing, reassuring tone. It was a voice designed to put one into a peaceful place. "Your daughter's father is being released as we speak. He should be down any second."

Danielle, somehow, felt she could trust this old fellow, but still held her ground.

"As soon as I see Jay, Leland is all yours."

"Very well, Danielle. Oh my, you'll have to forgive me, I haven't introduced myself. I am Dr. Thomas Hinske."

Phoebe shyly said, "You're the Cardinal for the center principle...virtue."

"Very good, Phoebe. We seem to know each other, but not really. I hope to remedy that, and show you, all of you, who we are. I wish I had been here sooner. I could have prevented all of this...unpleasantness."

Jay entered the room, breaking up the conversation and making a beeline to Danielle.

"Danielle, are you okay? I saw what happened. You were...Phoebe put the drug in your arm!"

"Father...look over here!"

Phoebe moved the chair. On the wall, a wet spot dripped down to the floor.

"Between Mother's skinny arm and the long needle, I shoved it clear through." She winked at Danielle. "At least I hoped it would go all the way through."

Danielle slowly removed the syringe from Leland's neck.

Jay picked Leland up and grasped his black shirt hard enough to rip his chest hair from its proper place.

The guards moved toward Jay, but the white-haired Cardinal stepped in between.

"Lieutenant, I'm afraid Leland couldn't help his behavior. You see, he has...."

Leland, spoke up.

"Schizophrenia...yes... I'm sorry Thomas. I promised I would tell you if it affected my work. Obviously, it has."

Jay let go of Leland. When he'd been working the Chicago beat, he'd never let anybody go. Crazy or not, he'd

held them until they were in constraints. Letting Leland loose
was not something that came easy.

50

Jay, Danielle, Phoebe, and Geezer became guests of the *Pentium Five* for the next few days. They soon learned of the extreme intelligence of Leland Paulson and the difficulty the other four had in reaching an understanding on his mental health. It was a mistake, a human mistake that would be studied and expounded on over and over. Furthermore, the Paulson's had hurt families, and those losses could never be fully recovered. The *Pentium Five* would compensate those that Leland and Ted Paulson had hurt, monetarily.

Jay still had his doubts, but he believed that the other four Cardinals did not know what had played out between Leland and Ted. As long as Leland was locked someplace where he couldn't get out, Jay would be fine. The other Cardinals assured him that Leland would be kept in a secure mental facility for the rest of his life. Jay promised to make sure they kept their word.

Had it been up to Jay and Danielle, they would not have stayed at the Quincunx Complex at all. But it was clear to them that Phoebe had a special kind of brilliance. She kept her calm and used her intellect to positively affect an impossible situation.

Phoebe didn't waste any time. "Did you meet the other Cardinals? They're wonderful, Mother. Two women control the department of love and trust. They seem to be able to use a much higher percentage of their brains than the average human. I'm learning so much it's like cheating. I'm soaking up so many mathematical and speculative theories, I'm afraid I'll bust." Then she winked at her mother. "But I won't."

Danielle was no slouch in the area of brain power, as well. Though she was proud of the attention her daughter was receiving, she was a bit envious. Danielle had been granted a safe and permanent removal from the sect, and she knew there was no going back.

"I think my favorite is Cyprian Jessup. He is the Cardinal for the Department of Wisdom."

Danielle smiled. "That comes as no surprise to me."

"Cyprian is Greek. He speaks dozens of languages and knows the history and tendencies of nearly all societies on earth. Because mathematics is a universal study, he's been able to use physics and reality to explore ways for all humans to reach their full abilities. He said he's not trying to make efficient robotic humans. He thinks he can help people to find their happiest level."

Danielle was impressed. "How deeply did he go into his findings?"

"He barely scratched the surface. He said he's simultaneously working on nearly five hundred other projects. It's all so exciting. And guess what? With all his knowledge and wisdom, he whispered something to me. He told me that the number five is not just a symbol for our sect. It is more than what we've learned. It shows up just about everywhere. We just have to look for it." She paused to let the thought of what she'd just said float around her. Then she realized her father wasn't in the room to hear her exhilarating news. "Where's Father?"

"He's been spending most of his time at the physical fitness complex in the woods, the one with the swimming pool. It probably isn't a surprise to you that the medical facility here is advanced. The medical research team is working with your dad to repair his leg. They've found a type of natural lotion that helps rebuild muscle. It seems to be working."

"Who's been working with him?"

"I'm not exactly thrilled with his therapists. They're both extremely pretty and extremely blond."

"Don't worry about it Mother. He only has eyes for you."

"It's not his eyes I'm worried about."

Phoebe and Danielle were seated in the lobby before a roaring fire. Whenever they emptied their glasses, they found them immediately refilled. Anything they wanted or needed was taken care of quickly. The two that were chosen to wait on them were very familiar.

Danielle put her feet up on the couch and instructed her two attendants. "The left foot is a bit tender today, Benny. You'll need to go easy on it. Earl, fluff this pillow. It doesn't feel right."

Phoebe laughed. "Don't work them too hard, Mother. They promised to run with me this afternoon."

"Jay might have the two blondes, but these young guys clean up pretty good once the makeup comes off."

"You know, Mother, they do have real names."

"I prefer Benny and Earl."

As they chatted, Geezer was in the next room with his own trainer. After the red lab's bath, brush, and manicure, Danielle wondered if they will have to change his name.

51

Jay, Danielle, and Phoebe left the Quincunx Complex and Connecticut feeling measurably better, both physically and mentally, than when they had arrived. They had each come so close to death that the future had become a gift. The outlook was bright, and even Jay had to admit that *The Five*, as a whole, could be onto something. He now understood why Danielle and Phoebe had become so obsessed with this strange, but interesting, group of people. Many of their beliefs and teachings were based on the thoughts of a man who lived during the sixth century B.C.E., yet at their core, their goal was to help humans excel.

On the plane ride back home, Jay looked up from his seat and wondered about his two favorite people, the girls to the left of him.

Danielle was slumped over, seemingly asleep.

Cyprian Jessup, Phoebe's favorite Cardinal, had given her sophisticated noise-cancelling earphones. She was told it held enough memory to store ten thousand seminars on various subjects. Phoebe was deeply concentrated on the study of wave structure of matter. She'd told Jay it was music so that he might be convinced she was a normal teenager.

Jay didn't believe either Danielle or Phoebe were typical. *What are they thinking? Will Danielle want to go back to work at her company? What about Phoebe? She isn't exactly a fit for the local high school.*

Danielle stretched her arm and yawned. She squinted and noticed Jay staring at her.

"What?"

"I think the question is, now what?"

Danielle's hair dropped over her eyes and she brushed it aside. "Is this discussion about the next few minutes or the next decade?"

"It isn't like Phoebe's worried about the clothes she'll need for her junior year of high school. She's at a much different level than a typical teenager. And you—what are you going to do with your life?"

Danielle didn't seem as concerned as Jay. Yawning, she said, "Speaking of the future, your plans aren't exactly set in cement."

Jay laughed. "We could open up a retail store. Everything goes for five dollars. That would be great karma."

"Sorry to kill your dream, but they don't build cash registers tall enough for someone of your size. You'd be all slumped over and laid up with back pain. Then I'd have to work double shifts. I don't even want to talk about holidays. We'd have to work through the holidays. Weekends! Kiss your weekends good…."

"Easy…I was just kidding." Jay blinked. "You're probably right. We'll put that one in our back pockets for now. How about…."

Danielle put her finger to Jay's lips. "Shhh…let's go home. We'll see how things play out. No need to rush into something. We'll figure it out."

52

Once they'd unpacked, Danielle and Jay agreed to let life happen. But life, they found, had a way of staying stagnant unless forced in another direction. Soon boredom chased them into the familiar and safe routines of the past. The Green County Sheriff's Department asked Jay to take back his old job as a Lieutenant, and Jay agreed.

Danielle returned to her role as president of Ponto's Canning.

As for Phoebe, she continued to listen to the lessons from Cyprian Jessup, the department head of Wisdom. She dreamed of going back to the woods of Salem and reconnect with *The Five*. September and the start of the local high school year was coming fast, but she did her best not to let that thought enter her mind.

On a humid and stormy day in late July, Jay sat alone in his dark kitchen. With only the dim light above the stove visible, he stirred his coffee and wondered how he was going to tell Danielle that he wanted to leave his job. It had been only a couple of weeks, but he knew this was no longer the path he wished to take. He wanted to ask Danielle to marry him, have whatever wedding she wanted, and settle into a life where he was his daughter's legal father, not just her biological one. But not like this. He was confident he'd find another career that could make his working life as much a pleasure as it had been back when Rufe was his partner and all seemed right with the world. When the time was right, he would attempt to set the course in the right direction and make them a family, but not now…not yet.

Long ago Jay had learned from his father that it was up to him to find the answers. No one was going to knock on his door and lay down the path to happiness and contentment. Then again…"

Jay heard someone at the front door. He was sitting in front of the TV, wearing an old light-green scrub he'd walked off with when he left the hospital after his leg surgery. His long cargo shorts hid some of the scars inflicted by Ted Paulson. His limp was slightly noticeable, but the pain only bothered him when running or sitting for a long period of time. With Danielle and Phoebe out for a drive to the mall, he didn't feel the need to dress up on such an undesirable Saturday morning.

It took a little while for Jay to recognize the man at the door. He wore a Stetson Temple hat and seemed to reflect the image of a very wealthy gent. The man tipped his hat forward, and rain that had collected in his hat poured onto Jay's bare feet. The man smiled with great delight.

Jay then saw the man's cane, and put two and two together.

"Same old Bernie…just as pleasant as ever."

Bernie Tennison was still quite blind from the attack that started everything. He was now also divorced, and despite the settlement with his ex-wife, quite rich. Between the money from the sale of his company, his own family inheritance, and the payoff that *The Five* had given all the victims, money was of little concern to him.

"What can I do for you, Bernie?"

"I wanted to thank you for finding the man who did this to me." He waved his hand over the sunglasses that he wore, rain or shine. "I know that finding him came at a price, and I'm grateful."

"You're welcome, Bernie. I'll make sure to tell Danielle and my daughter Phoebe you stopped by. I certainly couldn't have done it without them."

Bernie stood silently, leaving Jay a bit confused.

Finally Jay broke up the awkward moment. "Was there something else?"

"Well, yes, Barthus! There's a blind man on your porch. The pathetic fellow before you is wondering if you are going to let him stand here in the rain or invite him into your meager excuse for a home."

Jay opened the door, held Bernie's elbow, and moved him inside.

"Sorry, I thought this was a hello-goodbye thing."

Jay escorted Bernie to the kitchen and set him in a chair. He turned the ceiling light on and then wondered why he'd done that since Bernie couldn't see anyway.

Bernie started right in. "I'm divorced. The kids are with their mother. I've had plenty of time to figure out where I want to put my time and money."

"And where might that be, Bernie?"

"I want to catch bad guys."

"You what?"

"I want to go after unsolved murders. I sold my business for more than it probably was worth. I want to solve crimes, and I want you to do what you're good at. I'll worry about the money and the cases we take, and you can solve the crimes. You can call it what you want and hire who you want. Just don't take forever thinking about it."

Bernie had never been one to dawdle. He made his offer and headed for the door. The rain had let up a bit when Bernie walked out to his waiting driver. He didn't bother to turn around as he said, "I already have five or six customers, Barthus. One case is as big as the next. Victims' families need closure more than the police do...and they pay pretty well."

Jay thought back to what his father said about earning his way. *"Sorry Pop, but sometimes opportunity does come a knock'n."*

53

That night, Jay prepared his specialty; grilled pork tenderloin. He'd baked potatoes and carrots in tinfoil and brought the plate inside. Removing the baked beans from the microwave, he set them on the table just as Danielle and Phoebe walked through the door. They set their new fall clothes from the mall down, washed their hands and talked about the day in rapid banter.

Jay was amazed at how the two most intelligent women he knew could at one moment discuss abstractions of physics and, shortly thereafter, talk about the clerk at the clothing store with an ear piercing gauge the size of a silver dollar.

Jay polished off his dinner and opened a bottle of beer. He waited patiently while Danielle and Phoebe finished their own meal. During a brief pause in the chatter, he broke in.

"I had a visitor today."

They looked at him disapprovingly. He was unshaven and his scrub shirt was now heavily stained with barbecue sauce.

Danielle ran her gaze up and down the big man. "Whoever it was must have been impressed with your strong sense of fashion."

Jay twisted the cap off another beer. "It wasn't my ensemble that he came to see. In fact, he couldn't see anything. As a matter a fact, I greeted him completely naked," Jay lied.

To Jay's delight it worked, because Phoebe gagged.

"Danielle, do you remember Bernie Tennison?"

"I've never met him, but I know he was one of Ted's first victims. He was blinded, wasn't he?"

Jay thought back at the incredible pain that Tennison must have endured as acid ate away at his eyes.

"Well, Bernie sold his company. He wants to hire me as a kind of investigator."

Danielle let that sink in. "Who would you be working for?"

Jay smiled and held her hand. "Me, myself and I. Of course, Bernie would oversee things."

Danielle grabbed Jay's beer and took a drink. "Are you hiring?"

"What?"

"I don't want to run my company any more. I want out. We could do this. We could work together."

Phoebe spoke up. "You could both set your own hours. I wouldn't be tied here. I could learn somewhere else. There's a program in Connecticut."

Everybody fell silent.

Jay stood and took his beer back from Danielle.

"We have much to think over."

Phoebe won an argument that lasted several days. By the time she left Wisconsin for Connecticut she had her parents convinced, to a point, that perhaps she was right. They agreed to let her participate in the incredible opportunity to learn from some of the most advanced philosophers and mathematicians in the world. Yes, it was *The Five*. Yes, it was far away.

It was too far for a father who'd only known about his daughter's existence for less than a year. He'd grown to love her and wanted to make up for missed time, at least a small portion of it. And now she was leaving.

It was far for a mother that, short of occasional weekends spent camping with friends, was never away from Phoebe. Since Ted Paulson kidnapped her daughter, she'd never let Phoebe out of her sight.

Cyprian Jessup had sent handwritten letters to Danielle. Other letters were sent from those who would also mentor her daughter. The letters promised safety and protection.

Jay was dead set against it. But something that Danielle had been told made the decision a little bit easier.

It was mid-August. The sun beat down through thin clouds and the humidity seemed to be just what the mosquitoes ordered. After cutting the lawn, Jay's sweat covered his dirty t-shirt and the look of his worn-out blue jean shorts brought back memories of the seventies for his neighbors. Jay settled down in his backyard under a shade tree. The content of his six-pack cooler was currently all knotted up at three empty and three full. He'd been planning to break the tie, but his drowsy eyes were getting the best of him. He tried to finish an article in the sports section of the local paper, but after re-reading the third paragraph about another high-powered football team with NCAA violations, he'd nodded off. He awoke suddenly to the screech of an old, rusty lawn chair opening next to him.

Danielle sat and stared at him until his mind began to wrap itself around the present.

Jay took notice of everything about her—from the blue cargo shorts that fit her well, to the white button-down shirt that revealed just the right amount of cleavage. Jay counted the three undone buttons and smiled. He was indeed a lucky fellow.

"So what do you think?" Danielle said.

The wind, as slight as it was, carried her fragrance to him and it was impossible to think of anything other than making love to her.

"I don't think you could be any sexier than you are right now!"

Danielle gave Jay the stink eye. He made her mad because he couldn't read her mind. He made her disgusted, because he smelled like beer.

"I'm not talking about me, I'm talking about Phoebe. What's your opinion?"

His exciting moment of sexual fantasy disappeared in a flash. "Same as it always had been. No way in hell, at least not yet. She's only sixteen, for Christ's sake. I could barely brush my teeth at sixteen."

Danielle stood. "That I can believe."

"You still think letting her go was the best decision?" Jay asked.

"I called each of her mentors and asked them a question, including her favorite Cardinal, Cyprian Jessup. The reply I got from Cyprian was the most interesting. Do you want to hear it?"

"What does the Grand Poobah of Wisdom have to say?"

Danielle was going to say something about Jay's appearance reflecting the complete opposite of wisdom, but kept silent for the moment. "I asked each of them why they were interested in Phoebe. Cyprian said he was seventy-three years old and it had been increasingly hard to locate young people who have the complete package that Phoebe possesses."

"They sure like to use the sugar, don't they?"

"Are you saying Phoebe is not as talented as they say?"

"Of course not, she's remarkable."

"Cyprian went on to talk about the limited time he and some of the other mentors may have. He's worried that many of the projects that they have in the works may not reach completion. He believes that young people like Phoebe can keep *The Five* growing. He wants us to know that he didn't want Phoebe to come to Connecticut because of what they could do for Phoebe. It's all about what Phoebe can do for them. In other words, Jay...he told me the truth. Yes, Phoebe will learn things that very few in this world know about, but it is for mutual benefit. Phoebe brings something to the table that is rare these days...an unending curiosity and the brains to find the answers."

Tears began to drop down Danielle's cheek.

Jay hated it when she cried. "You miss her already, don't you?"

"Let's just say my frequent flyer miles will be going up in the near future."

54

With Phoebe gone to Salem, Danielle and Jay decided to tie up loose ends. If they were going to get serious about working together as investigators, the first order of business was to leave their current jobs.

For Jay it wasn't very difficult. There were still some people at the Sheriff's Department who thought Jay was at least partially responsible for the deaths of Captain Juul and Jim Ruferd. Though the facts were obvious, the rumor mill had shown itself to be a slow wheel to shut down. That being the case, Jay handed in his resignation. For the first time since college, he felt free from red tape, rules, regulations, and the incessant road blocks that had always seemed to clog up what really mattered.

Danielle had a much tougher time of it. Except for her stint in college, she had been with the company ever since her father hired her to clean out the stock rooms at age sixteen. She'd worked her way up in the company and, despite being the owner's daughter, she was well respected for how hard she worked and how well she had treated her employees. She knew almost everyone by name and made sure to say goodbye to all of them.

Bernie Tennison, Jay, and Danielle worked out the details together. The original thought had been to move to a large Midwest City with a large potential client base. But it was their rich benefactor who made the final decision. Bernie Tennison bought a large, dignified-looking brick building in Green County.

"We don't need to be in some crowded city. Our clients are not going to be typical cases. We'll take cases that defy logic and have ended up in a pile of dead-end files," Bernie reasoned.

So there it was. A month later the Vulca Detective Agency was ready for business. Bernie would not tell his two partners why he'd chosen the strange name.

Bernie was a detail-oriented man. He'd studied the likes and dislikes of his two new investigators. He'd learned what made them feel comfortable and what made them squirm. They each had completely different strengths and weaknesses; for this reason, he'd decided to set up separate offices. Each office was decorated and supplied according to Bernie's vision of his employees' temperaments. After all, sometimes the blind learn to see with more clarity than those with sight.

The entrance keys to Jay and Danielle's new office were sent in a Fed-ex envelope. The address, however, was not included in the package.

Danielle leaned against the kitchen table. "Now what? I want to see our new digs, don't you?"

"I've been bugging Bernie to let us see the place, but I couldn't break him." Jay looked inside the envelope again. Something was typed on the inside. He ripped it open. "Look— Bernie wrote a little note. It says, "Pick you up today!!"

As if by some weird stroke of perfect timing, a car horn beeped in the driveway.

Danielle and Jay raced out the door and saw Bernie and his driver waiting for them.

Bernie pushed a button and the back door opened. "Hop in, you two. I want to introduce you to your bat-cave, of sorts."

The car was roomy, and Jay had no difficulty getting himself inside. "You are a mysterious man, Bernie—with a hint of peculiar on the side."

As the car headed out of town, a blackened divider window shot down from the ceiling. The rear windows became dark as well. The only light to be seen was a crackling fire displayed on the divider panel. Jay realized they had become Bernie's captives.

When the car finally stopped, Bernie got out and opened the back door for his prisoners.

The sunlight temporarily blinded them, but it didn't take long before Jay and Danielle realized they were standing directly in front of Amalthea.

Amalthea looked as if it had never been abandoned. Gardeners were busy at work. The tower clock struck three and sounded perfect. The double door that symbolized *The Five* had been replaced with black and silver doors.

"One of the doors is carved with the image of Apollo, the other with Hercules. Vulca was an Etruscan artist from around 500 B.C. Some say he created many of the finest depictions of deities of the era. His works were admired more than gold. These doors are an exact likeness of his work. I want your work to be admired as well."

Danielle was smiling ear-to-ear.

Jay, on the other hand, wasn't nearly as elated. "This place doesn't exactly give me a cozy feeling, Bernie. What gives?"

"You'll grow to love it, Barthus. It all begins once we enter these doors. I know this place is overkill, but if you don't plan to expand, you'll never move ahead."

Bernie used his cane to push in Hercules' left eye. How he managed to hit it so precisely without sight was a puzzle to Jay and Danielle. The door opened.

"You'll have plenty of time to get used to the idea," Bernie said. He felt his watch. "Time's a-wasting. We have—that is—you have work to do."

Bernie knew the layout and walked briskly to the room at the end of the hallway. It was a basic conference room, except for the surveillance cameras and touch-screen on each of the four walls.

Bernie sat down at the head of the oval table.

"Danielle, I didn't change all of the rooms, but the five sided designs were not my style. I had most of them changed so that they only have four walls. Could you please touch one of the screens in front of you?"

Danielle did just that. A picture appeared, depicting a filing cabinet filled with manila folders. On each folder's tab was the name of a case.

"Pick one, any one, everybody's a winner here!" Bernie said in his best carnival voice.

Danielle touched the third folder from the top. The display brought up a picture of a dark haired man, perhaps in his thirties. Below the man's picture was a list of links to everything a detective would want to know about him and the case.

Bernie stood. "Which one did she pick, Pauly?"

Danielle and Jay looked at each other, sufficiently puzzled.

"Pauly?"

A voice came from the ceiling. "Sorry boss, I was busy. She picked the Butte Des Morts case."

"That'll be all for now, Pauly." Bernie seemed pleased with himself. "Pauly is kind of handyman. He'll be available 24 hours a day for various tasks. He lives here at Amalthea."

"If he stays up in the bell tower, can I call him, Quasimodo?" Jay laughed.

"I heard that," the voice from the ceiling said.

Bernie continued, "You picked a dandy, Danielle. It's our most recent case. This came to my attention just a couple of weeks ago."

Jay spoke up, not knowing if he should speak to Bernie or the ceiling. "Lake Butte Des Morts is a couple of hours north of us."

"That's right, Jay. Butte Des Morts means the "mound of the dead". The hill had been a burial for Native American corpses. In the early part of the 18th century they were killed in a battle against the French. There were other battles. They, obviously, were not treated well and it left later generations angry. In the mid-to-late 19th century, road crews moved the earth to make room for railroad beds. Shattered bones were visible as those corpses were mixed in with relics and gravel. This disgrace was visible for miles."

Danielle, who had Native American ancestry, hung her head.

"What about our victim?"

"Recently, city officials thought it would make sense to put in a permanent reminder of the spot. They dug the area to add a granite marker. Not surprisingly, they came upon a pocket of human bones. Most are believed to be from the Fox Indian tribes. That society actually precedes the French attacks. They think it might have been an original burial ground for the Fox Indians. Our victim was found mixed in with the other corpses. The kicker is…he was scalped."

Danielle stood and focused on the victim's face. She then turned and reached for the door. "You coming, partner?"

Jay wheeled his chair to the door and blocked the exit with his long legs. "Yeah, I'm coming. But I have something to show you before we begin this adventure of ours."

As Jay and Danielle made their way out the front door, they heard Bernie's voice echoing through the office speakers. "Don't be long. We have much to do...much to do, indeed."

55

Jay did not bring Danielle home. He drove her deep into the countryside. Once he was within a few blocks of his destination, he covered her eyes.

"You know I don't like blindfolds. When can I take this thing off?"

Jay removed the red headband that covered Danielle's piercing green eyes and grinned from ear to ear.

Danielle jumped out of the car and dashed to the sight in front of her. "A hot air balloon...I've always wanted to go on one. How did you know? I don't remember ever saying anything."

A long time ago, Jay had asked her father if Danielle had ever talked about something she'd never had the opportunity to do. "Oh, sometimes a guy just knows," he said.

There wasn't a cloud in the sky, and the temperature was a bit higher than a typical Midwest September. Danielle climbed into the cab with Jay. As they entered, the pilot exited and stood with a few coworkers.

"What the...what?"

"Don't worry about it." Jay reached in his pocket and unfolded his hot air balloon pilot license.

"When did you accomplish the training? How many trips have you made?"

"While I was rehabbing. And to answer your second question, this is my first attempt without my trainer."

"You sure like to give a girl that warm fuzzy feeling, don't you?"

"How's the wind, Mickey?"

"It's nearly perfect, Jay. Keep the radio on. We'll be here if you have any problems."

"You got it, Mick."

With that, Jay put his gloves on and let go of the ropes.

Danielle was both excited and scared as hell.

Jay lit the burner and turned a lever for lift-off. It wasn't long before they were looking down at a placid view of barns, pastures, and winding roads.

Danielle was speechless. She just stood leaning over the railing, taking it all in.

Jay had more up his sleeve than just a balloon ride. He had a destination and a burning question that was beginning to cause him pain and anxiety. From his vantage point, he could see where he wanted to go. He watched the altimeter and air temperature closely. He was doing everything he was supposed to do, but one thing kept creeping into his mind...speed. He wanted to get there fast, and his current mode of transportation wasn't doing the job.

At long last, he centered the craft over the appointed field. He lowered it to just the right viewing altitude and waited for a reaction. The slight wind didn't cause him any problems. He continued to wait.

Danielle was still taking in the flight itself, the beautiful blue sky, the fresh air, and the cows that crowded near a feeding trough. Then, suddenly, her bliss was momentarily disrupted when her loving pilot put his hand on top of her head and pointed it in a different direction.

When she saw, "Danielle, will you marry me?" carved into the cornfield below, she screamed and jumped into Jay's arms. The jump caused the balloon to jolt erratically, but Jay didn't care. All he knew was that his girl was kissing him all over his face, and that had to be a good thing. The crew on the ground broke the moment. The two-way radio blasted, "Was that a good scream or a bad scream?"

Jay broke in between kisses. "I think it was a good scream."

The radio exploded in congratulations. It was as if the home team just won an epic battle.

When Jay and Danielle gracefully reached the ground, the crew had Champagne open and ready. Danielle took a big swig out of the bottle, and then handed it to Jay. She then turned and walked toward her car.

The crew looked as puzzled as Jay!

"You know, you never did give me an actual answer," Jay shouted!

She shouted back, "You know, you never did give me an actual ring."

"I'm *working* on that!"

She turned, threw her jean jacket over her shoulder and smiled. "Then I'll be *working* on my answer."

ACKNOWLEDGMENTS

I thank Beth Jankowski, Craig Booher, and Rodney Schroeter, for their much needed editing work. I am also grateful to Patricia Crisanti (Salem Town Clerk) and Lieutenant Todd Olm (Appleton Police Department) in helping me with essential information in forming aspects of the story. Finally thanks to Joy LeClair, Nate Karth, and Kathy Popovich for reading the manuscript and making sure the story stayed on track.

I tend to do a lot of research in my writing. Sometimes it becomes vital to read through books that feed me enough information to formulate my path. Two of those books were: Divine Harmony (The Life and Teachings of Pythagoras) by John Strohmeier & Peter Westbrook and The Prose of Sir Thomas Browne edited by Norman Endicott.

Vic LeClair III lives in Wisconsin. He is the author of Nick Faber's Touch, The Nipishkoo, and Vesuvius.

Please visit him online at www.yourstoryastold.com

www.ingramcontent.com/pod-product-compliance
Lightning Source LLC
Chambersburg PA
CBHW051417170626
46809CB00006B/2194